A TASTE OF AMBER

'Punish me, please,' said Susan, her voice shy and quiet.

'Punish you?' Ginny echoed. 'How do you mean?'

I knew exactly what she meant, and the idea excited me even though I'd just come.

'Tie me up and spank my bottom,' Susan said, blushing at what she was asking for.

A TASTE OF AMBER

Penny Birch

This book is a work of fiction.
In real life, make sure you practise safe sex.

First published in 1998 by
Nexus
Thames Wharf Studios
Rainville Road
London W6 9HT

Typeset by TW Typesetting, Plymouth, Devon

Printed and bound by
Cox & Wyman Ltd, Reading, Berks

ISBN 0 352 33293 X

One

I should have let the games mistress seduce me in the first place. At least, that's what I should have done to avoid getting expelled from school. Instead I had told her to get lost and so found myself on the train home, wondering what I was going to say to my parents.

Not that it was as simple as that, but my refusal was the moment that counted. It really started a few weeks before. School was Bridestowe Ladies' College, a small, girls-only public school in the depths of rural Devon. It was the summer term and I was eighteen, a prefect and a model of responsibility and maturity to the juniors. To most of the teachers I was a successful product of the school: well-mannered, well-spoken and good at games, if a trifle wild and less scholarly than they might have wanted. To Miss Campbell I was a cheeky, sulky tomboy with a body I didn't know what to do with. She did, or at least she thought she did.

Unfortunately I was too innocent to realise this, even when she began to give me the occasional encouraging smack on my bottom whenever I was slow changing for games. She also used to talk to me when I was in the showers, but I thought my popularity with her was because I was good at sport.

It was in the shower that she finally made a move. Looking back on it, I realise that she must have planned the whole thing. She kept me talking all the way back from the games fields, then asked for help putting various bits and pieces away. The result was that by the time I got into the shower the other girls were already dressing.

Miss Campbell came into the shower with me, which was perfectly normal. Asking me to soap her back was less ordinary, but I thought nothing of it and complied, taking the bar from her and starting on her shoulders.

'Thank you, Amber, that's nice,' she said. 'Could you go a little lower?'

I did as she asked, rubbing the soap into the small of her back. I was feeling a little embarrassed, not because of our nudity or what I was doing, but because she was a mistress. Unlike many girls, I'd never felt comfortable about friendships with staff members. Such relationships are always unequal, with the girl very much the junior. Even at eighteen I liked to be the senior one in a friendship; bossy I know, but that's just the way I am. So was Miss Campbell, but she'd picked on the wrong girl to boss.

'Lower still,' she said gently as my hands began to go up her back.

If I went lower than I had done already, I'd have been soaping her bottom, and I was sure she couldn't want me to do anything so intimate.

I did the small of her back again and then, once more, started upwards. I still didn't realise that she was making a pass at me. I had no idea that she would get turned on by having me soap her, but I did see it as a gesture of status, like having me polish her shoes or do my ironing. Not that I was completely innocent. I already masturbated, and almost always over fantasies about girls, which I accepted as part of my personality. I'd also snogged both my closest friends and even played with one's breasts. The idea that Miss Campbell – thirty-odd years old and an authority figure – might want sex with me was something entirely different.

'Lower,' she repeated, only now it was an order.

'Miss . . .' I objected, looking apprehensively at the bare roundness of her bottom.

It seems incredibly naïve, but only then did I realise that she wanted me sexually. Actually, if she'd been a bit more passionate, she'd probably have got what she wanted. She was attractive enough: slim, elegant and strong-willed.

Another girl might have been excited by the situation; I could only see it as her wanting me under control. Her bottom did look enticing, though: firm and round and womanly. My instincts told me to go ahead, only my annoyance at being told what to do stopping me.

'Don't be silly, Amber,' she said, and it was the tone of her voice that finally spoilt her plan.

If she'd sounded excited, hopeful or pleading my hands would have gone to her bottom. I liked women's bottoms, and had often fantasised about caressing and smacking my friends'. As it was, she made it sound as if I was being disobedient. There was no way I was having sex with her in charge. I stopped soaping and stood back.

'I really don't think I should . . .' I started, determined to be firm but not feeling very sure of myself.

'Why ever not?' she demanded in the same tone.

'Because I don't want to,' I replied.

'Amber Oakley, you will do as you're told,' she snapped.

'No,' I answered.

'Perhaps a spanking would improve your manners?' she continued, now sounding threatening.

'No,' I repeated, outraged at her suggestion.

She turned on me, wearing the same look of righteous indignation she might have used if I'd refused some reasonable request. I stood my ground, making the situation a stalemate. I'm sure she would have dearly loved to take me around the waist, bend me over and spank me until I was begging her to stop, but she knew she couldn't physically do it. I was taller and heavier than her and if she tried she might well have ended up getting her own backside smacked instead.

She realised that it was hopeless, turning back to the shower and continuing to wash as if nothing had happened. I finished showering and dressed hastily, not exchanging another word with her.

I thought I'd handled the situation rather well, but I still felt bad about it, partly because the way she obviously saw me as an inferior had hurt my pride. Worse than that was the way it churned up all the adolescent uncertainties which I thought I'd resolved. Coming to terms with preferring girls to boys had provoked a fair bit of angst. A great deal more had been provoked by my urge to punish and humiliate my friends sexually. By eighteen I'd accepted both needs as part of me, but not the dimension Miss Campbell's behaviour had added.

My fantasies had always involved a mixture of sex and control, and most of them involved spanking other girls' bottoms. Given that I'd never spanked anybody, I had no idea where it came from. There was just something irresistibly fascinating about a girl's bottom being smacked as a punishment. It didn't mean I actually disliked other girls, just the opposite. I also knew that if I ever did spank a girl I'd want to hug and kiss her after I'd dealt with her, then go to bed. As it was, the strongest bit of the fantasy was not doing the actual spanking, but thinking of how the girl would feel as I took her pants down to get her bottom bare. She'd feel helpless, humiliated, about to be punished and unable to do anything about it.

And that was what Miss Campbell had threatened to do – to me!

There hadn't been official physical punishments at school for years, although one or two girls had been known to accept unofficial spankings in place of more tedious punishments. Not me though. The idea of lying over a mistress's lap with my skirt up and my pants pulled down was utterly unbearable. My bottom would be bare and my fanny would show from the back, and then she'd spank me. I knew I'd cry, which I do rather easily. I also knew it would turn me on. Whether I liked it or not, the idea of being spanked was at once terrifying and immensely attractive.

It had nearly happened, and I couldn't get it out of my mind.

This had the effect of increasing my sexual need and I started to play with myself more often. I'd do it late at night when it was safe, with the bedclothes down, my nightie pulled up to my neck and my knickers off. Instead

4

of thinking about sex with one of my friends, my fantasies would drift to what might have happened if I'd given in to Miss Campbell. In my imagination it would happen in the shower as it almost had, only I'd give in to the spanking and then she'd make me lick her between her legs while my bottom was all hot and red. Sometimes it would be different, perhaps with her spanking me in front of a class, with my gym knickers pulled down and my bottom bare for everyone to see. Worse still was the idea of being done on the games field in front of a visiting team. They'd all be laughing as I was pulled down over her bent knee. My skirt would come up and my pants would be taken down, despite my kicks and protests. Then I'd be spanked until I was blubbering. By then I wouldn't care what I was showing any more – fanny, bottom-hole, the lot. It was incredibly humiliating, and used to give me the most exquisite orgasms.

There was another detail – one that often came into my head just before orgasm, when I had least reserve. I'd be nearing my climax, imagining myself on my knees in the shower, Miss Campbell standing over me, her hand pushing my head into her fanny, and my tongue busy with her clitoris. Then, as I started to come, my mind would run off on its own, imagining her turning, putting her bottom in my face, and letting go of my head to pull her cheeks apart. She'd order me to kiss it and I'd know she didn't mean her cheeks or the rear of her fanny lips, but her anus.

I'd be looking at her bottom-hole from a distance of inches; a little ring of puckered pink flesh, slightly open in anticipation of my tongue. She wouldn't pull my head in and make me lick it – she'd expect me to do it voluntarily. I'd know that for me to accept would mark me as so far beneath her that, from then on, I'd be just a plaything for her, like a doll she could use when she liked. I'd do it, though; I wouldn't be able to help it – leaning forward, puckering my lips out as if I was going to kiss a friend. It wouldn't be a friend's lips I was going to kiss, but another woman's anus; the dirtiest, most servile act imaginable. Finally I'd kiss it, putting my face between her buttocks and planting a willing, unrestrained kiss right on the little hole.

Then I'd come, at first in utter bliss – my back arching and her name on my lips – then with a great rush of humiliation at the thought of what I'd come over. I'd lie there in the dark for a while, my nightie still up, hoping neither of my neighbours had heard me masturbating and wondering where such a dirty fantasy had come from.

I wanted to talk to my friends about all of this, but there were only two I was close enough to to admit such dirty thoughts. These were Ginny Linslade and Susan Wren, who were also the two girls I used to fantasise over when I wasn't thinking about Miss Campbell.

Ginny was the girl whose breasts I'd played with. Tall, blonde and curvy, she was extremely sexy and would have made a statue sit up and pay attention. We'd been friends a long time and she had accepted the increasingly sexual nature of our relationship with the same playful enthusiasm she brought to life as a whole. There was nothing false about Ginny; she was always open, straightforward and let her feelings lead her.

Susan was, in many ways, the opposite: petite, dark-haired and olive-skinned. She had only started her periods at seventeen and completely lacked Ginny's boisterous attitude to sex. On the other hand, it was she who had first asked me to kiss her properly. Very intelligent, shy and vulnerable, she saw Ginny and particularly me as protectors – a role I was more than happy to fill.

Somehow the moment was never right until one Sunday nearly a month after the incident with Miss Campbell. The three of us had been walking on Dartmoor and had bought a fair amount of beer to wash our lunch down. We ended up fairly drunk – too drunk to risk returning to the school – and so we chose a quiet spot among the rocks and sat down to chat with our shoes and socks off and our feet in the cool water of a brook.

Inevitably the conversation turned to sex and, as usual, it mainly consisted of Susan and I listening to Ginny. She was the only one of us who wasn't a virgin, having had intercourse with no less than three men. She'd also had plenty of less heavy encounters and had actually lost count of the number of men's cocks she'd sucked, or claimed to have sucked. Just one would have made her by far the most experienced of us. Susan had only ever allowed herself to be coaxed into taking a boyfriend's penis in her hand and I hadn't even seen one.

I had already come to terms with the fact that I preferred girls, but Ginny's vivid descriptions of sucking men's cocks still had quite an effect on me. Her father was a farmer in Wiltshire and she had two older brothers – a set up that seemed to give her endless opportunity for misbehaving. In this case she was telling us how she managed to entice one of the men who worked on the farm. The little flirt had waited until he was working in the yard beneath her bedroom window, then deliberately thrown the curtains open while she had no top on. Ginny's breasts were big and round and I could just imagine how the man must have felt with her flaunting them in front of him.

That was what she enjoyed most – to feel she was exciting, and the centre of attention. I suppose there's a bit of that in all of us, me included. Whereas I find it rather awkward if my body turns men on unintentionally, Ginny simply revelled in the effect she had on them. She was no tease, but felt almost a sense of obligation to anyone who had the guts to admit she turned them on.

That was what had happened in this case. He'd cornered her in the barn a couple of days later and made it quite clear that he wanted sex. Ginny had spent the next few minutes down on her knees in the straw with her blouse pulled open to show her tits and his prick in her mouth.

There was no way Susan or I would have done it, either of us would have probably kicked him and run for it. Not Ginny; she'd savoured every moment of having his erection to suck and played with herself while she did it.

'Did he come?' Susan asked, her voice a mixture of excitement and disgust.

'Right in my mouth,' Ginny answered with obvious relish.

I felt a little shiver go through me at the thought and exchanged glances with Susan. Ginny laughed, clearly delighted at our reaction. The idea of letting a man put his cock in my mouth really alarmed me. It seemed such a servile thing to do, yet, like the thought of kissing Miss Campbell's anus, the idea at once thrilled and repelled me.

'What does it taste like?' Susan asked.

'Cocks taste all masculine and really sexy,' Ginny answered. 'Spunk's salty and a bit slimy, but there's something about it that really turns me on.'

'Yuck!' Susan replied. 'It sounds awful.'

'You should try it,' Ginny suggested. 'You've got such a pretty face, any man would love to see you sucking on his cock, especially in your school uniform. You should ask someone. You won't get turned down.'

'I couldn't!' Susan protested.

'I'll ask, and then you can do it,' Ginny suggested. 'Come on, let's find a hiker or someone.'

'You really would, wouldn't you?' I asked in disbelief.

Ginny never answered because Susan said something that stopped the conversation dead.

'To be honest, I prefer girls,' she remarked in a small, embarrassed voice that sent a shiver right through me.

She was looking straight at me, her face the colour of a tomato. I was across the stream from her, Ginny sitting on a rock in the middle.

'Oh, I don't know,' she continued, turning away.

I thought she was going to cry, and felt really bad because she had had the guts to admit it and I hadn't responded. If I didn't take my chance immediately I knew it would be gone.

'So do I, Susan,' I said quickly as she started to rise to leave. 'You especially.'

She turned back, and there were tears streaming down her face. Ginny was looking on with an amazed expression. Susan obviously wanted a cuddle so I opened my arms for her, anticipating how her body would feel even as she stepped down into the stream.

What would have happened then I will never know. I wanted to take her in my arms and snog her, then cuddle

Ginny so that she wouldn't feel left out but, before she reached me, the sharp yap of a dog broke the trance. I turned to see a black and white mongrel trotting towards us, then heard its owner's voice from further away.

Susan stopped and Ginny hastily rearranged her skirt to cover the front of her panties. I stood up, looking in the direction the man's voice had come from. Standing on the rock I could see him, some way off and not actually heading in our direction. The moment had gone, yet the all-important admission had been made. When we'd kissed before, it had been in play, both of us pretending it was done out of curiosity. The next one would be unashamed passion; it was just a question of when.

Not very long was the obvious answer as we walked back in the general direction of school. There was a really intimate atmosphere between the three of us and we took each other's hands once we were on less rocky ground. I was in the middle, and itching to cuddle them both and let my hands explore their bodies. There would have been no resistance; just the opposite, in fact, but there just wasn't quite enough privacy.

We'd come round in a big loop. It was about four miles back to school, which would have meant that we'd have arrived respectably sober and in time for dinner. As it was, we were passing The Bear just as it was opening.

The pub was a great favourite with the girls, although it was unpopular with the school staff as it was happy to serve anybody old enough to be legally entitled to drink, regardless of petty things like school rules. Also, the course of an old railway ran some two hundred yards behind it and provided a route back to the school grounds that avoided the roads. We were hot, footsore and badly in need of a drink, so went inside without hesitation.

We were just at that stage of drunkenness when you haven't started to feel bad but have gone too far to realise that you ought to stop. Ginny ordered strong cider, flirting outrageously with the barman as he drew three pints of a dark gold fluid from a wooden barrel behind the bar. It was delicious; sweet, heady and intoxicating.

Not surprisingly we got drunk. However, it was the good sense of the barman in refusing to serve us a third round that was our real undoing. If he had, we'd have been too far gone to really do anything other than stagger back to school and go to sleep. The worst that would have happened was that we would have been punished for drunkenness. As it was, we came out of the pub in a thoroughly merry and rebellious mood; we were also very turned on.

As we started up the track I put my arms around the others' waists, then gave Ginny's bottom a squeeze as I helped her over the fence that led up to the old railway line. To get there we had to climb a steep slope to a section of viaduct, wet grass and loose shale making the going difficult at the best of times. In our condition it was next to impossible and extremely funny. It also meant that I could see up both of their skirts, the view of round bottoms in tight white panties completing the work the cider had begun.

I had to push Susan up to help her over the wall at the top, then followed, landing laughing on the grass between the two walls. Suddenly there was just the two grey walls, the thick stands of gorse that blocked off either end of the viaduct, and the sky; we were alone. Susan was on her back with her knees up and together, her sex pouting from between her thighs with the white cotton pulled tight against it.

'Would you two like to kiss me?' she asked, her voice shy and yet almost pleading.

That was it. I was fumbling at the buttons on her blouse with trembling fingers even as Ginny was pulling her legs apart. She gave a little squeak and a giggle, but made no attempt to stop us. In moments her blouse was open and her bra pulled up over her little breasts as she lay on her back with her legs up, Ginny fumbling under her skirt for her panties.

'Pull them off,' Susan gasped, lifting her bottom obligingly so that Ginny could peel her pants down.

Ginny took Susan's knickers right off, raising her legs and then spreading them open when the little scrap of

10

white cotton was no longer a hindrance. I leant down to kiss her, her tongue meeting mine as I put a hand to one breast. Susan's arms folded around my neck as Ginny went down between her thighs. I could see the brown puff of hair on her belly out of the corner of my eye, mingled with golden hair as Ginny put her face to Susan's fanny. She tensed and made a little choking sound in her throat and I knew she was being licked between her legs. Licked there for the first time and licked there by another girl.

Even in my drunken state I could hardly believe how rude that was – to actually kiss another girl's fanny – even though I'd fantasised about it often enough. Rude or not, I needed it myself, badly. I pulled back and knelt up rather unsteadily, watching Susan in her ecstasy as I struggled my panties off under my skirt. She lay there, clothing disarranged to show her fanny and titties, panties discarded to one side, an expression of utter bliss on her face. Ginny was kneeling between her legs, face buried between her friend's thighs, gorgeous bottom stuck up invitingly. It was like a ball under her school skirt: round, girly and far too tempting to resist.

I didn't know whether to straddle Susan and present Ginny with my fanny to lick, or to strip Ginny's bottom and bury my face between her thighs. For that matter, I could sit on Susan's pretty face and wriggle myself against her mouth until she started to lick. It was all too much; like having a huge box of chocolates and only being able to eat one.

Being a bossy little minx, what I did was take a firm hold on Ginny's waist and haul her round so that she was straddling Susan's face. She gave a half-protesting squeak as her lips were pulled away from Susan's fanny, but responded to my pressure and settled back to licking as soon as she had turned around. I moved to Susan's head end, breathing hard. Ginny's legs were splayed above Susan's head, her skirt hanging so that all I could see of Susan was her hair. I took hold of Ginny's skirt and pulled it up, revealing her panties stretched taut across her bottom, the material over her sex already sodden with

11

juice. Susan's eyes were locked on Ginny's rear view, her arms curled up around her waist. My fingers moved to Ginny's panties, pulling the gusset aside to reveal the dark gold of her fur – her sex lips moist and pink in the middle.

Susan moaned at the sight, only to be shut up as Ginny let her thighs slip apart and gave her friend a mouthful of fanny. I watched Susan start to lick. Ginny's panties were still held aside, and her bottom was spilling out around the taut edges of the material. Susan was licking Ginny's clitoris, and the pink flesh of her vagina was moist and open in front of my face. It was more than I could resist and, before I'd even thought of what I was doing, my face was against the softness of Ginny's bum and my tongue was working into the tight, fleshy hole of her sex. She tasted of girl – like my own fingers when I play with myself – her musky, feminine scent strong in my nostrils.

Ginny must have stopped licking Susan because she had started to moan and gasp, and I realised that she was about to come in our faces. It was much quicker than I'd have been, but then she was being licked by both of us. When she came she grunted and then screamed, totally abandoned in her ecstasy. I could feel the muscle of her thighs and bottom move as she pushed herself hard into us, giving a final choking gasp and then subsiding to lie limp on top of Susan.

I pulled back, my mouth full of the taste of my friend's sex. I wanted more and I wanted my own orgasm, my opportunity for it becoming clear as Ginny rolled off Susan to lie panting on the ground. Susan tilted her head back and looked up at me, her eyes big and moist, her mouth slightly open. Her tongue flicked out in a clear invitation and I moved forward, straddling her face just as Ginny had done. Her tongue found my clitoris – a truly wonderful sensation.

I sat up straight, squatting on my friend's face as she licked me, my head swimming with drink and sex, the sky and the grey stone walls of the viaduct spinning around me. I was in a haze of pleasure, unbuttoning my blouse and shrugging it off, then my bra. The air was cool on my bare breasts as I felt their weight and stroked my nipples. I wanted to be naked when I came and quickly unzipped my skirt and pulled it up over my head. Susan kept licking, her tongue circling my clitty with a maddening rhythm that was taking me slowly towards my orgasm.

After pulling off my socks and shoes I was stark naked; gloriously, utterly naked in the fresh air, caressing my breasts as the familiar spasms began in the muscles around my vagina. Ginny had sat up and was watching us, smiling at my uninhibited pleasure. I held my tits out to her, a wanton gesture that I hoped she wouldn't resist. She didn't, and crawled round behind me, taking a breast in each hand, stroking my nipples as I had been doing. That left my hands free, and so I edged forward, directing Susan's tongue to my hole and spreading my sex-lips with my fingers to get at my clitoris and start the little flicking motions that I always use to bring myself off.

I'll never forget that moment. The rich scent of sex mingled with the earthy smells of the moor and woods; Susan's tongue in my vagina and Ginny's fingers on my nipples; the air moving against my body, sensations of tension and burning in my muscles; the dizziness of drink mixed with the dizziness of approaching orgasm. I called out when I came, my vision going red as my climax exploded in my head, my balance slipping and only Ginny's arms stopping me from collapsing.

Then it was over, and my desperate need had been replaced with a sense of absolute fulfilment. I had no regrets, no guilt, no sadness – none of the things we are taught to believe should come with sex, particularly sex that involves tasting forbidden fruit. Well, I had tasted and eaten, and savoured every morsel.

Ginny and I hugged and then turned our attention to making Susan come. She was lying on her back masturbating, eyes shut, clearly intent on reaching orgasm. I cradled her head; her mouth opened eagerly under mine as our tongues met. Ginny was caressing Susan's breasts, leaving her to rub herself so that she could get it just right. From the pressure of her mouth against mine and the desperate passion of her kiss I could tell it wouldn't be long until she came.

I was wrong; she didn't come. Instead, she pulled away after a good few minutes of trying to get it right. I sat back, expecting her to say she couldn't make it. She was looking right at me with a curious pleading expression.

'Punish me, please,' was what she said, her voice shy and quiet.

'Punish you?' Ginny echoed. 'How do you mean?'

I knew exactly what she meant, and the idea excited me even though I'd just come.

'Tie me up and spank my bottom,' Susan said, blushing at what she was asking for despite the state she was in.

'OK,' Ginny answered, still sounding a bit puzzled, but with her normal enthusiasm.

'Do you want us to pretend you've been naughty?' I asked, hoping that I'd understood her fantasy.

'I have been. I've just let my knickers off for you,' Susan answered.

'That's true,' I replied. 'And licked us both between our legs. You certainly deserve a spanking.'

'Yes, please,' she sighed, making Ginny giggle.

Even in my drunken state I realised that Susan probably had some detailed fantasy in mind.

'How would you like it?' I asked.

'Over your knees,' she answered, starting to play with herself again as her fantasy built up. 'And call me names, and make me cry, please, Amber. Be prefects and punish me. I wish we got spanked at school, with our pants down and our bums all bare so everyone could see, oh I wish we did.'

She was rambling a bit and must have been even more drunk than Ginny and I, but she was also really turning me on. Ginny was sniggering and had the bright-eyed, mischievous look I knew so well. If she didn't really understand Susan's fantasy, then she was obviously prepared to join in for the fun of it.

'Shall we spank the little brat then?' I asked Ginny.

'Yes let's,' she answered eagerly. 'Roll her over on to her tummy.'

'Hang on,' I interrupted. 'Let's do it her way. Put your pants back on, Susan.'

She obeyed, hastily retrieving her knickers and putting them back on, then sitting down looking up at us. As Ginny was fully dressed, she looked every inch the commanding school prefect which, of course, she was. Tall, with her big breasts pushing her blouse out and her golden hair arranged around her shoulders, she almost had me wanting to go down on my knees with Susan and have my own bottom smacked. I was still in the nude and so didn't look so tough, but I was enjoying being naked and didn't want to dress. I also wanted to watch Ginny beat Susan before having my own go, and I wanted to be in control.

'Right,' I began, addressing Susan who was kneeling on the ground with her hands folded in her lap, her blouse still open and her titties bare. 'Wren, you dirty little tramp, we're going to punish you. Get on all fours.'

She bent forward into a crawling position, looking up at me and trembling.

'Face to the ground, bottom up,' I snapped, my voice rising as I warmed to the task. 'You're a filthy tramp aren't you, Wren? Masturbating out here where you thought you wouldn't get caught; lying there with your tits showing and your fingers in your fanny. You're disgusting! Well, I hope you enjoy having your fanny bare because you're going to be showing it while you're beaten. Take your pants down, now!'

Susan reached back and pulled up her skirt, exposing the seat of her knickers and the outline of her bottom inside them. She was trembling hard and her eyes looked moist as she hooked her thumbs into the waistband of her panties. Ginny reached down and planted a hard smack across Susan's thighs, making her yelp and producing a red handprint.

'I told you to pull your pants down!' I yelled as Susan hesitated.

She obeyed, easing them down over her bottom, revealing the crease of her bum and the little nest of fur around her sex, and settling them around her thighs. It

15

looked gorgeous, with the lips of her vulva pouting out from between her thighs and the darker spot of her anus showing, wrinkled and exquisitely rude.

'Do you feel like masturbating now, you slut?' I continued. 'Your bottom's bare; that's what you like, isn't it? Only it's not so funny when you're about to be beaten, is it? Do you realise you're showing your bottom-hole off to us, you little tart?'

'Yes, Miss Oakley,' she answered in a beautifully chastened voice.

'Oakley?' another voice cut in, and it wasn't Ginny's.

It couldn't have been a bigger shock if the viaduct had collapsed underneath us. We had been completely lost to the outside world; invisible but unfortunately not inaudible. The voice that had interrupted us was loud, authoritative and had a mild Scots accent. It was Miss Campbell.

We couldn't have been caught more red-handed if we'd tried. Susan had her bum towards the gym mistress: skirt up, pants down and cheeks so open that the view she was giving was just as rude as it could possibly be. I made a clumsy attempt to cover my boobs and pussy, but goodness knows why. Ginny just stood there, looking pathetic with one finger in her mouth.

I am not sure for how long we just looked at each other, but it seemed like forever. Finally Susan broke the spell by scrambling to her feet and trying to pull her panties up at the same time. Inevitably she ended up sitting on her bottom. She was blushing furiously, as was Ginny, and I could feel the hot flush in my own cheeks.

'I think you had better put your clothes on, Oakley,' Miss Campbell said.

She was trying to be icy and authoritative, but it didn't quite work. Since she had tried to seduce me she had treated me with cautious respect, aware that if I was pushed I might just complain. It would have been my word against hers, true, but mud sticks – especially that sort of mud. She had obviously assumed that I simply wasn't interested in sex. Now she knew I was.

All this went through my mind as the initial shock of being caught subsided. Lesbianism was the sort of thing that normally got girls expelled. True, crushes and minor encounters got ignored, but this was heavy – far too heavy for Miss Campbell to turn a blind eye to. On the other hand I was in a position to at least make her life difficult, and if she'd made a pass at me, there were sure to be other girls as well. Not Ginny or Susan, though, and so if anyone had a chance of talking us out of the fix we were in it was me.

Susan must have realised this immediately because she was looking up at me with pleading eyes and a shamefaced expression while she toyed nervously with a piece of twig. Ginny was a bit less quick and began to stammer an apology.

'Shh Ginny,' I said, reaching out to place a soothing hand on her shoulder. 'Could we talk please, Miss Campbell?'

Miss Campbell nodded and the three of them waited while I dressed. I took as long as I dared, thinking what to do. There were three options: give in to fate, blackmail or seduction. I have never been fatalistic; there's just too much obstinacy in me. I didn't like the idea of blackmail, either; not only was it wrong, but the complications would be endless. That left seduction and, if at the end of the day I ended up as Miss Campbell's little plaything for the rest of term, then it was better than expulsion. Besides, it wasn't as if I hadn't been fantasising over exactly that for the last few weeks.

When I had finished, Miss Campbell and I walked out on to the main span of the viaduct, leaving Ginny and Susan behind. When we were right in the middle I turned and leant back against the granite parapet. I didn't feel drunk any more, although I suppose I must have been, but I was very aware of the fresh wind blowing my curls across my face and the line of bare, craggy hills that made up the horizon. Miss Campbell spent a long moment with her back to me at the opposite parapet, also looking out across Dartmoor. I wasn't sure what to say, but it was obviously up to me to start off.

'I . . . I'm sorry about the other day,' I said.

She didn't reply and so I continued, reasoning that this was probably my one chance to get it right.

'I just wasn't ready,' I went on. 'And in the shower like that. Someone might have come in. I do like you, and I mean if . . .'

It was pretty clumsy and provoked no immediate response. She just leant her arms on the parapet and put her head back, as if trying to get herself fully in control. When she finally turned to face me I knew at once that it wasn't necessary to say anything more. She had been running and her straight, dark-brown hair was up in a pony-tail to keep it out of the way. Wisps of it were blowing across her face, which no longer looked stern, or even shocked. As a schoolgirl I had come to learn every grade of disapproving look, from the sort that says: 'Oh dear, well I suppose she'll grow out of it', to the full blown: 'What you need is your pants pulled down for a smacked backside, here, and now'.

Ellen Campbell's look was very different: warm, protective and with all the intimacy of one woman to another when both know that sex between them is a very real possibility. For a moment I thought she was going to come forward and take me in her arms. I would have responded but, instead, she gave me a brief, wicked smile.

'My cottage, after prayers,' she said simply and started back towards the others.

I followed, unable to resist watching the movement of her bottom in her tight running shorts. There was a fair bit of cheek showing, pink and soft around the edge of the green material. My fantasy came straight back to me: her bottom in my face, the cheeks open, my lips against her anus . . .

The rest of the day passed in a dream. Miss Campbell continued her run; Ginny, Susan and I walked back along the railway and reached school in time to shower and go straight into supper. There was an hour to pass after that, which I spent having an intense and rather surreal talk with Ginny and Susan. They knew everything, and talking

18

to them gave me the support I badly needed – at least until the moment I had to go and take prayers and turn the lights out in the junior dormitories. Finally the moment came. I gave Ginny and Susan a kiss each and left them in the corridor, turning them a last smile as I went through the fire door.

Outside the last light was fading in the west; a streak of rich purple over Cornwall. It was warm. Too warm to need tights under my school skirt. My uniform acted as a disguise, although I would have much preferred to change. Miss Campbell lived in one of the little cottages at the edge of the school grounds and, if anybody saw me on the way, they would simply think I was on an errand. As it was there was nobody about and I was soon walking under the scattered trees that sheltered the valley bottom. The cottage was half-hidden by a thick beech hedge, with only the roof visible in the twilight. The porch light came on automatically as I pushed the gate open, and she had opened the door before I got there. I went inside, the latch clicking behind me with a definite finality.

'Shall we have some wine?' she said.

It wasn't really a question; it was a statement. Her tone indicated to me that she still felt very much in charge, although not in the sense of being in genuine authority over me. Instead it was a very personal thing; a determination that in our relationship it was she that would be the senior one.

I accepted the glass although, after the afternoon's excesses, I was more in need of orange juice. She looked very different from her normal outfit of sports kit or sensible tweeds. A long sheaf of crimson velvet covered her from neck to ankle, clinging to her figure and restricting her walk to neat, precise steps. It was incredibly elegant and made me feel awkward and dull in my plain white blouse and knee-length skirt of dark-green tartan.

She was obviously well aware of this and, from the start, set things up to enhance her superiority. Firstly she motioned me, not to a chair, but to the sheepskin rug in front of the fire. I sat down cross-legged, acutely aware of the feel of wool against my thighs. Next, she placed the bottle where it would be me who poured when the time came to refill our glasses. Then she stretched herself out on the sofa, as languid as a Siamese cat and every bit as self-satisfied.

We talked for a while and my nervousness faded with the wine and her ease of manner. There was a faint scent in the air; a bit like burning leaves. It was quiet, too; very different from the chatter and clamour of school. Everything seemed rather unreal, in fact, only my uniform serving to remind me of who I was and what I was doing. That reminder served to start a delicious naughty feeling inside me: the knowledge that, however refined and adult my surroundings, my presence there made me a very bad girl indeed.

The conversation had reached a pause, both of us sipping our wine from the glasses which I had just refilled. She put down her glass with a deliberation that made me realise that this was it.

'Show me your legs, Amber,' she said, gently but in a tone that brooked no refusal.

My heart immediately went to my mouth. Taking the hem of my skirt, I lifted it, baring my thighs and the front of my panties. With my skirt rucked up I knew the bulge of my fanny would be very obvious. I also knew that there would be a tell-tale damp spot between my legs. She was looking at me from under half-lowered eyelids; a lady admiring a pretty pet.

'Undo your blouse,' she continued, and my fingers immediately went to tug the white cotton out of my waistband.

I lowered my eyes as I undid my buttons, my fingers trembling as each one popped open to reveal a little more of the pale flesh of my tummy. I reached the top and opened my blouse, then reached behind my back, acquiescing to the removal of my bra without having to be told. I fumbled at the catch, as clumsy as if it had been my first trainer bra and not the full-cupped type I'd been wearing for nearly five years. She gave me a small half-smile, cool and amused, making me hang my head to avoid her eyes. Finally the catch snapped open and I felt the increased weight of my breasts. Keeping my head down, I took hold of the cups and pulled my bra up. My naked breasts felt very big and very prominent as I eased my bra strap down one sleeve. They are quite big – too big to really hide – and I'd always been rather self-conscious about them. Now they were naked in front of the svelte, elegant Miss Ellen Campbell. They were plump and nude, along with my chubby thighs and rounded tummy.

'Puppy fat, how sweet,' she said, swinging her long legs off the sofa.

I could have cried. She really knew how to make me feel small, and it was turning me on, which made it worse.

'Off with your pants, darling,' she said.

I uncrossed my legs and lifted my bottom, hooking my thumbs into the waistband of my panties. As they came down over my bottom and my sex became bare I felt as if I was removing the last barrier between myself and my total surrender to her. She was standing over me, arms folded across her chest, her face set in an expression of lofty amusement. It was that which triggered my aggressive streak, otherwise she'd have had me on the floor exactly as she wanted. As it was I began to feel rebellious as I slipped my panties off my ankles.

'I'm going to spank you now, Amber,' she announced. 'Roll over on your tummy and lift your bottom for me. No, on second thoughts, kneel and put your head down. I want you to know how it feels to be in the position you made little Susan Wren get into.'

I began to obey, thinking of how rude Susan had looked kneeling face down with her bottom in the air. Miss Campbell wanted me the same way: utterly vulnerable with my pussy and bottom-hole on display. It's a wonderful position for a girl to be in – but preferably another girl. Her hand touched my arm to guide me into position. Somehow I knew that once I'd been spanked I'd be compliant. At least, it was always that way in my fantasies. If I didn't act now, I never would.

Grabbing her wrist, I twisted around and pulled. She was completely unbalanced and came down hard on the rug, squeaking in alarm at my unexpected attack. An instant later she had recovered herself and had put an arm around me to push me down. I resisted, and a moment later we had both fallen to our sides, each struggling to get on top of the other. We had both started laughing for some reason. Perhaps the release of tension; perhaps because we both knew that whoever lost was going to get a very red bottom from the other.

She was strong and fit and, for a moment, I thought that all my little show of rebelliousness had done was to ensure I got a harder spanking when it came. I was nearly naked, too, which didn't help. Nor did she fight fair, pulling my hair and scratching until I was forced to let go of her wrist. She had hold of me in an instant and then my arm was being twisted into my back. I turned with the pressure as she took a grip on my skirt, pulling it up so that my bottom was naked to the air.

'It was going to be a play spanking,' she gasped as she pushed me face down on to the rug. 'Now I'm going to take a switch to your fat behind!'

She tried to get a leg across the back of my knees, but her tight dress prevented her, making her loosen her grip for an instant. I gave a frantic lunge and pulled her down, her body sprawled across mine. She recovered quickly, our arms locking as she tried to renew her grip. For a long moment there was deadlock and then her arm began to go back and I realised that I was actually stronger than her.

Her lovely eyes were wide with surprise and alarm as I pushed her slowly down on to the rug. She was still laughing, but there was a nervous, uncertain quality to the sound.

'Now let's see who gets spanked,' I told her as I got my weight across her stomach.

Despite her struggles I managed to turn her over. If she'd told me to stop I would have done, but she just squirmed and giggled underneath me and I realised that it was still very much a game, for all that she had lost.

Besides, she had been going to use a switch on my naked bottom and I didn't see why she should get away with less. Once she was face down I sat my full weight on her back and started on my next task: baring her bottom.

She started to struggle again as she realised what I intended, but with me sat on her back and her arms pinned under my legs there was nothing she could do. Her dress was hard to get up; it was tight and pressed against the floor and rug. Her kicking didn't help either, with her high heels coming dangerously close to my face. I was determined, though, and soon had her calves bare, then her thighs. She was wearing stockings – sheer and lacy-topped – held up by suspender straps that cut into the soft flesh of her upper thighs. With her dress rucked up to the tuck of her bottom, I took a good grip on the roll of crimson material and started to expose my target.

'No, Amber, not bare!' she protested as the first swell of her bottom came into view.

I hesitated, but then continued. My pants had come off, and she'd told me to get into a position which left my most intimate secrets on show. At least she was going to be spared the indignity of showing her bumhole while she was whacked.

'Sorry,' I told her and started to lift.

Her little squeak of frustration as her bottom was exposed gave me the most delicious thrill. Her cheeks were already mostly out of her knickers – a high-cut black pair with a lace back that hinted at the dark parting between her buttocks. I had to pull them down; it was too much.

'Your pretty panties are coming down too, Miss Campbell,' I said, once her dress was up far enough over her hips to let me get at the waistband.

She squealed aloud as I said this and started to struggle desperately, pleading with me not to bare her bum. Her efforts to sound sincere were completely ruined by her · inability to stop giggling between protests. She couldn't unseat me either. I took her fancy knickers down slowly and methodically, peeling them over the smooth hump of her bottom and settling them around her thighs. Only when they were all the way down did she stop struggling. She then waited meekly to be spanked.

Her bottom was beautiful – small and round – a firm ball of flesh with skin as pale and smooth as cream. Just the thought of smacking those pale cheeks up to a glowing pink made my mouth dry and set my thighs trembling. I knew I was wet, and suspected that she would be too. On sudden impulse I pulled her cheeks apart, exposing the tight brown knot of her anus and the pink of her excited vagina in a nest of dark fur.

She obviously hadn't been expecting this because she gave a squeak of what sounded like genuine consternation, and clenched her cheeks tightly together. Thinking of her threat to switch me, I just laughed and planted a firm smack across her bare bottom. She squeaked and I gave her another, harder, and another. As I started to spank in earnest and her bottom warmed I found myself grinning. She was kicking her legs and squealing, and had started to give little sobs in between smacks. It was wonderful. Not just sexy, but really good fun – not to mention the blissful feeling of having a beautiful woman at my mercy.

Miss Campbell had spoilt my chance to spank Susan, so it was actually my first time, properly anyway. I'm sure it wasn't Miss Campbell's. She had started to moan and push her bottom up, making the cheeks part to reveal the swollen lips of her sex. Twice she had said my name, but it still surprised me when she spoke again.

'Beat me with the switch, Amber,' she asked. 'It's on the mantelpiece.'

I looked up to find a handle protruding from over the edge of the mantelpiece. I reached up and took hold of it; it was a wicked-looking implement of braided leather, about eighteen inches long. The business end was split into two thongs, like rats' tails. It looked exquisitely painful and an exploratory smack on my thigh proved that it was. It stung terribly, making two thin red welts despite the relatively gentle blow I had given myself. Realising that it was what she had intended to use on me, I found myself increasingly glad that it was me on top.

'You were going to use this on me, weren't you?' I asked as I tapped the vicious little whip against the reddened surface of her bottom.

'Yes,' she admitted, the sound as much a sob as a word.

I lifted the switch and brought it down hard across her bottom, making the flesh bounce and wobble delightfully. She squeaked and bucked beneath me, gasping with the sudden pain.

'Let me get my fingers to my pussy, please, darling,' she said.

I knew she was turned on, but her request still startled me. It was a frank admission of her need to come, and made me realise that I did too. I decided to refuse her request and get my full pleasure out of beating her before letting her play with herself. If we were to have full-blown sex, then I intended to come first, riding her back with one hand on my pussy while I whipped her lovely bottom.

It would have been great but, unfortunately, that was the moment the headmistress walked in on us.

Two

So I got expelled. If I'd let Miss Campbell have her way in the first place, things would have been different. We'd have been comfortably ensconced in a relationship and when she'd caught me with Ginny and Susan nothing would have happened. But it had, so there I was, staring morosely out across the flat grey waters of the Exe Estuary as I headed back towards London and the inevitably painful interview with my father. I was pretty depressed and not a little nervous but, beneath these emotions, I couldn't help feeling pride and a certain satisfaction.

The pride was because I had taken the fall alone in order to save Ginny and Susan from the same fate. Whether Miss Trent, the headmistress, actually believed that I'd been actively assaulting Miss Campbell I was not at all sure. I'd admitted to it, though, and nobody had challenged me. The fact that I'd had neither bra nor panties on at the time had been conveniently overlooked, and I supposed that Miss Trent had looked on expelling me as a sort of damage limitation. It's odd that sex is somehow more shocking than violence, but that's certainly how Miss Trent saw it. Miss Campbell, of course, had no wish to press charges and by mutual agreement we had declined to mention Ginny and Susan.

It had ended with Miss Trent getting a scandal of the smallest proportions she felt morally acceptable, Miss Campbell keeping her job, and Ginny and Susan not even being mentioned. Only I suffered, and my sacrifice was not quite as altruistic as it looked. Ginny's family owned a fair-sized chunk of Wiltshire and she wouldn't have been in the least troubled by being expelled. Susan was a different matter. She had a place at Oxford for the next academic year, and goodness knows what they'd have thought if the story had come out. I had done my A levels and knew my results would be at least fair, and that was the reason for my satisfaction.

My father had had my career mapped out more or less from birth. I was to be given a public-school education, kept firmly away from temptation, go on to business school and then join the firm of accountants of which he was a senior partner. The plan had now failed. All putting me in a remote girls' school had done was make me fall in love with the English countryside and turn my sexual thoughts towards my own sex. That wouldn't have mattered to his plans, even if he had known about it. As long as my results were good enough I would go on to college, lesbian or not. Getting thrown out of school for assaulting a mistress was a very different matter.

By the time I got to Paddington I had a lump in my throat which felt the size of a tennis ball. The short tube ride up to Highgate was spent thinking of clever things to say, all of them useless. I eventually decided on a policy of contrite stubbornness, and rang the doorbell with at least some determination.

As it was, it wasn't as bad as I'd expected. Dad was more exasperated than cross. My Mum defended me, as I knew she would have done even if I'd tarred and feathered Miss Trent. She had always spoiled me, though, her *laissez-faire* attitude being largely responsible for me ending up as such a tomboy. Dad knew I was just as stubborn as he was and, in the end, he had to admit defeat – at least temporarily. It was when his temper had cooled that he dropped the bombshell on me.

I had a godfather whom I had never met, despite having received the obligatory cards every birthday right up to my eighteenth. He was called Henry Gresham and had been at university with my dad. Knowing that I was about to leave school, he had called and suggested that I might like to work on his farm for the summer. My father had snapped up the offer like a shot, more than happy to get me out of the house and away from the enticements of London. The farm was in Hertfordshire, and that's where I was packed off to the following day. I had been banished.

Actually it wasn't nearly as bad as I'd imagined. I'd expected early mornings, porridge for breakfast, boiled mutton for dinner and church on Sundays. The truth was very different. Henry Gresham proved to be a large man with a red face and a permanently jolly manner. He knew I'd been kicked out of school and thought it was hilarious. He seldom got out of bed before ten o'clock and didn't expect me to, either, having a maid bring me tea and toast in bed. As for porridge and boiled mutton, Henry was a fanatical gourmet and every meal was a work of art.

His money had come from some astute racehorse dealing back in the seventies, and his farm was now given over to keeping rare breeds. All of this was handled by a manager, and Henry simply looked over it with a fatherly eye. He lived in the original farmhouse – a big red-brick construction set in a cluster of small fields and copses well away from the new buildings. I was even allowed to choose my room, selecting one that overlooked the woods.

I passed a happy two weeks exploring the area and basically mucking about, Henry never once demanding that I did anything other than by choice. The second weekend after my arrival, however, brought a cold front and rain; really dismal weather for July. Unable to continue my exploration of the local woods and streams, I retired to his library, spending the Saturday morning browsing through his huge collection of musty, leather-clad volumes.

The weather was no better after lunch, and so I returned to the library. Most of the books were technical tomes, many dating back to the eighteenth century. These were interesting enough, but didn't really fire my imagination. What did make me curious was a selection of tall albums on the highest shelves. They were bound in a distinctive dark green – which I knew was a favourite colour of

Henry's — and they looked personal. One of the covers even had an embossed picture that looked like a naked girl doing something with a snake. This fascinated me. Yet I hesitated, having no wish to make a breach of Henry's hospitality by looking through his private things. Besides, to get at them I would need to stand on a chair, and during the morning he had twice wandered in to fetch things from his writing desk.

On the other hand, he made a habit of taking a nap every afternoon and there was a good chance that I would be undisturbed. Feeling distinctly naughty, I wheeled one of the heavy armchairs across the room and climbed up on the seat, reaching for the books. Too late I realised that the fine layer of dust along their tops meant that my interest was unlikely to go undetected. Deciding the damage was done anyway, I pulled out the one with the girl on the spine, holding it up to get a better look at the picture.

She wasn't playing with a snake; she was tied to a tree. I opened the cover to find a title page with the legend: *Pony-Carting – Rushdean 1972*. I was immediately disappointed, remembering that one of Henry's interests had been pony-trap racing. I turned the next page anyway, expecting pictures of horses and buggies.

There were buggies all right, but they weren't pulled by horses. The first two pages had four pictures, each showing a lightweight trap with an elegantly dressed man either sitting in it or standing proudly by the side. It wasn't the men who had me open-mouthed and wide-eyed though, it was how the traps were being drawn. In all four cases a naked girl was harnessed between the shafts, wrists and waists attached to the traps, and reins leading from complicated leather bridles. Coloured feathers, polished brass ornaments, numbered plaques and, in one case, a scarlet rosette, added a subtle and humiliating touch to their bondage.

I turned the page with trembling fingers, scarcely able to believe what I was seeing. The album continued in the same manner, with picture after picture. Some showed racing, others some sort of show, yet others more complex sports, the details of which were not at all obvious. The only thing that unified them was that it was always the girls who were stripped and harnessed while the men, and a scattering of other women, remained fully, and immaculately, clad.

The whole thing was incredibly erotic, and I quickly found myself imagining what it would be like to have Ginny or Susan naked except for a few leather straps to keep them under control. Pony-girls, they were called: young women put in the role of horses for the amusement of their partners, and themselves. Their smiles and looks proved that. Coy or proud, decorous or mischievous, not one pony-girl looked hurt or angry.

Most of the men and dressed women carried whips and, as the album proceeded, it became clear that these weren't just for show. More than one girl had marks on her bottom. In one racing photo I could actually see the point where a whip was in contact with a soft, female bum-cheek. The camera had captured a small wave of flesh where she was being smacked; just the way Ellen Campbell's bottom had bounced when I took the switch to her.

The album was evidently the record of some sort of event, each photo being carefully annotated in handwriting that looked suspiciously like Henry's. Towards the end there were photos of some sort of ceremony, showing winning girls being awarded prizes. The losers suffered a very different fate, kneeling in the mud with their bare bottoms stuck up. The last two photos were the best of all: six pretty girls kneeling in a row, bottoms presented for punishment. The top photo showed them face on, looking shyly into the camera with their breasts dangling as they held their humiliating poses. This image had me wanting to put my hand down my panties, but the last was even better. It was the same scene, but viewed from the rear. The girls' bottoms were high, their knees apart, and their lovely cheeks open to show six fannies and six bottom-holes. Some were pert or petite, some full and meaty, but each glorious pair of female buttocks was marked with eight dark lines. The girls had been caned.

I was balancing the album with one hand, the other struggling with the button of my jeans. I desperately needed to touch myself, and I'd have sat down and masturbated on the spot if it hadn't been for the sound of a door closing somewhere in the house. I hastily slipped the album into place, climbed down, and dragged the chair back into position. I knew I was blushing furiously and turned to look out at the rain-sodden lawn in case Henry should come in and catch me with my cheeks flushed.

The album was obviously put together by hand and not something published in order to titillate its readers. It was real, and it was in Henry's library, which meant that, although he didn't appear in any of the pictures, it had almost certainly been him behind the camera. That meant that Henry liked pony-girls, which made a big change in my image of him as a friendly, slightly vague man. I'd been coming to think of him as a father figure, although more like Father Christmas than my own father, but all the time he'd probably been wondering how I'd look as a harnessed pony-girl with six red lines across the width of my naked bottom.

My teeth were chattering so hard that I was shaking. The thought of six girls being made to line up in the nude and present their bums for the cane was too much, especially when they'd been made to act as horses beforehand. That Henry had probably taken the photograph made it worse. None of the photos showed the girls being caned, so maybe he'd actually beaten them himself.

I had to play with myself. There had been no sound since the door had shut and I knew the maid was out. Tiptoeing to the library door I glanced into the hall and up the stairs. The door to the master bedroom was shut, which meant that Henry was taking his nap. The house was silent but for the gentle sound of the rain and the ticking of clocks. I decided to do it, and not in the safety of my bedroom but in the library with my legs apart in one of the armchairs.

I shut the door, feeling wonderfully dirty as the catch clicked into place. I was really going to do it – play with myself over pictures of pony-girls and come over the thought of caning them. Henry was asleep but, if he caught me, then maybe he'd serve me the same way; pull down my jeans and panties and cane my big white bottom as I knelt in his armchair.

A new blush coloured my cheeks as this last thought came into my head. I'd never before thought of Henry in a sexual context, but the idea of him beating me was undeniably exciting. Maybe I should go upstairs into his bedroom, admit my crime and beg for the punishment I so richly deserved.

He'd probably spank me first, I thought, as I sank to my knees on the floor and began to struggle with my trouser button. He was so big that he'd easily be able to take me across his knee like a naughty little girl. Then my jeans and panties would be pulled down and I'd have the shame of showing a bare bottom over a man's lap, helpless and kicking as he fondled me before starting my spanking.

I got on to all fours and eased down my jeans and panties together, imagining that it was him doing it. It felt so good with my bottom bare, and I found myself wishing that someone – anyone – was there to beat me. I slipped my hand back between my legs and began to play with my clitty, sobbing and gasping into the carpet.

A little voice inside my head was telling me to take it slowly, to take the album out and come over the thought of whipping the pony-girls. That would have been much more like my usual fantasies. But it was no good and, even when I tried to focus my mind on the thought of having Ginny and Susan like that, it kept slipping back to my own humiliation and punishment. My orgasm was approaching, swelling up and then fading as I tried to control my fantasy.

Finally I gave up, concentrating on how awful it would feel to lie bare-bottomed across Henry's lap – a contrite, tearful teenage girl about to be given the punishment most appropriate to her. He was nearly three times my age, which somehow made it all the more fitting that he should spank me. When he'd finished, and my poor bum was all red, he'd make me undress for the cane. Not because he particularly wanted to see me nude, but because it was better for my sense of remorse that I be naked. He'd make me touch my toes and my breasts would swing out under my chest embarrassingly big with my erect nipples betraying my excitement.

At that point my orgasm hit me. It was like an explosion, my back arching and my muscles going weak. I had my eyes tightly shut and my spare fingers clenched into the carpet, my head swimming with pleasure as the second jolt hit me. I knew I was gasping and panting, but was barely aware of my surroundings as my legs gave in and I collapsed on to my side to lie whimpering on the floor.

My first feeling as my orgasm subsided was one of utter shame. I had come over fantasies about men before, rarely, and fantasies about being punished before, notably by Miss Campbell. Never, though, had I come over the thought of being given a thoroughly humiliating whacking by a man, let alone an overweight fifty-something who liked putting young women in harness.

As I got somewhat unsteadily to my feet and began to arrange myself my shame gradually began to be replaced by a wry self-awareness. I'd done it and I hadn't been able to help myself, and the result had been among the best orgasms of my life.

I had had my much needed climax, but that didn't make my curiosity go away. After a quick wash and a change of panties I checked that Henry was firmly asleep and once more went into the library. This time I managed to find a sort of mobile step wedged against the end of a bookcase and hidden by a curtain. I pushed it into place and was soon, once again, engrossed in the albums.

The one I had picked first was the only one that told the complete story of one event. The others were more scrappy, but it didn't take me long to discover that my suspicions of Henry were correct. The third album I chose showed him exercising a blonde girl with freckles on a long rein. I recognised her as one of the girls from the first album and, on further investigation, it became clear that she was called Jean and must have been Henry's girlfriend.

33

Some of the photos showed parts of the farm in the background; rather a lot of them in fact. It was quite a shock to see the places I had come to frequent being used as pony-girl runs, spanking sites and scenes of other curious goings-on. Pony-carting was the mainstay of Henry's collection, but by no means its only subject. There were plenty of punishment photos: girls on their knees, over men's laps, over other women's laps, bent over tables, touching their toes and, in one case, a full photo-set of Jean receiving punishment bent over an upturned boat.

Most of the photos had been taken outside; not just the pony-carting ones, but plenty of tying-up and punishment shots as well as ones of Jean being naughty in public places. It astonished me to see how rude she was. Several showed her posing with her breasts or bum bare by the side of roads. One even showed her peeing in a ditch, with a cheeky smile on her face and a stream of golden pee running out of her open fanny. Oddly enough it was her delighted expression that shocked me the most. She'd obviously not merely allowed a man to photograph her in that most private act; she'd been actively showing off.

Uniforms were another thing of his. In addition to riding gear there were some military uniforms among the men, while several girls were in school uniform, abbreviated forms of military dress or, in one case, a little sailor suit with a skirt so short that it left the girl's panties showing.

I was already thinking of taking a more leisurely play in my bedroom but was determined to finish all the albums first so that I was really worked up by the time I started. I was also wondering how to enhance the experience. Seeing all those naked and half-naked girls indulging in strange and rude activities had left me feeling very innocent, not to mention inexperienced. I had thought that my own preference for my own sex and bottom smacking made me pretty adventurous, but some of the behaviour of Henry and his friends made my own look very tame indeed. I knew that I would never really dare to wake Henry and ask him to spank me, but I was seriously considering warming my own bum just to see what it felt like.

The second shelf proved not exactly disappointing, but there was something less open, less playful about the pictures in the first two albums I looked at. They were also newer, dating from the end of the seventies and the eighties. The scenes were different as well, showing big, empty warehouses that seemed to me a lot less fun as a place to play in than the fields and woodland tracks of earlier pictures. There was also a man who featured in almost all of the pictures. There was something disturbingly familiar about him. He had the typical seventies wide-boy look: a garish blue suit with wide lapels, a kipper tie in bright orange, and a flowery shirt. He also had a big, brush-like moustache, and it was that which made me realise who he was: Mr Rathwell, a client of my father's firm.

This stopped me dead. Mr Rathwell was a property developer and one of my father's best clients, which meant that he was a frequent dinner guest. He was also an oily, self-satisfied lecher who could never keep his eyes off me. Whenever he visited I tried to stay seated because of the way I knew his eyes were fixed on my bum when I walked. Of course when I was seated he'd stare at my boobs instead, and I had always made a practice of wearing baggy, shapeless clothes when I knew he was coming. He also had a knack of making half-sexual, half-insulting little remarks, phrased as jokes but always calculated to bring a blush to my cheeks.

Now here he was running pony-girl events. Up until then the idea had been fascinating me. Rathwell's involvement put a new slant to it. Henry was nice, friendly, open and kind. He had never pinched my bottom or tried to watch me in the bath, or any of the things he might have done while I was staying with him. More importantly, he treated me as an equal. True, he was in his fifties and seriously fat, but he was also really sweet natured. Besides, there was something about him that made the thought of being spanked over his lap exquisitely exciting, at least now that I knew what he had been up to when he was younger. Rathwell was very different. He was younger than Henry and kept his body in pretty good trim, but his personality was simply obnoxious. He was a creep, and the idea of him spanking me made me shudder.

Actually, the difference in their personalities was fairly evident in the photos, or so it seemed to me. At Henry's events everyone always seemed to be smiling and laughing, while at Rathwell's they were much more serious. Another major difference was that where with Henry the winners got a rosette and the losers got smacked bottoms, with Rathwell no one had rosettes and there was no evidence of what happened to the girls who lost. It struck me then that it wasn't so much what one did, but how one went about it. Henry was a true sensualist but Mr Rathwell merely thought he was.

It had just about stopped raining and, after my discovery of Mr Rathwell's involvement with Henry's pony-girl activities, I felt I needed a breath of fresh air. Pausing only to put on a pair of boots, I went outside, finding the weather fresh and cool. Everything about the farm now looked different, taking on a pattern that I had never before noticed. After seeing the pony-girl photos it was obvious.

The track that led from the main road was curved and sheltered from prying eyes by thick beech hedges and sections of densely grown wood. The oddly shaped tracks that ran through the woods had served as a run for exercising both horses and pony-girls. The big field behind the house was the main racetrack, the two strangely geometrical spinneys within it forming the centres of the course as well as being used for some of the more elaborate games they had played. The big field rose to a ridge with a thick hedge planted along the top, providing further shelter even though there was more of Henry's land beyond it. The yard was where they had put things together, the old stable blocks serving as well for pony-girls as they had once done for horses.

It was a masterpiece, and the effort Henry had expended on his obsession amazed me. I knew that he was fanatical about detail and not doing things by half, but his creation was none the less astonishing. It also looked completely innocent to anyone who didn't know what was going on, like myself before that day. I had assumed that the shapes of the woods and the way the fields were laid out was just the way things had once been, with small, irregular fields in place of big, orderly ones. Possibly it had started like that, as many of the trees were fully grown and must have pre-dated Henry by hundreds of years. Most were younger and clearly planted on purpose.

Another thing revealed by the pictures was why certain trees were commoner than others. The two spinneys – one circular, one rectangular – were mixed birch and hazel, both trees which I had just learnt provided ideal switches for girl's bottoms. Nothing seemed innocent any more and, as I explored, I began to realise just how naïve I was. Trees set on their own had once been used as hitching posts or to tie girls to for whippings. Henry's collection of ornamental grasses such as bamboo and pampas had once provided canes, green and pliable for the bottoms of losing competitors. The stile that separated garden from fields had once served as a whipping block. The heavy iron rings set in the stable walls had once tethered naked, excited women.

Had it been anyone other than Henry who had created this monument to perverse sex, I think I would have been terrified. As it was he had been the perfect gentleman to me and I couldn't imagine him ever behaving otherwise. The pictures also showed that, whatever had happened, however many girls had been punished, however many stripped and humiliated, all of it had been done with their full consent.

By the time I had finished exploring I had made up my mind. My curiosity was just too strong. I was going to have to ask Henry about it.

How to go about it was a very different matter. When I got back indoors he was taking tea and had a place already set for me. I joined him and sat sipping tea and wondering how best to broach the subject. From what I had seen he hadn't done anything for at least ten years, which made my task harder. The idea of bringing the subject up and finding that he was now against it horrified me. There was also the problem that he might find my interest intrusive or resent my having inspected his albums.

These considerations stopped me from saying anything over tea and, afterwards, he retired to his study to work, leaving me at a loose end. I went out again, my mind full of strange images as I walked out across the big field and into the woods. I still wanted to play with myself again, and even went so far as to choose a sheltered bit of wood where I could pull my top up and play with my nipples. It was really too cold, though, and for some reason I didn't feel quite safe, so I ended up returning to the house feeling thoroughly frustrated.

I went to my room, but found that Brenda – who was Henry's maid and general housekeeper – was hoovering outside. As she had a habit of popping in to talk to me without warning, that scotched my plan of stripping and treating myself to a leisurely hour of really wanton masturbation. Instead I contented myself with writing to Ginny and Susan describing my discoveries of the morning. This turned me on even more and, by the time Brenda came in to tell me that dinner was ready, I was absolutely bursting.

As always, dinner was a complex and formal affair. Brenda had gone home and Henry had cooked. He was a good cook, providing all sorts of delicacies of which I had never heard. This was all very well, but it meant that he was forever going back and forth to and from the kitchen and it was impossible to pin him down to a conversation long enough for me to get the subject round to pony-carting.

Finally we finished and retired to the drawing room. Henry poured himself a large glass of Armagnac, did the same for me, and then sprawled himself in his favourite armchair. He looked thoroughly content, the picture of a man without a care in the world, also homely and safe. I had drunk the best part of a bottle of wine and was feeling bold, even reasoning to myself that there was no way he could be anything but delighted by my interest in his sex life.

He moved his legs into a more comfortable position, giving me an unintentional view of the bulge in the front of his trousers. It looked impressively large although, as I had never seen a man's cock in the flesh, it was hard to make comparisons. He turned towards me and I looked away, hoping that he wouldn't notice my blush.

'Horrible day,' he said evenly. 'One would hardly think that it was July. I hope you found something to do with yourself?'

That made me blush again, thinking of how I had played with myself on the floor of his library and fantasised over him spanking me. If he noticed he gave no sign, merely throwing me a questioning look.

'I was reading in the library,' I said and then decided to take the plunge. 'Henry, do you know someone called Mr Rathwell: Morris Rathwell I think it is?'

'Yes, dreadful man,' Henry replied, giving no sign that there was anything odd about my question. 'He's one of Charles's clients, isn't he?'

'Yes,' I answered, with a lump rising into my throat. Charles was my father although, even at eighteen, I never called him by his first name. The way Henry used it so casually made him seem dreadfully senior. My resolve faltered. Fortunately his next question gave me an opening that it was hard to back out of.

'I bought a field from him,' Henry was saying. 'Twenty years ago it must be, but we never did get on. Why do you ask?'

'I . . .' I began, almost chickened out, and then took the plunge. 'I saw some photos of him in the library.'

I stopped. Henry was looking at me in surprise. It didn't seem likely that his library contained any other photos of Mr Rathwell, so he had to know what I'd been up to.

'I'm sorry,' I stammered hastily, suddenly wondering what I'd done. 'I didn't mean to pry, I just . . .'

'No, no, please,' he interrupted. 'I don't mind at all. As long as you don't, that is?'

The tone of his question registered surprise, disbelief even, and I suddenly realised that his attitude was anything but what I had expected. He didn't see me as a nosy child who'd been interfering with his personal things; he saw me as a well-mannered young woman who should have been both shocked and defensive on discovering that he had once made a practice of treating women like horses.

For a long moment neither of us spoke. Then Henry started to laugh and I couldn't help but join in. Finally he stopped and took a good-sized gulp of his brandy, shaking his head as he turned to me.

'Well, you do surprise me,' he said. 'There was I worrying whether I should hide certain things from Charles's sweet little daughter, and all the time you've been reading them. You don't even seem shocked.'

'I was a little,' I admitted, 'but it all looked really good fun, and then I worked out how you'd arranged the grounds for your pony-carting events. I couldn't resist asking about it.'

'I'm delighted you take such an enlightened attitude,' he answered. 'Might I even dare ask if the idea of being a pony-girl appealed to you?'

'More a driver,' I said, noting a new, and wicked glint in his eye and then a slight flicker of disappointment as I stated my preference. 'I'd be prepared to give it a try, though. I don't believe in doing things to other people that you're not prepared to have done to yourself.'

'A fine philosophy,' he said, brightening immediately, 'but not one that is shared by the regrettable Morris Rathwell. I do hope you're not thinking of joining his pony-girl club?'

'Does he still do it then?'

'I believe so, but if you want to play, I recommend getting a group of your own friends together. Rathwell is not really quite the thing.'

'Why? I mean, I know he's a creep, but that's just because of the way he behaves to me.'

'I can imagine,' Henry sighed. 'He is crass, coarse and mercenary. He lacks style and imagination and, frankly, does not deserve to be part of such a wonderful sexual diversion. Let me explain and perhaps you'll understand better. Here, have some more Armagnac.'

I held out my glass and let him fill it, then sat back, eagerly awaiting what he was going to tell me. I'd done it and was feeling thoroughly pleased with myself. What's more, Henry's attitude to unusual sex seemed no different from his attitude to everything else, which was somehow reassuring.

'It began in the late sixties,' Henry started, 'when I met a girl called Jean. You probably saw pictures of her in my albums. Before she met me she'd been with this fellow in Carlisle, and his great thing was to ride her around with her wearing a bridle. It was pretty makeshift by all accounts, but she'd developed a taste for it and so when they broke up and she came up to London, she wanted a partner who'd treat her the same way. We met at a party and ended up in bed. I was a bit surprised when she wanted to be mounted and taken from behind with a strap held between her teeth, but I've never been one to turn down a bit of fun, so I went along with it. You don't mind me describing things like that in detail do you?'

'The more detail the better,' I assured him. Actually I had been picturing him taking the freckled blonde girl whose photos I'd seen from the rear while she held a leather strap between her teeth. It made an enticing picture.

'We got on well and moved in together a few weeks later,' he continued. 'The fantasy developed slowly over the next year. I made a proper bridle for her, and a girth strap with a saddle of sorts. I was a heavy chap, even then, but she could take my weight.'

'Did you spank her?' I asked, slightly surprised at myself despite the ease with which the question had come out.

'Oh yes,' he answered. 'I've always felt it perfectly normal for a healthy young man to want to smack his girlfriend's bottom. Unfortunately not all girls agree. Jean was quite keen, though, especially if it was done as part of her pony fantasy. I bought a riding whip for the purpose

41

and often used to give her a few strokes to jolly her along before I mounted her.

'Anyway, when Jean and I had been together a year or so I inherited the farm from my uncle Ralph and we moved in. Things went well, and both of us were keen to see if we could find other partners to take our fantasy a step further. We advertised discreetly and, after several failures, managed to get a small group together. We used to meet here or at another farm called Rushdean.'

'I saw the album,' I said, remembering the name from the first book I had looked at.

'Ah yes. August seventy-two,' Henry said wistfully. 'That was a good meet. Maybe the best. There were eight couples and, at the end, we lined up six of the pony-girls and switched the lot of them. You must have seen the pictures?'

'I did,' I answered.

'And you liked them, I take it?'

'It really excited me,' I admitted. 'Did you do the caning?'

'Some,' he answered. 'Each of us gave each girl one stroke. Ah, six beautiful bottoms all in a row. So pretty; especially when they'd been whacked. Not a sight I'm likely to see again, I fear.' He paused, sipping his Armagnac thoughtfully as he remembered the scene.

I was wishing I had been there, although it had happened before I was born. The thought was making me excited and, from the way the bulge in his trousers had expanded, I could see that he wasn't exactly indifferent either.

'So,' he went on, 'we continued, with three or four meets a year of varying size and success. It was a proper little club by then and I started to lay out the grounds to create an ideal venue for our meets. By seventy-five things were really at their peak, in terms of numbers anyway. Really we should have stayed small, because with more people it was impossible to make sure everyone knew each other well enough to really let ourselves go. Morris Rathwell joined about that time, and soon proved one of our most enthusiastic members. He was the first one who hired a girl as his pony instead of bringing a genuinely interested girlfriend. We'd never let single men in before but, after that, the club decided to let anyone in who could bring a willing girl. That spoilt it for me, as it meant huge meets at which half the girls were only there for the money. The number of people who turned up at the farm was beginning to attract attention as well, so I finally put a stop to them using it.'

'That's a shame,' I put in, feeling that I ought to say something sympathetic as Henry obviously felt strongly about what had happened.

'Very true, my dear,' he sighed, 'especially as it was the cause of Jean and I splitting up. We'd been together twelve years and I was pretty upset. For some reason she blamed me for the way everything had got out of hand, and perhaps we'd both changed over the years. Anyway, we parted company in eighty-two and I stopped going to meets. By then Rathwell had taken over and was running them in warehouses which his property company had temporary charge of. He'd introduced betting, spectators and an entry fee; big prizes, too, in place of our pretty rosettes. More than half the girls were professionals as well, so it wasn't really my thing anyway. I suppose I could have found another pony-girl if I'd tried, but after Jean I didn't really feel like it and so I just drifted away. I've been to Rathwell's as a guest once or twice since – just to try and recapture the spirit – but it's really not the same.'

'Maybe it could be again,' I suggested, sorry that the end of the story had left Henry rather morose.

'I fear I am too old and fat,' he answered. 'Yet, and I say this without the slightest intention of pressuring you, should you wish to so indulge yourself I would be more than happy to lend advice and the experienced hand of a mature pony master.'

He looked at me, hopeful but not at all demanding, and very different from the greedy, lecherous looks I remembered from Morris Rathwell. With his combination of pathos, gentility and the offer of indulging myself in such an exciting sexual fantasy, he had me unable to resist.

'I'd love to,' I answered. 'Maybe I could bring a friend up and you could help us train?'

'You have no idea of the effect that offer has on a poor old man,' he answered, drawing his breath in and expelling it. 'Were I less of a gentleman I might be forced to make a suggestion I might later regret.'

Well, that was one way of putting it. It was hardly surprising that he was excited, and I could see that his cock was stiff in his trousers. I also knew he wouldn't push me into anything I didn't want to do. With the wine, the brandy and my earlier frustration, I was just about ready to play.

'You never know, I might accept,' I said quietly.

'You mustn't tease,' he replied, but his tone was very different from his actual words.

He moved, making a quick movement to adjust his cock inside his trousers as he did so.

'Maybe I could help you with that,' I said, borrowing the line Ginny had used on her farm labourer boyfriend. I know she'd have said it confidently, though, while my own voice sounded small and urgent.

'Would you really?' he answered, moving so that he was turned fully towards me.

I nodded, a tiny, nervous gesture, but enough to convey my willingness. My fingers were shaking as he started to unbutton his fly, my eyes riveted to his crotch. I'd never even seen a man's cock before and now I was going to help him come. I didn't even really know what to do, but didn't want to admit my innocence and could only think of Ginny's vivid and joyful descriptions of what she'd done with her various lovers.

I slid off my chair on to my knees, still watching as he undid the last button and started to open his fly. The bulge inside his pants looked enormous; a great hump underneath the material. I swallowed and moved forward as he pulled the front of his pants forward, revealing first a thick brush of hair and then his penis. There was a heavy roll of flesh around the neck, exposing the brighter pink of the sensitive-looking head. The shaft was solid and covered

44

in veins under the dark-pink skin – a sight at once obscene and delicious. It also looked huge; far too big to fit inside a girl's vagina. Of course that's ridiculous, as it was nothing like the size of a baby's head, but this was my first time and it was actually quite scary.

He pushed his pants further down, pulling his balls out, then taking hold of his cock and rolling the fleshy foreskin fully off the head. I moved a little closer, not sure if his action was a specific invitation. Maybe he wanted me to take it in my mouth, in which case I was willing. Anything as long as he didn't expect to fill my vagina, or worse, my anus, which I was sure wouldn't be able to accommodate him.

I smiled at him and licked my lips, pulling my top up as much to postpone the moment when I had to take his cock as to show him my tits.

'Beautiful,' he breathed, starting to pull harder and faster at his cock.

It was now fully erect, standing up over his balls like a great pillar, incredibly male and absolutely terrifying. The foreskin had stretched back, leaving the head swollen and glossy with the pressure. His hand was wrapped around the shaft, his fingers not quite meeting his thumb, moving slowly up and down and squeezing with each stroke. I found myself stroking my nipples, each little bump of sensitive flesh nudging my fingers in turn and producing a sharp prickle of pleasure. He slid forward on the chair and opened his legs, pushing his cock out to me in a clear invitation.

Still uncertain about touching it or taking it in my mouth, I edged forward on my knees and wrapped my breasts around it. As my soft flesh enfolded his rock-solid erection I found myself against a man's penis for the first time. It felt great, hard and urgent between my boobs, as he began to push it in and out between them.

'Oh, Amber, you are lovely,' he breathed as I squeezed my breasts together more firmly.

The head of his cock was nudging my neck with each push, while my face was pressed against his waistcoat, his

45

great belly soft and fleshy beneath it. I'd done it, I'd let his cock touch my flesh; an act that broke down my final reserve. I felt deliciously dirty, wanting to do something even ruder. All of a sudden I badly needed it in my mouth. I rocked back on to my heels, looking directly at the erection I had promised to indulge.

I felt as if I was being hypnotised, drawn towards the bloated penis that was pointed directly at my face. My mouth opened and I leant forward, hardly believing what I was doing even as I gaped to take the head into my mouth. I tasted it, salty and rich with a flavour I had never imagined, rubbing my tongue against the turgid flesh. It slid in until I couldn't take any more and I began to suck, moving my lips up and down his shaft as I remembered Ginny explaining how it should be done.

Part of me felt detached, amazed, even horrified, at what I was doing. Everything in my upbringing made the act of sucking a man's penis seem debased; a dirty act that was also an admission of the girl's inferiority to the man whose cock she was sucking. At a more animal level it was absolute bliss, rocking slowly back and forth with that great cock sliding in and out of my mouth, my breasts heavy in my hands with the nipples hard between my fingers.

Despite my best efforts to take it all in, there was still a lot of cock sticking out of my mouth, and Henry now moved his hand to the base of the shaft, making a ring of a finger and his thumb and starting to masturbate himself into my mouth. He had started to groan, which I guessed meant that he would come soon. Too soon for me; I had a lot of sucking to do before I was satisfied.

I drew back, leaving his cock shiny and wet with my saliva, an inch in front of my face. Again, borrowing a leaf from Ginny Linslade's book, I poked my tongue out and traced a slow line up the underside of his penis, then kissed the top and began to nibble ever so gently with my teeth. He sighed and then gave a sharp intake of breath, which made me think I had overdone it with my teeth. I pursed my lips around the head of his cock, sucking to make it better.

His hand closed gently on the back of my head, pushing me down. I went with it, allowing his cock to slide deep into my mouth. He grunted and jerked hard into me. Suddenly, and completely unexpectedly for me, my mouth was full of something warm and slimy which tasted of salt. I gagged as the head of his erection nudged the back of my throat, the come filling my cheeks and then spurting out around his shaft. He let go of my head and took his cock in his hand, jerking at it frantically even as I pulled back. A second jet of come erupted from the end even as it left my mouth, catching me in the face, then a third, splashing on my top and breasts.

My mouth was full of it and it was trickling down my chin, soiling my top and dribbling on to my breasts. I felt utterly dirty as I began to rub it into my nipples, wet and sticky against the hard buds of flesh. He had lain back, his breath coming hard and fast, his cock already deflating as he watched me play with my breasts.

'Come if you like, don't mind me,' he said in between gasps.

I was far too excited to care about showing off in front of him. I lay back, pulling my trousers down to get at my pussy. My panties followed, down to my knees, as I lay on my back with my legs rolled up, bottom and fanny pushed out towards him. I pulled my legs right up, my knees touching my breasts as I put my hands between my legs and began to masturbate. I felt beautifully rude and unashamed as I did it in front of him, one hand keeping my pussy lips open, the other teasing my clitty with little flicks. I could taste the male come in my mouth and feel it on my face and breasts. My top was soiled and now my jeans and panties probably were too. My legs were up and my fanny wet and ready in front of him. He'd even be able to see my bumhole – wrinkled and dark in between my full bottom-cheeks – begin to pulse as I knew it did when I came.

Then I was screaming out, coming under my own fingers, my mouth wide open in my ecstasy, my tongue covered in Henry's sperm. It went on for ages, peak after peak, until I couldn't stand it any more and stopped rubbing at myself. After that I could only lie exhausted on the floor, breathing almost as hard as he had been.

Neither of us spoke for a long time. We were both lost in our own thoughts. I did feel a little shame, but not enough to make me want to cover myself or run out of the room or anything silly. It had felt so natural with him; uninhibited and easy, and the exact opposite of how the social conscience that had been so carefully drummed into me dictated I should have felt. True, it wasn't the first time I'd gone against it – after all, it also forbade fancying other girls – but it felt great to have broken the code of respectable behaviour so thoroughly.

I finally got up, walking to the bathroom with my trousers and panties held up at thigh level. Henry gave me a big, cheerful grin and then followed. We washed together without hesitation, Henry's first words after our sex being a half-jocular apology for the state of my clothes. I replied with a shrug and a smile.

'Where, if I may ask,' he said a moment later, 'did you learn to give fellatio like that? Not at Bridestowe Ladies' College, I'll warrant.'

'Sort of,' I replied. 'Actually, I'd never even seen a man's cock in the flesh before this evening. I've listened to plenty of descriptions, though, from my friend Ginny Linslade. She's the one who's going to be my pony-girl.'

Three

'I had supposed that your pony would be some lucky boyfriend,' Henry remarked the following morning as we ate breakfast. 'And while I'm bound to say that after yesterday evening your preference for girls came as something of a surprise, I admit to being delighted.'

'Wait until you meet Ginny,' I replied around a mouthful of bacon and egg. 'Then you'll be more than delighted.'

'I can hardly wait,' he answered. 'Term ends next week you say?'

'Yes. I'll write to her this afternoon,' I promised. 'I'd ask my friend Susan, too, but she's off on a Caribbean holiday her parents booked as a present for getting into Oxford.'

'Very impressive,' he admitted, raising his eyebrows slightly. 'Do you know I've often found that it's the really clever ones who have the most extravagant sexualities. The dirtiest minds, to put it another way.'

'Perhaps,' I answered, uncertain if my own – more limited – experience supported his idea.

'It is frequently the case,' he insisted. 'Although not an invariable rule. Given that you prefer girls, I trust that I didn't impose on you in any way last night?'

'No, no,' I assured him. 'I don't dislike the idea of sex with men. I just . . . oh, it's hard to explain. I don't really think of you as a man anyway. Whoops, sorry, that sounds really bad.'

'I shall take it as a compliment,' he answered, 'if only because I think I understand what you mean. It is perhaps not the physical man for whom you feel distaste, but the actual reality of the great majority of modern males. I would personally like to think that I do not belong in their ranks.'

Henry had put my outlook more or less exactly into words, helping resolve the uncertainty over my true feelings which had afflicted me since puberty. Thinking over what he had said, I lapsed into silence. Inevitably my train of thought led back to the present situation and the prospect of further exploring the world of pony-girls.

'Henry,' I said after a while, 'do you think we could go along to one of Mr Rathwell's events, just as spectators?'

'I'm sure we could,' he answered. 'But please, Amber, do be careful of Rathwell. He is certainly not above threatening to tell your father unless you allow him some sort of sexual favour. Charles, while one of my oldest friends, is not the sort of man to lightly accept what he would doubtless see as perversion in his daughter. What he would think of me for corrupting you while *in loco parentis*, I do not care to imagine.'

'You're right,' I admitted, 'but he couldn't really expose me without exposing himself as well.'

'Ah ha, a good point,' Henry replied, 'but would you risk calling his bluff? Remember that he puts a considerable amount of business Charles's way. As he is a most valuable client, Charles is unlikely to argue with him.'

'I'm not so sure about that,' I responded. 'Daddy's pretty hot tempered, and obstinate, too. Still, it would be a risk so I suppose we'd better not.'

'Do not be so hasty, my dear,' Henry continued. 'Morris's events are pretty big nowadays by all accounts and he is hardly likely to be looking for his accountant's daughter in the crowd. A black wig to cover your distinctive tawny curls, some make-up and a leather domino to hide your eyes, and he'll never notice. I shall call him after breakfast and find out when the next event is planned.'

As soon as we had finished eating we went into the study. Henry eventually managed to find Mr Rathwell's number. The answer came quickly and I stood by Henry's chair listening to our end of the conversation.

'Morris, good morning,' Henry began. 'This is Henry, Henry Gresham. Yes, nearly two years. Very well thank you. Now, Morris, tell me, you are still running the pony-girl club, aren't you? Splendid, splendid. When's the next event? Yes I'd like to come – Fifteen pounds? What, even for the man who introduced you to pony-carting? Oh, very well, if you insist. No, two, I'm bringing a friend. A young woman; she's eighteen. Oh, a bit over medium height, shortish hair, very pretty. I'm not sure, quite large. Well I'd guess 36C, not that I see it matters. Fairly slim, not more than twenty-six inches at a guess. Very fine, well rounded. Look, Morris, never mind my friend's figure, when is the next meet? The twenty-eighth? Excellent. Hmm. No, just as spectators. Five thousand! Good heavens Morris, I have to say, you don't do things by halves. Very well, I'll put a cheque in the post. The nerve of the man; he actually insisted we pay admittance! Me!'

The last remark had been addressed to me and not to Mr Rathwell, Henry turning to face me as he put the phone down.

'I'll pay for my ticket if you like,' I offered.

'No, no, I wouldn't hear of it,' Henry replied. 'It's just that he has the nerve to charge me. I mean, if I hadn't introduced him to pony-girls in the first place the wretched man wouldn't even have a club. When I ran meets here they were free, and for friends only. I'd never have thought for an instant of charging to attend. He's expecting about three hundred people to turn up at some huge warehouse in the Lee Valley. He's been advertising at clubs apparently. God alone knows what sort of people will be there. Worst of all, he's charging five hundred pounds as a stake for the main race and offering five thousand to the winner!'

'Five thousand!' I echoed.

'So he says. Fair-sized prizes for other places as well,' Henry continued. 'The mercenary little toad. I never thought I'd see the day.'

Henry was evidently upset, although I wasn't quite sure I understood why. After all, the fact that Mr Rathwell had commercialised pony-carting to such an extent didn't stop Henry from enjoying it in a more playful form with Ginny and myself. Also, an idea was already taking shape in my mind. Ever since I had arrived at Henry's I had been becoming more and more fond of the country life and the idea of business school had been becoming more and more repellent. My idea was to try and set myself up with some sort of trade that allowed me to stay in the country. My father would be furious, but there would be nothing he could do about it short of cut me off, which my mum would resist bitterly. The problem was that I had only a few hundred pounds to my name and such ventures need finance. Five thousand pounds might not be enough to buy an existing business, but it would be sufficient to get me started on something new, especially with the contacts I had been making while at Henry's.

All this went through my mind while Henry fumed over Mr Rathwell's commercial exploitation of the pony-girl club. I shared his dislike of Morris Rathwell but, as Henry had pointed out, at a big meet there wasn't any real reason why I should have any contact with him. This would be true even if I was racing, because Henry could do all the talking and I could race in disguise. On the other hand, it didn't seem a tactful moment to broach the subject of wanting to race to Henry. Instead I decided to make a suggestion that would take his mind off Mr Rathwell. It was a fine day, if a little cool and, being Saturday, we were alone on the farm.

'Would you have time to show me your cart and the harness Jean used to wear?' I asked.

'Certainly I would,' he answered, brightening immediately. 'Allow me one more cup of coffee and we'll see what we can do.'

I waited while he drank his coffee, fidgeting under the table in my impatience. After the previous evening there was no uncertainty between us, and we both knew that I would probably be spending most of the morning naked and perhaps end up with a few stripes across my bottom. Not that we'd slept together. He hadn't suggested it and I hadn't felt ready for something that would certainly have meant the loss of my virginity. Possibly it had something to do with my revelation that I preferred girls to men, but I think it more likely he simply didn't want to push me. I had, after all, done exactly what I offered: eased the head of sexual tension that he had built up while we talked by helping him to reach an orgasm that he had evidently needed very badly.

He finally put his cup down and rose from the table, dabbing his lips with a napkin as he pushed his chair back. I got up, too, and followed him to the scullery where we put on boots as the ground was still a sea of mud from the previous day's rain. He took a large, rusty key from a hook on the wall, found a can of oil on a window ledge, and we went outside.

The yard – which had once been the scene of such strange and wonderful sexual activity – consisted of the rear of the house and two blocks of stables on either side. The fourth side was open to the big field, and brick arches joined each stable block to the main house; one leading to the garden, the other to the drive. Following Henry, I entered the left-hand stable block and stood patiently while he tried to open a door. Eventually the lock gave in, the door creaking open to reveal a dusty chamber hung with cobwebs and illuminated by a yellowish green light coming through the single, algae-spattered window.

Inside was what I immediately recognised as one of the carts from Henry's pony-girl photos. Unfortunately it was in less than good condition, rusting metal and peeling paint spoiling its once elegant design. The harness hung on the wall and was in little better shape. The leather was dry and worn, the brass tarnished and dull. It all seemed to me rather sad, like the ghost of something that was once vibrant and brisk. I expected Henry to feel the same, only more strongly as it had once been his pride and joy and would also undoubtedly invoke memories of Jean. As it was he was surprisingly cheerful, inspecting the equipment

53

with what was evidently an experienced hand. I soon found out why.

'You mentioned last night that you would be interested in trying the experience yourself,' he remarked, rather too casually.

'I'm game,' I admitted, 'but all this tack is a bit past it, isn't it?'

'Nothing that a bit of elbow grease and a lick of paint won't put right,' he answered. 'It was a tradition with the club that the girls always kept their tack in tip-top condition, acting as grooms as well as ponies, as it were. You have rather too dominant a personality to slip easily into the role of pony-girl, but I feel that after a few hours of polishing and painting you might find yourself in a more submissive frame of mind.'

'Maybe,' I answered doubtfully, 'but I'm not sure. I generally like smartening things up, and it doesn't make me feel submissive.'

'True,' he responded, 'but then, if you're willing, we would add one or two touches in order to add a little spice to what would otherwise be a boring task.'

'Oh yes?' I queried.

'Indeed,' he continued. 'For instance, I might demand of you that before lunch you turn this room into the immaculate pony-girl stable it once was. You'd work freshly spanked and naked and, when you had finished, I'd make an inspection and dish out some suitable punishment for any inadequacies I might note. Just an idea, of course, but I would enjoy it immensely.'

'I bet you would,' I answered, looking around me at the mess.

Remembering Susan's fantasies of punishment and humiliation I'm sure she would have loved to have been in my place. Personally I wasn't so sure, especially with the prospect of some unspecified punishment at the other end if I didn't come up to Henry's expectations.

'What would my punishment be?' I asked.

'Whatever you fancied,' he answered with a shrug. 'I would suggest, say, a stroke of the cane for every imperfection and another for every ten minutes you take over three hours.'

I didn't reply, quite eager for the spanking but wondering how it would feel to be caned if I messed up. I had seen the way Ellen Campbell bucked and squealed under the little quirt I had whipped her with. On the other hand she had been in ecstasy, begging me to whip her harder. By the end she had been so turned on that she'd wanted to play with herself while I whipped her. Would I feel the same? It was very tempting to find out, and if she could take a whipping then why not me?

'I'll do it,' I told Henry, 'but be a bit gentle with me. I've never even been spanked before, not properly.'

His face lit up with a beaming smile that made him look more like Santa Claus than ever. It was all too obvious that he was delighted at the prospect of giving me my virgin spanking.

'Excellent,' he said. 'There is one important point, however, that you should know if we are to play such games. I will ignore all your cries and pleas, even tears, but should you say the word red, I will stop immediately. I always used the word amber, after traffic lights, to mean slow down. In your case I think yellow would be a more appropriate word.'

'Fine,' I agreed.

'Good,' he answered. 'In that case I think we'd better get started. Fetch a chair from the scullery.

'Yes, sir,' I answered, giving him a deliberately cheeky curtsy.

A weak fluttering feeling had started to build in my stomach. I was about to be spanked over Henry's lap and it would undoubtedly be with my bottom bare. I'd put a skirt on that morning and that would shortly be being lifted; but it was the thought that he would then pull my pants down that redoubled the butterflies.

I ran for the chair, placing it in a dry patch to the side of the door. Standing by it with my hands folded in my lap, and my head hung, I waited for him. It was the pose I'd always imagined Susan being in when I fantasised about

55

spanking her. Now I was doing it, and I was about to get the same treatment I had always wanted to give her. I resolved to take it well, allowing my feelings to show but not making an undignified display.

Henry approached, his expression one of cool amusement as he seated himself. He patted his lap, kind but authoritative. I obeyed his gesture, glancing at his face and then lowering myself across his lap with a reluctance that was not completely fake. His arm curled around my waist, pushing down the small of my back and fixing me in place. I hung my head down and shut my eyes, intent on the physical sensation of what was happening to me. My skirt moved against the sensitive flesh of my thighs and I realised that he had hold of it. Despite my willingness this came as a shock, and a little shiver passed through me.

I had always tried to appear mature and controlled in front of Henry, and I'm sure he didn't realise just how inexperienced I really was. Certainly he seemed entirely indifferent to the feelings of shame and panic that were welling up in me as he lifted my skirt. When I'd sucked his cock I'd been fairly drunk, which had helped to keep my inhibitions down. Now I was feeling the full humiliation of my position, and the disgrace of making a sexual display of myself.

He lifted my skirt slowly and, by the time I knew my pants were showing, I was almost in tears. I was trembling, too; I was feeling a mixture of sexual excitement and utter shame far stronger than I had imagined it would be even when masturbating over being spanked. It was no fantasy now, but reality. His thumb was in the waistband of my panties, pulling them open so that he could see down the back of them; easing them slowly down, exposing my bottom inch by inch. The edge of the elastic popped over the tuck of my cheeks and I knew I was bare. I could feel the air cool on my nakedness, and Henry's eyes burning on to my nude bottom.

He settled my panties around my thighs, chuckling to himself as he adjusted his position to force my bottom higher into the air. For some reason it felt very fat and very prominent – a wobbling ball of flesh that I could do nothing to hide or protect. The urge to cry had retreated, but I was breathing heavily, almost panting, as I braced myself for my beating.

Henry's hand came to rest on my bum, pushing in as if to test my texture. The hand lifted and I started to whimper and kick in anticipation of the slap. It didn't happen, which made it even worse. I knew I wasn't being very brave. In fact I was being pathetic, especially when I thought of how blissfully Susan had offered her bottom to Ginny and myself.

Instead of commencing my spanking he put his hand back on my bottom and began to stroke. He was very gentle and I found myself soothed by the light caresses on my bare skin. He did it as if he were stroking a cat; long motions that ensured my whole bottom got an even share of attention. Sometimes he'd cup a cheek and squeeze it, and occasionally his little finger would brush my crease, nudging the hair only an inch from my anus. This began to make my pleasure rise faster, but also increased my humiliation. I began to wonder if he'd pull my cheeks open to inspect the little hole, or maybe spread my legs to show off my fanny as well. Actually, I wasn't sure that it wasn't already showing; it's hard to know when you're head down over someone's lap.

'Oh well, I suppose I'd better be merciful,' he said, abruptly halting his exploration of my bum.

I thought he was going to let me down and I immediately got a sharp pang of disappointment. That wasn't what he meant, though. His grip changed and, an instant later, his hand landed hard, right in the centre of my plump, naked seat. I squealed in shock, only to get another smack a bit lower and even harder. The third landed and then the fourth – too close together to allow me to compose myself – then more in a hard, relentless rhythm that immediately had me kicking and squealing. It stung crazily and I quickly lost any hope of retaining the slightest shred of dignity. I knew my legs and bum-cheeks were opening as I thrashed, and that Henry was being given extremely intimate flashes of my fanny and bottom-hole. I didn't care, though, just as long as my desperate wriggles reduced the pain of my spanking.

I could feel the shocks going right through me, but especially my sex. As he continued, the pain receded, a warm throbbing feeling replacing it. My bottom felt hot and deliciously sexy as he continued to slap at my bouncing cheeks. It was really starting to arouse me, making me feel warm and yielding. I knew my squeaks and protests had turned to sighs and uninhibited grunts of pleasure and, at that moment, would gladly have submitted to a heavier beating or the penetration of my mouth or vagina, even of my anus, with anything short of a cock.

Henry stopped suddenly, pushing me off his lap to sprawl on the ground. My bottom was burning and throbbing and I couldn't help pushing my hips back and forth as if hoping for entry. He made no move to take advantage of me and I returned slowly to my senses, getting to my feet and pulling my pants back up under my skirt.

'Thank you,' I said, still somewhat breathless.

He smiled back. His face was quite red, as was the palm of his hand.

'My pleasure,' he replied, shaking his hand ruefully, 'although I fear that even with a bottom as well upholstered as yours a hand spanking is not entirely painless to administer. Maybe I should have used a hairbrush.'

'Another time,' I answered, blushing at his reference to the size of my bottom.

'And so to work,' he continued. 'You will find that having been spanked adds greatly to your enjoyment of the task, as will your nakedness.'

I remembered that I was supposed to do it in the nude and quickly began to peel my clothes off. I handed each item to Henry, finishing with my bra and panties. Even though he'd seen everything and had just spanked me, I still found myself blushing as I bared my breasts to him. I then hesitated and turned my back to him to take off my pants.

'Very pretty,' he remarked as he took my discarded knickers. 'Now put your hands on your head and turn around.'

I obeyed, blushing red as I showed off for him. He admired my naked body with a casual, almost proprietorial expression, although I'd half expected him to take his cock out. He evidently had more control as, once I had turned around a couple of times, he told me to stop.

'Stick your bottom out. Let me see how red it is,' he said.

I did as I was told, showing him the effects of my spanking.

'Very pretty,' he repeated. 'Put your boots back on, go and look at yourself in the mirror, and then you had better start work. Oh, and put a ribbon in your hair.'

I followed his instructions, running up to my room to fetch a big red ribbon and then going into the bathroom to look at myself. My bum showed a deep pink in the mirror with occasional darker marks on the crests of my cheeks. The spanking had brought goose bumps up, too, making my poor bottom look sensitive and thoroughly beaten. I admired myself for a while, even bending down and opening my cheeks to show my fanny and bumhole. I had to admit that I looked sexy; at least my reflection was certainly adding to my already considerable sexual high.

Naked but for Wellington boots and my red ribbon I went back outside. Henry was still sitting in the chair, but had fetched a couple of things while I was upstairs. One was a book on pig keeping, which he was reading with a nonchalance that I hoped was at least partly put on. The other was a long, wicked-looking cane with a crook handle which immediately put a lump in my throat. He caught my look of apprehension and returned a sinister grin.

I'm obstinate, and don't back down easily, but just for a moment as I looked at that sleek, threatening implement designed specifically for girls' bottoms, I wondered if I could handle it. As it was my bum was warm and rosy and, as Henry had predicted, I felt pliable and submissive.

Maybe if I hadn't been so turned on it would have been different, but I doubt it.

'We'll start from now, shall we?' he said, glancing at his watch. 'I make it eight minutes to ten o'clock. I'll be generous and give you until one before your penalty time begins, but if you delay my lunch, then woe betide you.'

I hastened to my task, trying to figure out the best way to do it even as I ran for the stable. Inside was truly filthy, with the grime of years mixed with cobwebs, mud and old leaves. The obvious first step was to get everything out and clean the room, then I could worry about making it all spick and span. I wasn't going to chicken out, but if I could avoid the cane by fair means I certainly would.

Two and a half hours later I realised that I was going to do it. The room was scrubbed and clean and the fittings on the walls painted glossy black, as were the metal parts of the pony-cart. I had done the woodwork in a mid-green, as it was the only other paint I could find, yet the pony-cart certainly looked smart when I had finished. I had oiled and polished the harness, leaving the leather supple and shiny and the brassware gleaming. There were one or two places were corrosion and age had made a really good finish impossible but, as it was nearly thirty years old, I felt I had done a pretty good job. I'd had to lay it out on the floor because of the wet paint, but I didn't feel that I could be criticised for that. There had also been various posts, stakes and oddly shaped bits of wood at the back. I had no idea what they were for, but cleaned them and painted them black anyway. Odd flakes of old paint remained here and there, so I had used the green paint to imitate the patterns as best I could.

Personally I was considerably less smart than the room and gear. I was running sweat for one thing, the day having become considerably warmer since I'd started. I was also fairly liberally smeared with paint and mud, not to mention oil, brass polish and various cleaning fluids. Still, no part of my orders said I had to be clean, and so I contented myself with hosing off the worst of it before making my final inspection. I had done everything possible, leaving nothing that could be fairly criticised.

I declared myself ready for inspection at exactly one o'clock, Henry rising from his chair and sauntering over to the stable. He had collected a notebook and pencil earlier and now held these as he looked at the results of my three hours of hard work.

'Hmm, fair,' he remarked, tapping his pencil against his chin. 'Sadly I'm afraid it is not good enough for you to escape a beating.'

'Why?' I protested.

'Well, for a start my racing colours are crimson and black,' he answered. 'This green colour is quite inappropriate and in fact is the colour I used for the front door.'

'I couldn't find anything else!' I protested, feeling distinctly piqued at the injustice of his criticism.

'Don't be a brat or it will be two strokes per error,' he chided me.

I shut up, looking on as he went over things and feeling increasingly sulky as he tutted and hummed to himself.

'Right,' he finally announced, drawing a line under the column of ticks he had made in his notebook. 'First there is the use of the wrong colours. Second, the paint is still wet –'

'Hey!' I interrupted.

'Amber,' he replied warningly.

I shut up again as he continued.

'Third, you have not put everything back in place. Fourteen objects in total, tut tut, Amber. Item seventeen is then the flat tyre on the cart and I feel I should add two strokes for corrosion on the brassware: one because you did the lock but forgot to polish the key, and one for your surly, petulant attitude. That makes twenty-one, but I think twenty-four is a better number, don't you?'

'No!' I protested. 'I couldn't help any of those things, and you've no right to add three strokes just because I'm sulky about getting the cane when I haven't really done anything to deserve it. It's not fair!'

'A single word will release you from your obligation,' he reminded me.

I looked at him, feeling the tears start in my eyes at the sheer injustice of what was about to happen to me. He was looking down at me, stern and self-satisfied, certain of his right to put the cane across my bare bottom. I felt humble and weak, a bad girl objecting to a just punishment simply because she doesn't want it. I thought of backing down but I couldn't. Standing naked and filthy in front of him, my bottom still pink where he'd spanked me, I realised that I did actually want the cane. The tears were running freely down my cheeks as I got down on my knees in front of him.

'Well?' he asked, tender yet still forceful.

'Beat me, please,' I sobbed.

'That's better,' he answered. 'Now kiss my boots.'

I obeyed, putting my lips to each shiny toe cap and tasting the mixture of leather, polish and mud.

'Good, you're learning,' he continued. 'Now crawl out into the yard.'

Once more I obeyed, following him on all fours as he strolled out into the bright sunlight. Most of the mud had dried, but he made sure that I ended up in the middle of a fair-sized puddle of it. My tears had stopped, to be replaced with an intense feeling of trepidation as they dried on my cheeks. Henry kicked my boots gently, making me open my thighs and present him with my parted bottom.

'Down,' he ordered. 'Put your breasts in the mud and pull your back in.'

The cool water touched my nipples as I responded, stopping with my face an inch from the surface. I arched my spine, knowing full well that the action made my bottom part yet further and would fully reveal my fanny and anus to the man who was about to cane me. It felt shameful and dirty but also so good, unrestrained and somehow irresponsible because, after all, I was only doing as I was told.

If I was accepting of making an exhibition of myself, then the thought of punishment was hard to take. He walked away and I watched his retreating legs out of the corner of my eyes. My heart gave a jump as he picked up the cane and flexed it experimentally. He was really going to do it – beat my poor red bottom and leave me with twenty-four welts to teach me to do as I was told and do it properly. At a deep level I knew it was fantasy play, but it felt real and it wasn't going to make the caning hurt any less.

As he walked back I found myself kicking my feet in the mud in the agony of anticipation. He came to stand next to me, gauging his stroke. The cane tapped my bottom, right in the middle. I closed my eyes and gritted my teeth. There was a swish . . .

And nothing. Henry had deliberately cut the cane through the air to make me think it was going to land on my bum.

'Bastard!' I whispered, teeth still clenched against the expected pain.

'Now, now,' he remarked. 'Temper, temper.'

I had relaxed a tiny bit, only to catch the first real stroke of the cane full across my bottom when I was least expecting it. I yelped and bucked, instinctively reaching back to rub my stinging bottom. I could feel a roughened line where it had raised a welt and, for some reason, this really turned me on. I got back in position and stuck my bottom up, again bracing myself while I thought of the strange feeling of the line of roughness on my own flesh.

The second stroke was worse; perhaps because I was a expecting it, perhaps because it was harder. Looking behind me I realised that he was being a lot softer than he need have, applying the strokes with only about half the swing he might have done and not really putting his weight into it at all. Realising this, I found myself wanting it harder, but didn't know why. The third stroke landed, again making me squeal and jerk. Half of me was begging him to stop, incredulous at why I should allow myself to suffer such pain and humiliation. The other half wanted more, and harder.

'Harder please, Henry,' I whispered, looking at my tear-stained reflection in the puddle beneath me.

My mouth was slightly open, my eyes wide and wet with

tears. It looked really exciting to see myself like that, and another thought immediately came into my head: the need to see someone else in the same position. The next stroke caught me and I gasped at the impact, then again at the next, harder still and immediately afterwards.

He started to cane me properly, then – hard, rhythmically and methodically – always waiting just long enough between strokes to allow me to get back into my proper position when my legs kicked out or I wanted to feel the growing cluster of marks on my poor, whipped bottom. By twelve I was whimpering; by eighteen my face had gone into the mud and was covered in it; when the twenty-fourth fell my knees were as far apart as they would go and I had slid a hand back between my legs, intent on finding my clitty and taking myself to orgasm.

'Twenty-four,' he said merrily, 'and well taken for a beginner.'

'Carry on, Henry,' I begged, starting to rub at my clitty.

'Tut tut, my girl, we'll have none of that,' he answered, running his fingers over my bottom to feel the welts. 'This was just to get you in the mood. Now I intend to give you some basic pony-girl training, so it's time you got into your harness.'

'Please,' I said, 'I want to come.'

'Patience,' he answered, but smacked the cane across my bottom again anyway.

'Please, Henry, cane me,' I pleaded, still rubbing at myself. I didn't want to come without the added thrill of the cane smacking against my unprotected bottom, but knew I'd do it anyway.

'Oh, very well, you have been a bit of a brat so I dare say you deserve it,' he said, planting another hard stroke across my cheeks.

I started to concentrate on my orgasm as he once more began to cane me. My bottom was on fire, but it was all pleasure now, a burning sensation that made me dizzy. Being called a brat had added to it, triggering a fantasy I'd previously enjoyed. I imagined myself a stable girl, which I really had been the previous summer. The owner had decided to punish me for cheeking him and had made me strip and work in just my wellies. Then he'd made me kneel nude in front of all the other staff, and had beaten me with them all watching in delight and laughing at me.

I started to come, yelling at Henry to beat me harder as my orgasm rose up inside me and burst, flooding me with a sensation as blissful as any I had had before and compounded by the pain in my bottom. The cane struck again, making me scream from the unbearable intensity of it all, then it was past and I was relaxing, sinking slowly down on to the mud only to have the cane strike again.

'Ow!' I squealed, the stroke creating real pain across my already heavily punished bottom. 'Stop, Henry! Red! Red! Red! I've come!'

'Sorry,' he remarked, 'I thought you were right at the peak.'

'No,' I managed, letting my body collapse into the welcoming cool of the wet mud. 'That was . . . that was something else. Thank you, Henry. Thank you for teaching me.'

I trailed off, completely exhausted by my experience and really not feeling up to playing pony-girls at all.

'You don't really want to harness me up now, do you?' I asked.

'No, no, I was just teasing,' he answered. 'I wouldn't really deprive you of an orgasm and, besides, it's time for lunch.'

'Good,' I sighed. 'My bottom is burning all over. Is it all right?'

'It's not bleeding, if that's what you mean,' he answered. 'You took a good forty strokes, though, and you shouldn't expect to sit down comfortably for quite a while. Still, you'll find that the ache brings pleasant memories and I'll enjoy watching your beautiful bottom all the more while we train this afternoon. For now I'll get the hose so that you can wash yourself before coming into the house, then I'll make lunch while you clean up properly. I'd advise putting some antiseptic cream on your bottom, too. It's not really wise to rub a freshly caned bottom in the mud.'

65

'Good idea. I will,' I answered, climbing unsteadily to my feet.

'Oh, and one other thing,' Henry said as he reached the hose reel. 'Remember that if you put yourself in a position where escaping punishment relies on being perfectly behaved, you'll never, ever get away with it. The pleasure of seeing your face when you realise it's all been in vain is just too great.'

'I'll remember that,' I said, promising myself to make good use of the same technique when I got my hands on Ginny. I had genuinely been in a sulk when I found out that I was going to get caned, and the emotion had added a delicious extra layer to the whole experience.

Saturday lunch was something of a ritual with Henry and consisted of a spread of delicious things like quail's eggs, York ham carved from the bone, cherry tomatoes and ripe cheeses, all washed down with a dry, delicate pink wine that he favoured. I took mine sitting on a cushion, an act which reminded me of what we'd been up to despite Henry calling a break in our play so that he could concentrate on lunch. Personally I'd have been happy to stay naked and act as his maid but, as always, he insisted on doing the preparation and serving himself.

By the time I'd finished I was in a happy, sleepy mood; feeling naughty but not very energetic. Henry of course hadn't come, but I couldn't imagine that he had really been indifferent to playing with me and wasn't at all surprised when he asked very politely if I'd mind taking his cock in my mouth. I got on my knees without hesitation, giving him a leisurely suck while he sipped his wine. It felt naughty and rude but really quite a natural thing to be doing and I suffered none of the qualms of the night before. He took me by the hair when he was about to come and I swallowed obediently, tolerating the slimy, salty sensation of his come for the sake of his pleasure.

We sat, talked and sipped wine for a long time after that, only deciding to continue my training when the heat had begun to fade from the day. Most of the conversation had revolved around how to get the best out of the fantasy and so, when the time came, I was already pretty excited at the prospect of being put in harness. Henry had explained how it generally took more time and care to get someone who normally preferred to dominate into a submissive role. That had been the idea of the morning's activities – or at least partially.

The sheer complexity and technicality of it all fascinated me almost as much as the sexual potential. There seemed to be a term for everything, either adapted from the world of horses and carriages, borrowed from the language of sexual deviancy, or just made up. Beforehand I hadn't even known the use of the words dominant and submissive to describe people who enjoy giving and taking respectively. These seemed to be very basic while, on a more detailed level, I had learnt that the thing I had whipped Miss Campbell with was technically a quirt, that a switch was a different implement of punishment but also someone who enjoyed both domination and submission, and even that the almost unimaginably dirty act of peeing on someone for erotic pleasure was called either urolagnia or watersports. Henry also had a pretty good idea of what makes girls excited; at least dirty-minded girls and from a perspective that was both dominant and male.

He was certainly right about one thing – since having my bottom whipped I'd been much more pliable and eager to be told what to do. This was just as well as, when we went over to the stables, I got my first taste of really being under someone else's physical and mental control. As before I stripped to my boots, only now feeling a good deal less self-conscious about it. He put me in the bridle first. This was a sort of cage made of leather straps that buckled into place to secure my head with a leather bit in between my teeth and a set of reins hanging down my back. Just wearing it was enough to set me shivering again and when he had fixed the upper strap to my hair with my red ribbon, I pushed the bit out with my tongue to ask Henry to fetch a mirror from the house. All I got was a smack on the back of my thighs for talking with the bit in my mouth, which he had already told me was forbidden.

'One more word and I'll cane your thighs,' he remarked casually.

I shut up, waiting while he fixed the rest of the harness on to me. First there was a belt that encircled my waist, clinching me in very tightly so that my chest was forced out and my hips somehow seemed wider. Leather wrist-cuffs followed, designed to clip on to the shafts of the cart but also to fasten together. Henry pulled my arms behind my back and locked the cuffs, leaving me unable to protect myself except with my feet. Matching ankle-cuffs took care of that, hobbling me so that all I could do was stand there waiting for my legs to be released. The feeling of helplessness was really strong, and combined with my sense of being on display and the tingling ache of my recent whipping to produce an extraordinarily intense sexual awareness. Henry heightened this further by coming round in front of me and taking a leisurely feel of my breasts about which I could do absolutely nothing. He felt them exactly as he wanted to, weighing and kneading them in his hands, rubbing my nipples erect with his thumbs, and then going back behind me to bounce them as if testing a pair of melons for quality.

After a full minute of this I badly wanted to touch myself but, of course, I couldn't. Instead I whimpered and shook my head in the hope that he would be merciful. He wasn't, and instead laughed, slapping my thighs again just for the hell of it. He threw my reins over a ring set in the wall, which I knew meant that I wasn't to move; not that I had the choice.

I was left squirming my thighs together to try and get some friction to my clitty, while Henry opened the upper half of the split-level doors nearest me and then went outside. The cart was where I had left it, drying in the sun along with the other pieces of newly painted gear. He dabbed his finger on the underside of the seat and looked at it, shaking his head sadly. I could see the green mark and knew that the paint was still wet, which presumably meant no pony-carting until the next day. Henry shook his head and gave the flat tyre an exasperated kick, then walked out of my range of vision towards the opposite stable block.

There was nothing I could do but wait. For all I knew he'd gone off to have his afternoon nap while the paint dried. He usually went to his room after lunch, but today had had me suck him off and had then sat drinking and talking with me. The amount of wine I'd drunk was something I was beginning to regret, not because of the mild buzz I was getting from the alcohol, but because my bladder was beginning to feel full. My waist belt made it worse, constricting my tummy and pressing on my bladder. It only had a couple of settings and had obviously been custom-built for Jean, who was a fair bit smaller than me.

By the time Henry reappeared I was beginning to wriggle – not with sexual frustration but with the need to pee. He hadn't retired to bed but had put on work overalls and was carrying a great armful of equipment. I tried to get his attention but didn't dare push the bit out for fear of getting my thighs caned. My bottom was aching and sore and he had already explained that a whacking on the thighs was a good deal more painful and not nearly as sexy. 'Bums for caprice, thighs for correction,' he had said, and I didn't want to dispute his dictum, especially if the forty cane strokes across my poor behind had merely counted as caprice.

I was about to call yellow and ask to have my ankles and wrists unfastened long enough for me to relieve myself when Henry went back inside. He had set up a pair of blow heaters which were aimed at the underside of the cart, with an extension lead trailing back towards the kitchen door.

'Just nipping into Hertford for a repair kit,' I heard him call from outside my range of vision.

'Hey!' I called, frantically trying to get the bit far enough out of my mouth to shout properly.

It was too late. Even as I called I heard the door of his Land Rover slam. A moment later the engine started. I was alone, in bondage, and badly in need of a pee.

Henry's departure did more than merely add to my frustration at the prospect of wetting myself. It also made me feel far more vulnerable. I began to realise how safe it felt to have Henry around. Not only was he big and solid physically, but he owned the land and everyone who came to the farm deferred to him. It wasn't likely that any of the farm workers would visit him on a Saturday. If there was a crisis they would always phone first.

Now it was different. Henry wasn't there to fend off callers and there was just a chance someone might come by. I had met his workers, mostly coarse, earthy country boys. If any of them found me harnessed up and obviously involved in some sort of kinky game it seemed very unlikely that they would hold themselves back. All they'd have to do was tip me over into a kneeling position or roll me on to my back with my legs up and they'd have unrestricted access to my virgin fanny. Maybe there'd be more than one and they'd take turns, putting their cocks in me one by one until I was sore and dripping sperm from my open, soggy vagina. Ginny had once said that if she was too wet and open men sometimes expected to put it up her bottom, not that she had let anyone. I wouldn't have the choice, and I could easily see a man preferring the tightness of my anal ring to putting his cock into a vagina already wet with my juice and his friend's sperm. I'd always had a thing about my anus, finding the idea of men wanting to put their cocks up it even more alarming than the idea of having my virginity taken. It was a dirty thing to do as well; unbelievably so.

I tried to calm myself, realising that I was almost certainly getting in a fuss over nothing. Nevertheless I shuffled along until I could see only a small angle of the yard and the big field beyond it. If my fears of molestation were groundless, then my fears of wetting myself certainly weren't. The strain was becoming unbearable and, before long, I was having to stamp my feet up and down to stop it happening. My ears were strained for the sound of Henry's car and my fanny was clenched tight as hard as I could manage. I heard a sound in the distance – a car engine. Relief flooded through me, only to fade as the sound passed, leaving me sobbing in frustration. I bent forward a little because it eased the pressure, sticking my bottom out as – for the third time that day – tears of frustration began to well up in my eyes.

Then it just happened. There was a damp feeling between my thighs. I squeezed desperately but it was already trickling down my legs, warm and wet on my skin. I'd wet myself – a realisation that filled me with embarrassment. For a moment I managed to control my stream, creating a sharp pain in my tummy. It was too much for me and I let go. My pee sprayed out from between my tightly closed thighs, splashing on the floor behind me and running down my legs and into my boots. I made a last despairing effort to control myself and then gave up, filling my boots to the ankles and making a huge puddle on the floor beneath me. Despite the shame of what I'd done, the feeling of relief was exquisite. As the gush slowed to a normal stream and then a damp trickle I found myself sighing in pleasure.

I was only crying a little but I'd done it and now it was too late. Henry was going to see me standing in my own puddle and, when he did, he was bound to want to put me through some new and humiliating punishment; painful too. It would probably be my thighs. A thought that made me shiver. At that moment I heard the sound of another car. This one came down the drive, and after a moment of panic thinking it might be someone else, I heard Henry's deep voice calling out to me.

He came into the stable to check up on me, glancing first at my tear stained face and then at the puddle on the floor.

'Are you all right?' he asked, sounding desperately apologetic.

'I suppose so,' I answered weakly. 'I'm sorry, I just couldn't help it.'

'No, no,' he insisted. 'I should be apologising, not you. I should have realised you'd need to pee after all that wine. Shall I release you, or would you just like a hug?'

It was that question that broke down any final reserve I might have had about submitting myself to Henry. He didn't dismiss my accident as trivial and demand that we

71

got on with it, nor did he assume that as I was a bit upset I necessarily wanted to stop playing. Instead he gave me the choice. I asked for a hug and he immediately put his arms around me, stroking my hair and soothing me without any regard for his boots and overalls getting wet with my pee.

'I used to love making Jean wet herself,' he said as he finally stepped away, 'and I admit I was going to ask how you felt about it ...'

He trailed off, evidently hoping for a response.

'I'd do it again if you wanted,' I answered, not entirely sure about my own feelings but with a lot of my embarrassment taken away by his response. 'Can I be a pony-girl now please?'

'Of course,' he responded. 'As soon as I've fixed the puncture and as long as the paint's dry.'

When he had unfastened my ankles he took my reins and led me out into the yard. A brief hose down cleaned my legs and feet and there I was – stark naked but for my harness and waiting to be put through my paces. It felt glorious; the ache in my bottom and the memory of everything else we'd done during the day combining to take me so far out of myself that I really did feel as if I was owned and under Henry's orders.

He tied my reins to a ring and went to hammer one of the posts into the ground in the centre of the yard. This done, he picked up a long coil of rope and attached one end to my bridle. Walking me behind him with the rope thrown over his shoulder, he went to the post and attached the other end of the rope to a groove near the top. It was obviously an exercise post, designed to warm me up.

'Run round until I'm ready for you,' he ordered as he walked clear. 'And I want to see smart neat steps: walk, trot and high-step as I explained to you. Five laps of each.'

I set off, trying to remember the way I was supposed to walk. He had explained, but I hadn't expected to be told to do it without him there to instruct me and I couldn't remember exactly what I was supposed to do. Instead I did my best to imitate the straight-legged gait of a walking horse. This earnt a murmur of approval from Henry and then a smack on my legs for trying to be clever.

He went to fix the cart, leaving me to my warm-up. I completed the five laps of each gait, trotting and high-stepping to the best of my ability, relishing the feeling of being under orders but wishing I could see myself from Henry's position. When I stopped, my thigh muscles were a little warm and my breathing a little deeper. I was pretty fit, yet Henry looked as if he weighed a good twenty stone and the prospect of pulling him in the cart made me think that I was going to get a good workout.

When he had finished repairing the cart he pronounced the paint dry and began to peel off his overalls. Underneath, to my surprise, he was in full riding gear, lacking only the traditional pink coat. He did look magnificent – every inch the master – and I felt a flush of pride in being his pony-girl. He had also secreted a riding crop somewhere, which he was now tapping against one highly polished boot as he walked towards me. I gave a little whinny, now thoroughly in my role. Henry smiled and stopped to admire his prize.

'You are beautiful, Amber,' he said, and I could tell that he really meant it.

'Stamp once if I may photograph you,' he continued. 'It would be nice to have a record of your first time as a pony-girl.'

I stamped, eager to record the moment. He walked back to the house and returned with a camera, taking several shots of me from different angles before he was satisfied. He concentrated on my head and full-length views, finishing with a couple of close-ups of my welted bottom. Only then did he untie me and lead me over to the cart.

I found myself trembling hard as he took my wrist-cuffs from behind my back and fixed them to the eyes at the ends of the shafts. It was now fixed to me, something I was obliged to pull if I wanted to move, exactly like a draft animal shackled to its load, which was what I was.

'Kneel,' Henry ordered sharply, waiting until I had knelt down in the dust of the yard before climbing over the shaft and settling himself into the seat.

'Rise,' he commanded, 'then walk on.'

I stood up, expecting the strain of at least a proportion of Henry's not inconsiderable weight. To my surprise it was no great effort, and, when his crop tapped lightly against my right buttock in the walk signal he had told me about, I started off without difficulty.

He walked me around the yard at first, allowing me to get used to responding to the feel of the bit in my mouth and the way it tugged to change my direction. The feeling was truly extraordinary. All the human freedoms that we take for granted had been denied me. I was naked, casually naked as if it was of no consequence whatever that the most intimate areas of my body were on show. I was forbidden to speak, I was attached to a cart which it was my job to pull, and my least movements were being dictated by my master.

True, I'd had to be beaten and humiliated before I could really get my full pleasure out of being a pony-girl but, now that I was there, the experience was all the better for it. Henry had certainly judged me well, but then I probably wasn't the first strong-minded woman he'd put between the shafts.

When he decided that I was following his instructions adequately, he turned me out into the big field, aiming for the gap between the two spinneys. This was slightly uphill and harder work. By the time I reached the gap I was panting and sweating profusely. He turned me to the left, angling me around the circular spinney, then giving me a touch of the whip as we started downhill. He was very gentle, giving only light flicks to guide me, which was just as well considering the state of my bottom.

I broke into a trot, moving easily but scared that if I went too fast I'd be unable to stop the thing. Henry was more confident, flicking the reins against my back and repeatedly tapping my bottom until I was almost running. I doubt if I could have controlled my rush if he'd steered me into the yard but, as we approached, I felt a tug at my left cheek and took a long, low arc to the side, passing the end of the stables and moving back up the field towards the tip of the rectangular spinney.

I'd been surprised how easy it was when I started; now on that second uphill run I realised I'd been wrong. Beyond the spinney the ground rose more sharply, climbing to the ridge and the tall hedge that barred the view from the fields beyond. By halfway I was really straining, digging my toes into the soft grass and grunting with the effort. Henry urged me on with flicks of the whip, which quickly began to smart against my bruised and sweat-soaked buttocks. It was sheer obstinacy that drove me on, though, and I made the ridge. I thought he'd rest me but, instead, he turned me into a sort of pocket where the hedge doubled back on itself. I made the final effort, collapsing gratefully to my knees as soon as Henry gave the order. My muscles were aching with the strain and I was panting hard, too exhausted to wonder what he had in mind for me.

'Face to the ground,' he ordered.

I put my face in the grass, lifting my bottom, acquiescent to the whipping I expected to receive. It would be my thighs, I knew it. The idea obviously tempted him and soon they'd be as red and sore as my poor bottom. I'd behaved well, but that wasn't important. If he wanted to beat me, he would – just for fun. He had climbed out of the cart and was tapping the riding crop against his boot. This was it.

'At this point,' he began, 'it is traditional for masters to whip and then mount their pony-girls. In this case, however, I intend to forgo the pleasure of your vagina. You are wet and undoubtedly ready for entry, as I'm sure you know, while years of riding at Bridestowe have left you with no hymen to speak of.'

I'd thought that there was nothing left that he could do or say to humiliate me. That did, remarking casually on the intimate details of my anatomy and the fact that I was not obviously virgin.

'As I'm sure you also know,' he continued, 'your delightful anus tempts me, but I have no wish to hurt you and so will restrict myself to giving you a brisk thrashing and then take my pleasure between your magnificent buttocks. If you have no objection?'

I shook my head, actually meaning that he could do anything to me he liked. I was ready to be fucked and, at that point, I think I'd even have let him try to put it up my bottom. If he wanted to put it between my bum-cheeks instead then that was up to him, just as long as I could play with myself.

'You may masturbate if you wish,' he said, as if reading my mind.

He released one of my hands from its restraining cuff at my hopeful nod. I quickly put it back between my legs and started to dab at my clit. It felt good, my tiredness making the sensation feel as if it was coming through a fog in my head. Only when I had begun to sigh and push my bottom up expectantly did he start to crop my thighs, lightly at first and then harder. It stung, and when I cried out after perhaps the eighth stroke he stopped abruptly and I heard him move behind me.

An instant later something thick and hard settled between my bum-cheeks and I knew that he had put his cock between them, using the crevice of my bottom as a slide to masturbate in. His balls started to bang against my fingers and his hands closed on my hips. It was beautifully rude, with him humping my bottom, his belly resting on me and his shirt and jodhpurs rubbing against my sore skin. I stuck my bottom further up, keen to have his shaft in contact with the most sensitive areas of my rear, especially my anus.

It worked, and I started to come with him rubbing vigorously against me, stimulating my fanny lips and bumhole just as I was stimulating my clit. I squealed with pleasure, clamping my teeth on my mouthful of leather, dizzy and faint with sensation. My vision went completely red for a moment as I climaxed. There was a wet feeling between my bum-cheeks; his cock was sliding faster and more easily. He was groaning and I realised we'd come together even as the slimy feeling touched my bumhole. I still had my hand on my fanny, and the sheer filthiness of having male come rubbed into my bottom-hole triggered a second spasm. I screamed this time, biting hard on to my bit. Only Henry's grip on my hips kept me upright, and he held me there until he'd fully drained himself between my cheeks, only then pulling back. I collapsed on to the grass, only vaguely aware of him unfastening my other cuff.

He stripped me slowly, leaving me completely nude in the warm grass, aware only of my aching, satisfied body, the green of the beech leaves around me, and the blue of the sky above. I must have fallen asleep within minutes, but I don't remember it.

Four

When I woke up that afternoon in the little enclave of beech hedges it was to find Henry with tea set out on a tray just as if he'd been serving it in his drawing room. We drank and talked, discussing the day. I didn't even bother to dress, although he'd brought me my clothes, which shows how relaxed I was.

Later, I realised that something felt fundamentally different. I suppose a critic might have said that I'd soiled myself; lost my innocence. Actually I'd never been that innocent, just inexperienced. The true difference was that I'd now done what previously I'd only imagined and in consequence felt more alive and self-confident than I ever had before. One might have thought that doing such submissive things would have had the opposite effect, but it didn't, perhaps because it had, after all, always been my choice.

We rested all Sunday, with me doing nothing more energetic than giving Henry's cock a leisurely suck after lunch. He retired for his nap after that, leaving me to walk in the grounds. I felt myself drawn to the hedge enclave, where I lay on my front in the grass, completely secluded from the rest of the world. After a while I pulled my dress off and lay back down to sun myself. I was nude underneath, having decided to do without panties because of my tender bottom and then taken my bra off when I'd sucked Henry so that he could roll my dress down and feel my breasts.

I was soon thinking about what had happened the day

before, and how it would have felt if I'd surrendered my virginity in that very place. I'd been willing and, at eighteen, felt it was about time, yet knew that if I wanted Henry to do it I would be able to choose my time and place at leisure. Feeling thoroughly happy, I began to stroke my bottom, feeling the still-smarting skin and delighting in the afterglow of a good whipping. My fingers soon went down between my cheeks, touching my anus and then slipping inside so that the tight ring closed on the top two joints. Rolling to the side I put my other hand between my legs and began to masturbate, bringing myself off very slowly as I imagined how Henry's cock would have felt inside me.

Over the next week I masturbated more often than ever before. The bruising on my bottom made me constantly aware of my sexuality and, each time I touched myself or caught sight of my rear view in a mirror, I'd want to come. In the end I had to force myself to do it no more than twice a day because my fanny was getting sore. Keeping Henry entertained also kept my interest in sex up and, after each dinner when Brenda had gone home, I'd suck him or strip for him or put myself in a rude pose for him to come over.

We managed a bit more pony-girl training in the evenings and, by the following Saturday, I knew most of the terminology. I was also considering making my own harness to replace the old and ill-fitting set that Henry had made for Jean nearly three decades before. We spent most of the day training and rolling the track through the woods to make it once again fit for pony-carts. I enjoyed myself and had a lovely orgasm at the end, tied to the training post, which I was discovering – the hard way – also served as a whipping post.

My heart wasn't really in it, though. I had something else on my mind. Two hundred miles away in Devon, term was finishing at Bridestowe Ladies' College and Ginny was coming up by the morning train on Sunday.

I collected her from the station myself, and we fell into each other's arms and kissed so fiercely that we drew a look of disapprobation from the ticket collector. We couldn't stop talking as we drove back to Henry's farm, and I even stopped in a lay-by to show her my bottom. Henry had used a training whip on me, leaving long, thin red lines. There were only twelve of them, laid over the now-fading marks of the previous week's much sterner punishment. Ginny was delighted and a little shocked, wanting to touch and offering to kiss me better. I let her, putting my hand inside her blouse as our kiss turned into a full-blown snog. I think we'd have had each other then and there if a car hadn't come past but, as it was, we rearranged ourselves amid fits of giggles and I drove on.

I had been a bit concerned that she might be unimpressed by Henry, but she accepted him with her normal easy-going enthusiasm. Being a farmer's daughter she in fact had considerably more in common with Henry than he and I, and were discussing unusual pig breeds within minutes of meeting.

She was also full of enthusiasm for the idea of trying our hand at Mr Rathwell's race, especially when the sum of five thousand pounds was mentioned. Her optimism was a great deal higher than Henry's or mine. We had intended to go to the meet, size up the competition and compete only if we thought we had a realistic chance. Ginny had no such reserve. Instead she pointed out that she was young and fit and that if Mr Rathwell had been running the club for a decade or more then most of the pony-girls would be older and were probably housewives or had sedentary jobs during normal life.

This conversation was held over lunch, with Henry making the occasional noise of uncertainty and me remembering how many times Ginny's boundless enthusiasm had landed us in trouble while we were at school. Finally Henry pointed out that as he still had the records of all the race times from when they had been held at the farm, it should be easy to determine whether or not Ginny and I stood a chance as driver and pony-girl.

Even Ginny had to accept that a practical test was the best way to find out how good she was and so, in the mid-afternoon, we went into the yard. Henry had brought a deck chair out, which he set up and lowered himself into, producing a large and antique stopwatch and a notebook. That seemed to suggest that it was up to me to get Ginny ready, so I braced myself to try and make a good job of my first time as a pony-girl mistress and ordered Ginny to strip.

'What about footwear?' I asked Henry as Ginny began to peel her clothes off with a nonchalance that made me envious despite my increased acceptance of my own sexuality.

'I imagine that anything goes,' Henry answered. 'Some girls always liked spike heels. They look sweet but are totally impractical for racing. Barefoot's not a good idea in case someone's toes get run over, so we always used to be practical about it.'

'Keep your trainers on, then,' I told Ginny.

'Sure,' she answered, kicking her jeans-shorts and panties off her leg to leave herself nude but for her socks and trainers.

She looked gorgeous, and she knew it. I couldn't help but stare, my attention making her giggle and then put her hands on her hips and stick her tongue out at me. Ginny at eighteen outshone just about anyone. A little taller than me, and golden haired where I'm tawny, her figure was all curves: very full breasts, a soft, slim midriff, hips that would have been too wide on a shorter girl, long, well-formed legs, a wonderfully full, rounded bottom and a neat fanny hidden in a nest of dark gold hair. Her bright eyes and perpetually cheeky look added the final touch to her beauty, and having her naked in front of me had my fingers itching to take her in my arms.

Remaining cool and aloof, as I had been taught that a good mistress should, I told her to put her hands on her head and then walked slowly around her. It was less than a month since the day she and I had been caught having sex together with Susan Wren, but where Ginny's naked body had once been a daily sight in the school showers, now it was a treat. It was also mine to play with, something that made all the difference and which she clearly accepted without reservation.

'What do you think?' I asked Henry.

'Well, she's certainly all woman,' he answered. 'Her legs are fine, and her muscle tone looks good.'

I reached out and squeezed Ginny's thigh, finding it firm underneath despite the rounded, feminine shape.

'But her breasts, while magnificent, might tend to make running awkward. They must be bare, remember. Still, we shall see.'

I cupped one of Ginny's breasts in both hands, running my thumbs up over the nipple. She closed her eyes, purring with pleasure as I stroked her. My own breasts pretty well fill my hands, but each of Ginny's took two hands to really get hold of. The feel of her in my hands was lovely, but I had to agree with Henry; in a long race they would become uncomfortable, which would be a disadvantage. It had been the same with long-distance running at school, and then she'd been allowed to wear a top. Indeed it had been compulsory to wear a top, I corrected myself.

'Mr Rathwell holds his events indoors, doesn't he?' I queried.

'Yes,' Henry answered. 'This one's in some huge warehouse in the Lee Valley.'

'Will that mean that the race isn't too long?'

'Yes, undoubtedly. Taller, stronger pony-girls might have an advantage.'

'We might be all right then. She can't help her boobs bouncing when she runs, but she shouldn't get sore over a short course. At school she always used to get teased about her curves. You don't think her bottom's too fat, do you?'

I gave Ginny's bum a playful smack, making one cheek bounce and wobble for Henry's assessment.

'Plump bottoms may be unfashionable,' he answered after a pause, 'but at the end of the day a ripe pair of cheeks is arousing and always will be. Besides, nobody could accuse her of not holding it well; her cheeks appear wonderfully buoyant, one might almost say pneumatic.'

'I agree,' I added. 'Still, no more flattery or she'll start giving herself airs. Let's give her a little practice and then try some times.'

I went to fetch the cart and harness, hoping that our intimate discussion of her body had left Ginny with the tingle of humiliation that had added so much to my own experience. Knowing her, it hadn't, but I was keen to at least try and give her the same depth of experience I had enjoyed myself.

The harness was as tight on her as it had been on me, especially the bridle, which fitted awkwardly among her mass of hair. As I struggled with the straps and buckles I determined once more to make a new one, certain that I could not only create a better fit but improve on Henry's design. Ginny submitted to being harnessed up without a murmur, only the increasing stiffness of her nipples betraying her underlying feelings. Only when she was fully harnessed and kneeling in the dust of the yard did she look at me and give any hint of how she felt.

Her lower lip was trembling a little, while her eyes were big and slightly moist. There was a flush to her cheeks and upper chest, and I knew that for all her poise she was strongly affected by the experience. I moved forward to stroke her hair and she leant her head against my thigh, rubbing her cheek against the material of my jeans in a gesture that was at once submissive and affectionate. It was that which brought home to me the full extent of what we were doing. Ginny was strapped up and otherwise quite naked and defenceless, kneeling in the dirt at my command. Far from feeling angry or degraded by the experience, she was eager to be soothed and caressed by me and, presumably, just as eager to obey my commands and taste the sting of my riding whip.

If being a pony-girl was exciting, then having one of my own was better, although I had yet to test the more intimate pleasures that my position as Ginny's mistress would allow me. Being beaten produces a strong mental sensation as well as the obvious physical one, and I had to admit I thoroughly enjoyed it. I fully intended to beat Ginny and make her come, and hoped that the almost purely mental thrill of punishing her would make my own orgasm as good as those I'd had under Henry's discipline.

83

Thinking of Henry reminded me not to leave him out, a topic I'd already discussed with Ginny while we washed before coming out.

'Be a good girl and I'll let you lick my fanny and maybe even suck Henry's cock,' I addressed my pony-girl, remembering the way Henry had so successfully teased me with the prospect of punishment and sex. I determined to give Ginny the same treatment. 'Behave badly and it's the cane for you.'

Ginny nodded, then put her head down as I mounted the cart.

'Rise,' I ordered, putting my feet on the rest bar.

She rose to stand, her beautiful bottom within reach of my whip and immensely tempting. The commands had been explained to her, and all that remained was to flick the whip against her right cheek and we'd be going.

'I'll take her for a quick warm-up first,' I called to Henry, flicking Ginny's bottom.

She walked forward, towing me easily behind her. I relaxed, or at least as much as I could with the sight of her in front of me. Angling her up the big field and around the circular spinney, I took in the sensation of driving a pony-girl for the first time. The cart felt stable, although it took a minute to get used to it. Ginny had no difficulty pulling me, not even on the slope. As I weigh perhaps half what Henry does this wasn't so surprising.

Moving her down the slope at a run was mildly exhilarating, but even at a sprint we moved far more slowly than a real horse would have pulled a buggy. I took her round again and on the second lap began to appreciate something that Henry had told me but which I had not really understood.

Controlling a pony-girl produces a slow, steady build-up of sexual tension. Just seeing a beautiful girl in her harness is exciting, as is the thought of controlling her. Actually doing so makes one's pleasure build and build, reaching a peak far greater than if one had merely satisfied one's initial lust. I suppose the same is true of any form of drawn-out sex play, but it is especially effective with a

84

pony-girl. It's fun to drive a pony-cart anyway, but there is the constant view of one's pony-girl's bare, bouncing bottom. She can be made to pose, too, perhaps kneeling in a position that not only looks exquisitely humble and submissive but parts her buttocks to reveal her fanny and anus. She can be caressed and teased, and can do nothing to dictate where her mistress's fingers go or how intimately she is fondled. Then there are the more subtle expressions of dominance, such as feeding her by hand, watering her from a bottle, and putting her in ribbons and other pretty things. Finally she can be mounted, still in bondage, and brought to orgasm.

Of course, mounting her really takes a cock to fill her with, which I naturally didn't have. Not that I would have to go without my ultimate pleasure, and various ways of making the best of Ginny's tongue were going through my head as I steered her in a last circle and drew her to a stop beside Henry.

'What course shall I take, then?' I asked.

'It seems sensible to go for a short one on the flat,' he answered. 'Take her out through the arch that leads to the drive, around the house, and back through the garden to here. That was always our short sprint course. Jean always used to manage about a minute and a half, but that was pulling me, so you'd better be able to do better than that.'

'What was the record?' I asked.

'I'll tell you when you've tried it,' Henry answered.

'Fair enough,' I told him. 'Rise then, Ginny.'

She rose again and responded to my rein and whip commands until I had her lined up at the point indicated by Henry. At the touch of my whip she took off at an impressive pace, sprinting down the drive so fast that I had to clutch the sides of the pony-cart. Turning across the front of the house nearly spilt us, but she managed to control our weight. The tyres crunched on the loose gravel where the car was parked, little stones flying up to either side of us.

I remembered to urge Ginny on as she made for the narrow arch that led into the garden, but still didn't feel secure about letting go with my hands. I knew I wouldn't look very elegant or commanding hanging on for dear life but, fortunately, there was nobody to see. For all the mental control of being in charge of a pony-girl, physically one actually feels more secure when in harness, which I suppose must also be true with real horses.

Ginny took the arch at full speed, brushing clematis against my face. Beyond was the garden, a large lawn studded with round flower beds and crossed by a geometrical design of pressed gravel paths. To get to the far arch by paths we needed to make for the centre of the lawn and turn sharply back on ourselves. I pulled at the reins to steer Ginny to the right, but she took no notice, instead bumping the cart up on to the lawn and making directly for the arch.

'Hey! Not on the lawn!' I called, once more nearly getting unseated by the bump when we crossed from path to grass.

Ginny took no notice, sprinting straight for the arch, turning hard through it and crossing the imaginary line by Henry's chair at full speed. Only then did she slow, wheeling the cart around and responding to my reins when I drew on them to bring her to a stop.

'Fifty-eight seconds,' Henry remarked, snapping the case of his stopwatch shut as he rose from the chair. 'A good time, but if you will excuse me I believe I heard Amber say something about the lawn.'

'You're in trouble,' I told Ginny as Henry's broad back vanished through the arch. 'From me as well as Henry, disobedient girl. Kneel and stay in position.'

Ginny knelt, allowing me to climb out of the cart and follow Henry into the garden. As I had expected, two ruts ran across the lawn where the wheels had sunk into the earth that was still wet from the application of a sprinkler.

'Sorry about that,' I said, walking up beside Henry and putting my arm on his shoulder.

'It's no great matter,' he replied, returning my friendly gesture with an arm around my waist. 'Indeed more than one race has been won by the same manoeuvre. If you look carefully you will see that the lawn still dips a little despite years of rolling.'

'We don't need to tell Ginny that, though, do we?' I suggested.

'My thoughts exactly,' Henry replied. 'Does she have any particular favourite fantasy we could turn into a punishment?'

'Not as such,' I admitted. 'She's really into showing off and being the centre of attention. She used to attract the lads at her farm by making sure they got a glimpse of her in the nude or something, as if by accident.'

'Something of an exhibitionist, eh?' Henry replied. 'Well, I know what do with girls like that. What about physical punishment and so on?'

'I'm sure she'd be willing to try, but I don't think things like sexual humiliation get to her the way they do to me. It wouldn't be fair to say her tastes are simple, but they're more down to earth, perhaps. Still, I'm sure she'd enjoy having her bottom warmed, and I'd enjoy doing it to her.'

'Then do so,' Henry answered, 'and tell her it's her punishment. Try the course twice more first and, after you've beaten her, take her around the estate but make sure you're at the place where the track doubles back by the copper beech at . . . let me see . . . four-thirty.'

'Fine,' I agreed. 'What are you up to?'

'That,' Henry announced, 'is not for you to worry about. Just make sure she knows the stop word.'

We walked back to the yard, finding Ginny still kneeling obediently on the ground. Other than my brief and hot-tempered use of the quirt on Ellen Campbell's bottom, this was my first chance to punish a friend. On the other hand it was something I'd always fantasised over and, if spanking Susan had been my favourite fantasy, then giving Ginny the same treatment came not far behind.

'Right, young lady,' I told her as Henry and I approached. 'Two more circuits and then I'm going to teach you not to disobey me. You'll also have to atone to Henry for driving across his lawn.'

Ginny bowed her head, a gesture so submissive and

yielding that I began to wonder if she had been picking things up from Susan. I knew that they'd been to bed together a couple of times after I'd been expelled, and that Ginny had more than once given the smaller girl the spankings she craved. From Ginny's behaviour it looked as if she also might have caught the bug of enjoying physical punishment on her own bottom.

After not two but three more circuits Ginny managed to record a time under a minute without using the lawn as a short cut. We tried once more but she was obviously beginning to tire and was slower. Henry then told us that the best-recorded time was forty-nine seconds and that for beginners we had done extremely well. That improved my confidence, especially as it was Ginny's first time as a pony-girl.

'Time for your punishment, then,' I announced when she was once more kneeling in the yard, only now breathing hard and slick with sweat. 'Before I start you should know that to stop it you just have to say the word red, or yellow if you want me to slow down. Now, I'd really like to teach you a lesson by thoroughly humiliating you, but I know you'd just enjoy it if I made you suck Henry's cock, and you're going to lick me later anyway. Instead, I'm going to give you a good, old-fashioned spanking and then a few strokes of my whip to give you something to remember.'

I unfastened Ginny's wrist straps, pulled her to her feet and marched her into the scullery. Henry followed, making himself comfortable against an old-fashioned mangle as I pulled a chair out and gestured for Ginny to get over my knee. She went down, lying over my legs with her hands touching the ground on one side and her feet on the other. I put my arm around her waist in the same way Henry had used to hold me down when he first spanked me. Ginny sighed as I put a hand on her bottom. Her flesh was damp and prickly from her exertion, her bottom full and fleshy, the cheeks a little open to show a tuft of golden hair between them. She was shivering, and so was I as I wobbled her cheeks under my palm. The sensation of having her over my lap was exquisite. Nude but for her harness, her lovely bottom stuck up for my attention, posed for me to punish at my leisure.

'You're so lovely, Ginny,' I said, forgetting to be dominant in my sheer lust for her, 'and I'm going to spank you so hard.'

With that I set to work, bringing my palm down hard on my friend's naked bottom. She squeaked and her bum bounced, then again as my hand smacked down a second time. I tightened my grip on her waist and delivered the third, then the fourth, delighting in the way her bottom wobbled with each smack and was growing pink from my attentions. I set in with a will, making Ginny kick her legs up and down and squeal out protests through her gag. It was great, my sole regret being that I hadn't had a chance to take down her panties and make her suffer the shame of having her bottom laid bare. Actually that would have had little effect on Ginny, but I would have enjoyed it anyway. The physical sensation of being soundly spanked was certainly having an effect on her, though, with her legs kicking up and her body writhing under my restraining arm. Her whole bum was red, the cheeks now coming further apart as she wriggled. I smiled up at Henry, who returned a satisfied grin as he stroked a very conspicuous bulge in his trousers with one hand.

'Yellow! Yellow!' Ginny finally squeaked through her mouthful of leather. 'Amber, you're so rough! Ow, my poor bottom!'

'Sorry,' I said, 'but you deserved that, and I did so enjoy it. Let's see how you enjoyed it.'

I slipped a hand between her legs without warning, drawing a squeak from her as my fingers found the dampness of her fanny and then a long sigh as I slid my two longest fingers deep inside her. She was wet, swollen and ready from the excitement of what I had done to her.

'You're soaking, you dirty little tramp,' I chided her. 'Well, there's only one cure for that.'

'Amber!' she squealed as I set to work again.

Only when the palm of my hand started to get sore did I finally stop, rolling Ginny off my lap to lie panting on the floor, her bright-red bottom stuck out towards Henry. Spanking her had turned me on so much that I was ready to come, despite not having once touched myself. Throughout the pony-carting I'd been getting slowly more and more worked up, and now I was at boiling point. Another detail from my fantasies suddenly sprang into my mind, and it was something that might successfully humiliate Ginny.

'Play with yourself,' I ordered, standing up.

Ginny didn't need telling twice, immediately rolling on to her back, opening her legs wide and starting to masturbate shamelessly in front of us.

'Show her your lovely cock,' I told Henry.

Ginny pulled her head up, continuing to rub at herself as Henry undid his fly and pulled out a nearly erect penis. I stepped over and took it in my hand, tugging at it until it was rigid in my hand.

'That's huge,' Ginny breathed in awe.

'Is it?' I asked Henry.

'So I'm always told,' he replied.

'It is,' Ginny assured us. 'Slip it in me for a bit, please, Henry.'

'My pleasure,' he answered.

He went slowly down on his knees, his cock rearing up towards Ginny's open fanny. She reached forward and took it in her hand, stroking and pulling, then putting the head to her vagina as he moved forward. She groaned loudly as it slid inside her, rolling her legs up and catching her own ankles. Henry began to move into her, pushing her thighs back against her tummy with each forward motion. I could see it going in, Ginny's sex stretched wide where the great thick shaft went into her. Her eyes were shut and her mouth was clamped around her bit, biting hard into the leather. Looking at her beautiful face with its expression of absolute ecstasy added an urgency to my intentions and also an exquisitely rude detail.

'Don't come in her!' I demanded, struggling to get my trousers down.

'I shan't,' Henry puffed, taking hold of Ginny's legs and starting to fuck her slowly and evenly.

She sighed, opening her eyes again as I pulled off my panties and boots together. Turning her face to me, she pushed the bit out of her mouth and stuck her tongue out to me, her eyes fixed on my bare fanny.

'Like I said,' I addressed Henry, 'don't come in her; pull out and come on me.'

He moved back, his cock popping out of my friend's fanny to stand proud and glistening with her juice. It was more than I could resist not to taste it and I went down, opening my mouth for him to guide it in. The flavours of cock and fanny mingled in my mouth. I sucked greedily for a bit before pulling back and mounting Ginny, presenting Henry with my naked upraised bottom spread wide in front of him.

'Come all over it,' I demanded.

'I'll spank it if you don't stop being bossy,' he answered, and the next instant a hard smack landed on my bum.

I looked around to find that he was masturbating himself over my bottom while he spanked me, gently but firmly. I started to kiss Ginny, our tongues meeting as my bottom bounced under another slap. Ginny's arm went around me, hugging me into her as I was spanked. It was gorgeous being held lovingly and beaten at the same time but, before I could really get into it, I heard Henry groan and felt his come splash between my open bottom-cheeks, warm and wet.

Rising and turning before Ginny had a chance to realise what I was doing, I positioned myself over her face, paused an instant to let her appreciate what was about to happen, and then sat squarely down on her face, spreading my bum-cheeks as I lowered myself. She gave a muffled squeak and then was silent, unable to protest with my bottom on her face.

'Lick it,' I ordered, 'and you're not to come until I have.'

Henry had sunk back on his haunches and was looking on in delight as I rubbed my come-spattered bottom directly into Ginny's face. Her mouth was against my bottom-hole, her hands going back to her fanny.

'Is she doing it?' he asked.

'Yes,' I answered, gasping the words out as Ginny's tongue tip began to lick at my anus.

I started to dab at my clitty. Ginny was actually doing it, licking my bottom, her tongue eagerly lapping up Henry's sperm. I paused to pull my top and bra up, needing to bare my tits so that I could play with a nipple. The tip of Ginny's tongue was actually in my bumhole, wriggling about to give me the most exquisite sensation.

Henry watched as the two of us played with ourselves, both fannies spread before him, both of us with our bodies naked and aroused, one girl licking his semen from the other's bottom. He had left his cock out and was playing with it, stroking his balls and working a thumb up and down the shaft. Ginny's tongue was well inside me and I was starting to come, the muscles of my bottom contracting against her face. I transferred my attention to her fanny as my climax began. One hand was cupping her plump mound, golden hair spilling out around her palm, two fingers holding her vaginal lips apart so that she could use the knuckles of the other hand to rub at her swollen clitoris. My own vagina started to pulse, my anus tightening, actually around Ginny's tongue. Her pretty, kissable mouth was open around my bumhole, smeared with sperm and my juices. The firm pink tongue that had been intertwined with mine moments before was now pushed into my anus, probing me, filling me.

I screamed Ginny's name as I came, pressing myself hard against her face, my head thrown back in ecstasy. It happened twice more, smaller peaks with my screams of pleasure subsiding to gasps and then sighs. Ginny immediately started to rub harder at her own clit, licking at my bottom ever more fervently. My bottom-hole felt so sensitive that it was hard to stay in place and let her lick it, but it would have been cruel to dismount when she was about to come. I didn't have long to endure it, though. Her legs came up and squeezed together around her arms, I felt her taking a desperate breath beneath me, and then her tongue was pushed back inside me and she was coming, bucking under me, licking as if she was trying to eat me and thrusting her hips up in little jerks. If she knew just what a sight she was making in front of Henry then she obviously didn't care, no more than I had done moments before. Finally her jerks and squirms stopped and I climbed off, grinning at Henry. He raised his eyebrows in return, clearly impressed.

'I told you she was dirty,' I remarked, proud that my friend had lived up to the image I had built of her.

We had made the rudest, most uninhibited display in front of him, getting completely carried away and doing things that would have been unthinkable had it not been for the slow build up of pleasure provided by the pony-carting. Ginny and I discussed this while we washed. She admitted that she hadn't really seen the point at first but had been willing to play on the grounds that anything I was so keen on had to be worth a try. Actually being put in harness had converted her, making her realise not only how good it felt to be under the control of a lover but also how much opportunity it gave for showing off. The aspect of making an exhibition of myself had been only a minor part of the thrill for me, and it was evident from what Ginny was saying that her pleasure, while no less intense, was very different to mine. We agreed that it takes imagination to appreciate pony-girls as a form of erotic play, but given that first bit of imagination the possibilities are endless.

Only when Ginny was admiring her pink bottom in the mirror did I remember that in the heat of our passion I had completely forgotten to whip her. So far I wasn't making a very good pony-mistress, not only getting carried away much too easily but forgetting to administer promised punishments. According to Henry, really dedicated mistresses never exposed their bodies and never allowed themselves to show true intimacy in public. He had also admitted that he considered this attitude pedantic, and I agreed with him. To have spanked Ginny, then caned her and just carried on pony-carting, would have been a waste. I'd needed an orgasm, and it seemed logical to me that a genuine mistress would take her pleasure how she liked and in front of whom she liked. That sounded good anyway, although the truth was that I'd been feeling incredibly sexy – not to mention dirty – and had been unable to resist going with my desires.

Henry had thanked us politely and retired to his room, presumably to sleep. Whatever mischief he had been planning in the woods was obviously off and so I made tea and we went out to drink it on the lawn. When we had finished and were relaxing on the warm grass I asked her if she wanted to continue anyway and she readily agreed.

She was stark naked, while I had thrown only an oversized T-shirt over my head, so it was the work of a moment to put her back in harness. We drove off at a leisurely pace, now doing it more as something friendly and intimate rather than specifically erotic. The day was still warm, but less bright, making the idea of being naked particularly satisfying. Feeling thoroughly relaxed and safe, I stopped the cart halfway up the big field and peeled my top off, throwing it over the back seat before driving on. It felt great pony-carting completely nude, the fact that it was technically against the etiquette of the thing only adding to the fun.

We drove to the top of the big field and along the hedge, then into the woods at the end. Most of this was old woodland with great beeches meeting over our heads. The woodland smells, dappled light and cool air all helped to create a soothing atmosphere. A little, sensible part of my brain was telling me that to an outsider we would look pretty strange. The sight of a naked girl harnessed to a cart and driven by another, equally naked, girl through an English beech wood might well be considered odd, even surreal. To us at that moment it seemed completely natural, a pleasant way for two intimate friends to spend the afternoon. True, there was an erotic element to it, and I certainly hoped that we'd look arousing to any but the most priggish of people, but we were content to keep that aspect of it as a pleasant undertone.

I knew it was roughly half past four and so drove towards the place Henry had told me to be simply for curiosity's sake. It was the part of the track most distant from the house, and formed a sort of hairpin shape in an arm of the wood. The tip of the wood was cut off by a railway cutting, although the trains ran well below the level of the wood and so could see nothing. I knew about the railway, and had guessed that Henry's plan might involve it in some way. I wanted to try and work out how, and so stopped Ginny by the copper beech and had her kneel while I stole carefully through the wood towards the cutting.

A track led from the tip of the double back to the edge of the wood, then turned to run parallel with the tracks to a field. I supposed that he might have suggested driving Ginny along it so that she would come out in view of the railway at the exact moment a train passed. The passengers would have had a fine view of her in the nude, not to mention me driving her, but would have been unable to do anything about it. It would have been the perfect piece of exhibitionism, but would also have required precise timing.

I reached the point where the track turned and I could see the railway. It emerged from a tunnel a couple of hundred yards to my right, passed my vantage point and then levelled out on to flatter ground. Once the cart had been turned down towards the field it would have been impossible to hide.

I turned back, wondering if I should simply make Ginny drive out to a point where she would be seen and wait until a train passed. The sense of anticipation as she waited to be displayed would be superb, and just the sort of thing she liked. Then however many people happened to be in the train would get a good view of her breasts and fanny as she stood harnessed to the cart, making an obviously deliberate display of herself. It was too good to resist but, as I approached the cart, I heard the sound of an engine coming towards us along the track. My first thought was that it was Henry playing the fool, then I glimpsed red through the trees. Henry's Land Rover was a typical dull blue-grey, but his estate manager's four-by-four was red.

There was no time to put my T-shirt back on, nor to

undo Ginny's wrist-cuffs. One thing Henry had impressed on me was that the estate workers must know nothing about what we got up to. Of course it was possible that it was actually Henry, but there was no way I was hanging around to find out. Ginny was already on her feet, and I grabbed her reins and pulled her along the track I had just come down. There was no choice, as one side of the hairpin was visible from the other. We just managed to get out of sight in time and froze behind a huge beech, waiting for the car to pass. Only then did I discover that my T-shirt had fallen off the back of the cart.

Ginny was giggling but I was near panic, which got worse when the car's engine died and we heard the door slam. It had parked at the apex of the hairpin, which could only mean that the manager was going to come down the track we were on. The idea of being caught in the nude was bad enough, but my real concern was for Henry. I was sure it couldn't be him, as we had left him snoring in his room and, in any case, it was hard to see how he could have got hold of the estate manager's four-by-four.

I ran towards the railway, pulling Ginny after me. We came out of the wood and were faced with a stark option. There was no cover at all down the track, but a dilapidated wooden fence was all that separated us from the railway cutting. I started on the buckles that held Ginny's wrists, praying that we hadn't been heard and that the manager wouldn't walk too fast. One came open, then the other, and she was free.

'Lift it over!' I hissed, taking one end of the cart.

We hauled the cart over the fence and dragged it behind a stand of broom that hid us from the track. Unfortunately it left us in clear view of the railway, the short tussocks of grass on the cutting slope making it impossible to hide. Ginny just kept giggling, but I was in a serious frenzy, crouched low behind the broom bush but painfully aware that I was making a fine display of my bottom should a train pass. It was a local line and hardly busy, but I had a horrible suspicion that Henry hadn't picked on half past four at random.

I was right. Even as I peered cautiously out from behind the bush the tracks started to sing and I heard the sound of a train approaching. I crouched down as far as I could and hid my face, thinking of the eyes of the passengers staring at my bare bottom. Ginny was laughing and I peeped between my fingers to find her standing up, waving her hands at the train and showing everything. Turning to look, I saw the last two carriages rush past, several faces staring open mouthed through the windows. I was blushing furiously and thinking of how public exposure was very different from showing off to Henry and Ginny when a voice called out above the noise of the train. My humiliation was complete. Not only had I been seen naked by a good fifty people, but we were about to be caught by the farm manager.

My face must have been the colour of a beetroot as I looked up, only to find not the manager, but Henry beaming down at us from the fence. Ginny was in fits of laughter, and it didn't take much to realise that I'd been set up.

'We didn't feel that it was right for you to get away with it completely,' Henry announced as he climbed over the fence. 'So Ginny and I worked out a little game for you while you were out of the room after lunch.'

'You two . . .' I started, then trailed off wondering why Henry was holding not only my top but a coil of rope.

'Er, Henry,' I began, only to have Ginny grab my arms and pull them tight behind my back.

Well I suppose I deserved it. I'd been playing mistress all day and even bossed Henry around quite a bit. What I'd forgotten was that while Ginny might delight in being my pony-girl and being spanked by me, her fantasies did not revolve around being my sexual plaything. They must have decided quite early on that I needed a lesson, and now I was going to get it.

I was laughing and struggling half-heartedly as they dragged me to the fence and pushed me down over it. My T-shirt was used to tie my hands behind my back and the rope used to bind my waist to the top rail. Henry had brought ankle-cuffs, which he attached to me and then to two fence posts. Lastly I had the bridle put on and a pair of my own panties stuffed in my mouth to shut me up. The position left my legs wide open and meant that the next train would get not just a view of my bare bottom but everything, fanny and all. This was utterly humiliating and was all I could think about while Ginny gave me a brief lecture on not being so bossy and then proceeded to take the riding whip to my bottom.

She gave me a good whipping, ten for spanking her so hard, ten for making her lick my bumhole and ten for the fun of it. Each stroke bit into my bottom and would have had me squeaking if I hadn't been so well gagged. Henry watched me beaten with an air of immense satisfaction that added to my humiliation, while Ginny laughed at the sight I made with my bottom stuck up as she whipped it. Thirty strokes left me whimpering and sobbing over the fence and feeling thoroughly contrite for having been rough with her. She stopped, glancing at Henry and then sinking to her knees behind me.

'Ten minutes,' Henry said as Ginny's lips kissed my smarting bottom.

'Tell me when it's five,' Ginny replied.

Her kisses moved around my bottom, covering my hot, welted cheeks, working slowly down the line where they meet and then going to my fanny. I sighed as she buried her face in me, her tongue working on my clit. Henry came forward and took my bare breasts in his hands, working on the nipples to help me come. Not surprisingly, it didn't take long. The sudden comedown from being Ginny's mistress to hiding from the supposed farm manager had left me feeling vulnerable. Being tied and whipped with the chance of being seen by people in a train had intensified the feeling and turned it into an erotic one. Having my breasts molested while Ginny licked me really put the cap on it, and had me wriggling and biting on my mouthful of damp panties and leather in no time at all.

I started to come and Ginny put her hands on my bottom, exploring the burning cheeks even as my orgasm hit me. Being upside down the blood had gone to my head and I nearly passed out at the point of climax. For all my excitement I felt extremely sorry for myself and thoroughly punished – a strange mixture of feelings but a very nice one.

'A bit less high and mighty in future, Miss Amber,' I heard Ginny say as my climax faded, 'or you'll get more of the same.'

Five

That first day more or less set the scene for the days that followed. Ginny was more than willing to play, but made a point of maintaining a balance between us. This meant that, while it was nearly always her between the shafts of the pony-cart, as often as not I was the one who ended up with a sore bottom or on my knees with my face buried between her thighs.

With Brenda's daily appearance in the house it was impractical to try the course out except in the evenings, and we got most of our practice in among the woods and copses where there was no chance of us being caught. We also went to bed together but Ginny always left before we went to sleep. This was a shame, as I felt that I wanted to share a bed with her and wake up with her in my arms. It wasn't until the Friday night that I had the chance to do so.

The weekend was spent training more seriously and, by Sunday evening, we had managed to clock a time of fifty-two seconds, which even Henry had to admit was enough to make us contenders for Mr Rathwell's event. The actual race was now only a few days away, and the rest of the week was spent in mounting excitement.

We repainted the cart in Henry's crimson and black colours, replaced the wheels, trained in the woods each day and put Ginny on a red-meat diet. As I had promised I would, I had re-designed the harness and made two customised sets for Ginny and myself. I had used a soft leather – supple but thick – making eight-inch-deep waist-belts that hugged our midriffs and attached to the shafts of the cart at either side. Straps rose from back and front, crossing between our breasts. These placed the load on our shoulders, making control easier. The new wrist-cuffs were thicker and more elaborate, the bridles a simple set of four straps, the bits and metal cheek-rings. Smaller rings allowed our hair to be put up. This left mine in little tufts which Henry assured me looked sweet, while the effect gave Ginny a great mane of rich blonde curls tumbling down her back. I had also used nickel-plated steel fittings in place of brass, an innovation which I felt made for a smarter look although Henry felt it was out of keeping with tradition.

Getting the leather had meant a trip to a leather warehouse in Whitechapel and, while we were in London, Henry had taken us to various shops to get me an outfit that would prevent Mr Rathwell from recognising me. The day before the race I got fully kitted up in front of the mirror. Looking at myself I could hardly believe it was me, and was sure that Mr Rathwell would never connect the wicked, leather-clad mistress I now appeared with the rather cold and haughty daughter of his accountant.

I had chosen a leather corset that took my waist down to twenty-two inches and laced at the back with scarlet cord. This pushed my breasts up and together, a chemise of soft leather leaving a good slice of each showing. My shorts were of the same leather, hugging my bottom and pulled tight against my fanny. Knee-high boots fastened with a line of straps and sporting four-inch heels set my legs off, while a black wig concealed my distinctive curls. Instead of buying a domino I had opted for a top hat with a veil, effectively concealing my face from all but the closest inspection. Gauntlets completed the ensemble, leaving me looking very kinky, very fierce and very unlike Amber Oakley.

Just wearing it made me feel really good, and I jumped on Ginny to give her a playful spanking. This ended in a fight on my bed, which I won and took my reward by sitting on Ginny's face while she nuzzled my fanny through the tight leather. Restraining myself with some difficulty from going further, I let her go and we went downstairs to show off to Henry. He was suitably impressed and gave the opinion that Mr Rathwell would be far too scared of me to dare a close inspection.

The next morning we rose early and breakfasted well before loading the cart into the back of the Land Rover. Ginny and I helped each other dress, our excitement rising as we transformed ourselves into mistress and pony-girl. Her muscles had firmed up over the time she had been at Henry's, and she could now pull him up to the ridge without needing a rest at the top. Having done the same myself I knew how hard it was, and felt seriously confident in our ability to win. She also looked delectable in her new harness, full make-up and carefully groomed hair tied with crimson ribbons. It seemed unlikely that any other girl there would be quite so beautiful. Mr Rathwell was bound to be jealous of myself and also Henry – a thought that pleased me immensely.

Ginny and I put on long coats over our gear and we left Henry's farm. I'd only been there a little over a month but, as we left the leafy lanes of Hertfordshire and entered the great sprawl of the London suburbs, it felt as if we were entering another world. Not only that, but knowing how we were dressed under our coats and what we were up to made me feel both special and naughty.

The warehouse in which the meet was being held proved to be a great squat structure of red brick supporting a roof of corrugated plastic. It looked pretty squalid and drew a few disapproving remarks from Henry, as did the process of having to queue, then be checked by security and finally show our tickets at the reception.

'I never thought it would come to this,' he complained as we entered the main body of the warehouse.

I understood how he felt, but was determined not to let it dampen my spirits. An oval area had been kept clear in the centre of the warehouse floor, pillars supporting the roof forming a line down the middle with a plastic fence linking them. Motorway cones delineated what was presumably the track and another plastic fence held back the crowd.

The crowd was what really had Henry complaining, and I was forced to agree with him. For a start there were a good five males for every woman present. Only a handful of people were dressed in pony-carting outfits, and a good many hadn't even troubled to smarten themselves up. Even with our coats on Ginny and myself stood out from the crowd, and I found myself immediately feeling less happy. Henry was right, Mr Rathwell had turned what had been an exclusive and elegant erotic sport into a sordid, commercial shambles.

A hot-dog stand, betting booths, portable lavatories and a make-shift bar all added to the overriding impression of squalor, although the last at least allowed us to get hold of a much-needed drink. Having done this, we started to look round, quickly finding the place in which we wanted to be. An area at the end had been fenced off for competitors, with a pair of heavy-set security guards making sure that the rest of the crowd stayed out. Within the enclosure things were more as I had imagined them to be and, once Henry had managed to get us in and we had started to chat with other genuine enthusiasts, I quickly began to feel at home.

I also began to feel notably less confident of our ability to win. The first people to approach us were a couple who obviously took the sport very seriously indeed. Ginny and I had taken our coats off and were standing there in all our finery when I saw a girl look over to us, tap her boyfriend on the arm and start towards us. She was a good three inches taller than me and combined power and elegance in a way that I had never before seen. Slim hipped and moderately small breasted, she lacked the opulent beauty of Ginny, but looked far the better runner. Her legs were extraordinarily long and appeared to be pillars of solid muscle, every one showing as she walked. Her jet-black hair was coiled on top of her head in a functional bun and held in place with a bright-yellow clip: otherwise she was stark naked, a simple-looking harness of yellow-and-black rope-work dangling from her hand.

Perhaps, even more ominously, her boyfriend was no more than five foot three and lightly built into the bargain, putting the finishing touches to a team that seemed very likely to be unbeatable.

'That's a brilliant harness. Where did you get it?' she asked as they approached.

'I made it,' I admitted proudly.

'You made it?' she echoed. 'It's great. Do you do commissions?'

'I suppose so,' I answered, not only flattered but keen to get to know her.

'Great,' she continued. 'I'm Vicky, by the way, Vicky Belstone. This is my boyfriend, Todd Garvey.'

'Amber Oakley,' I replied without really thinking. 'My pony-girl is Ginny and this is Henry.'

Todd shook Henry's hand and gave me a polite bow, but his eyes were on Ginny. Considering his face was more or less level with her naked chest I could see his point. The five of us chatted for a while, with Henry taking their names and addresses for future reference. Todd's interest grew when he discovered that Henry was the Henry Gresham who had founded the club, which cheered Henry up considerably. My worry was that by revealing my true name to Vicky and Todd I might have dropped myself in it, a worry that was further compounded by Todd's next remark.

'Morris will be green with envy when he sees you,' he addressed Ginny. 'Not that Melody and Harmony aren't cute, but he hates to think anyone other than him can ever get a pretty girl for themselves.'

'Melody and Harmony?' Henry queried.

'His team,' Todd replied, jerking his thumb over his shoulder. 'The two black girls over there. They're good but not in Vicky's class. Besides, Morris has four stone on me.'

I followed the direction he had indicated, noting two girls so similar that they might have been twins. They certainly looked impressive, full figured and with bold, dark eyes in faces that looked naturally confident, almost insolent. Both had cloaks of pale-blue silk thrown over their shoulders, but I could nonetheless tell that they were powerfully built. As Todd said, though, they were clearly not in the same class as Vicky and I felt confident that Ginny could at least hold her own against them.

'He only uses a pair to show off,' Todd was saying. 'I actually think he loses a little speed that way.'

'That is generally the case,' Henry agreed, 'though of course in a race where stamina is of the essence a pair is an advantage – particularly cross-country.'

'Cross-country?' Vicky queried.

'We sometimes used to race cross-country,' Henry answered. 'On lonely routes and with the girls in bikinis. If you're genuinely competitive about pony-cart racing there's nothing to compare with it.'

'I'd like to try that sometime,' Vicky responded. 'The idea of being outside appeals to me, too. We've trained in isolated woods occasionally, and it always gives a special thrill.'

'We always had meets outside,' Henry said wistfully.

'Morris says it makes the meet impossible to control,' Todd put in. 'He certainly wouldn't make as much money. There must be well over three hundred spectators in here, never mind us lot. Here he is, actually.'

My heart skipped a beat. Todd was looking behind me, undoubtedly at Morris Rathwell.

'Henry, Henry, you old dog,' I heard a voice that I immediately recognised. 'What do you think, then? Come a long way from your little efforts on the farm, haven't we? Well, I say, is this your new pony? Smashing tits, love, why didn't old Henry introduce you to me before?'

'Morris Rathwell, Ginny. Ginny, Morris Rathwell,' Henry said rather formally.

'Pleased to meet you,' Rathwell continued, with my back still firmly presented to him. 'I'm sure we'll get better acquainted later. Henry's a lucky old dog I must say. Oh, hi Todd, Vicky.'

This was it. I had to turn around and, having given my real name to Todd and Vicky, I could hardly use another one now.

'Morris, hi,' Todd responded, Vicky not answering at all but turning away.

'I'm going to have a chat with Trisha,' she informed her boyfriend. 'Are you coming?'

'Sure,' Todd replied, following Vicky who evidently had no wish to talk to Mr Rathwell.

I was saved, at least for the time being, and turned to face Mr Rathwell.

'Be a love and get some drinks in,' Rathwell was saying as he held out a fifty-pound note to Ginny. 'Do you still drink that brandy, Henry? Mine's Bacardi and Coke — a double – and don't forget the change. Oh, and who's this?'

'My driver, Mistress Evangeline,' Henry said without a pause.

Well, it was a bit of a mouthful but not bad for the spur of the moment and, for an instant, I thought we'd got away with it. Unfortunately I hadn't counted on Ginny. She was walking towards the bar, smiling at the various men who were ogling her naked body. Suddenly she turned back and looked right at us.

'What do you want to drink, Amber?' she called.

'Amber?' Rathwell echoed, looking at me more intently.

Ginny realised what she had done and put her hand to her mouth in shock, which destroyed my last chance of avoiding recognition. Rathwell looked from one of us to the other, then to Henry.

'Not Amber Oakley, your goddaughter, surely?'

'I . . .' Henry began, but Rathwell had turned and lifted my veil without the slightest warning.

I was looking directly into his face.

'Well, I'll be damned!' he exclaimed. 'Miss Amber prim-and-proper Oakley, a pony-girl driver!'

There wasn't a lot I could say, so I just shrugged and then rather pointedly rearranged my veil. Rathwell couldn't find anything to say either, for once, and it was left to Henry to try and rescue the situation.

'We, ahem . . . we felt it perhaps unwise to advertise her new-found role too widely,' he told Rathwell. 'I trust that you would not be indiscreet? Were Amber's tastes to become common knowledge it might prove awkward.'

'Fucking right,' Rathwell answered. 'Old Charlie'd blow a fucking fuse!'

'Exactly,' Henry agreed.

'No, no, you don't have to worry about me,' Rathwell continued. 'What, rat on my old mate Henry's god-daughter? No way, especially when it would mean she and young Ginny wouldn't be up for a laugh after the meet. I'm giving a little party, just a few of the better girls and my closer friends, if you get my meaning.'

He could have put it more crudely, but not much. The deal was clear. Ginny and I joined in whatever after-meet party he was planning or he told my father about me. It didn't take much imagination to guess what was going to happen at the party.

'Sorry,' Ginny addressed me as she returned to us.

Henry coughed, turning a look of disgust towards Rathwell.

'Morris,' he began carefully, 'without wishing to use strong words such as blackmail or coercion, I must point out that you and I both know the ultimate consequences of what you appear to be suggesting.'

'Henry, Henry,' Rathwell answered, 'you mistake me. All I'm suggesting is that the three of you might like to come along to my private party after the meet. If Amber and Ginny choose to unwind a little while they're there, perhaps show their host a little gratitude, well, that's up to them.'

Henry snorted. It was hard to judge whether or not Rathwell was bluffing. He had manoeuvred me into the position of having to make a choice of my own free will, but also of knowing that if I didn't pleasure him in some way that he always had the option of turning nasty. It wasn't blackmail – there was no direct or specific demand – but the ball was in my court and I had to judge how to play it. The cunning bastard had Ginny and I effectively trapped.

'Let us put that in the form of a bet,' Henry said thoughtfully.

'Maybe, maybe, I'm always interested in a gamble,' Rathwell answered.

I stayed quiet, sure that Henry had something clever in mind, something that would make Rathwell think he was on to a good deal but snatch the prize away at the last instant. Whatever he did, it would also have to leave Rathwell sufficiently pleased with himself not to go to my father, which made for some tricky balancing.

'We had originally intended to enter your main race,' Henry began. 'On seeing the competition I was becoming less certain. However, I feel that if you are willing to forgo our entry fee, we might agree to something. Perhaps our attendance at your party if your team manages to beat us? Assuming you're competing that is?'

'Sure I am,' Rathwell answered, 'but no way am I taking those odds. How about if they win they get off scot-free and keep the five grand. If they beat my team I only get to fuck Amber.'

'You can't do that; she's a virgin!' Ginny protested.

'Ginny . . .' I sighed.

'All the better,' Rathwell started, then seemed to think better of it. 'No, fair's fair. I'll settle for a blow job if they don't win but beat my girls. However, if we beat them I get the whole works.'

'You expect to have sex with me?' I demanded.

'I'd sure like to, doll,' he answered.

'No way!' I snapped back.

'I'll do it,' Ginny put in, then turned to me. 'After all, I dropped you in it.'

'No, Ginny . . .' I began, only to be cut off by Rathwell.

'When I say the works I mean both of you,' he said.

'No way,' I repeated.

The prospect of his cock in my mouth was bad enough, although it was a risk I was prepared to take. Actually letting him fuck me was out of the question. On the other hand, whatever we accepted had to leave Rathwell satisfied either with whatever he got or that he had lost fairly. At the end of the day the question was: what was the most intimate service I was prepared to risk having to perform for him?

'How about this,' I said, speaking slowly and choosing my words. 'If Ginny and I win the race, we take the five grand and we'll come along to your party, but I promise nothing. If we don't, you can cane me at the party; as many strokes as the position we come in at. Well?'

'On the bare?' Rathwell demanded.

'I suppose so,' I replied.

I knew I could take a caning and, while it would be humiliating, there was no actual contact involved.

'Fine,' he said, 'but if we beat you then I get a blow job from both of you into the bargain.'

I hesitated, glancing at Ginny, who shrugged. I considered his offer. Todd and Henry, who seemed to know what they were talking about, both felt that driving a two-in-hand would put Rathwell at a disadvantage. Rathwell was confident, but then he was always confident.

'Fair enough,' I answered him.

'Nice,' he replied, smirking broadly.

I retired to the bar with a heavy feeling in the pit of my stomach. The chances of us winning were very slim indeed and, even though Vicky Belstone clearly detested Rathwell, she was unlikely to give up the chance of such a large prize merely to score off him. It wasn't certain that she would win, in any case. Three of the carts that were now setting up in the enclosure were pulled by men and, athletic-looking ones at that. I hadn't known this was acceptable, but it was pointless to complain.

It seemed likely that Ginny and I could finish among the first five or so, and probably beat Rathwell. The odds were that I'd end up taking three or four cane strokes at the party, which I knew I could take physically without difficulty. Mentally it was a very different matter. They'd pull my shorts down and discover that I had very girly flowery panties on underneath. Those would be pulled down, too, and then my bare bottom would be whacked in front of a fair-sized audience. Doubtless they'd jeer and clap and call the strokes out until I was finished with, and for the rest of the party I'd be sitting on a sore bottom. The marks would be visible where my shorts left my bottom-cheeks bare, so I wouldn't even be able to cover my shame properly.

The thought made me shiver, and gave rise to an even more worrying concern. Whenever Henry or Ginny had beaten me the experience had put me in an excited and grovellingly submissive state. Even the thought of my near-inevitable public caning had a similar effect, and I was distinctly worried about how I'd behave once beaten.

Henry had gone to fetch the cart, leaving Ginny and I to prepare ourselves. She was profusely apologetic about revealing who I was to Rathwell, but I made light of it. It was, after all, me who had made the initial mistake and it would probably have come out anyway. Besides, Ginny was looking forward to the race immensely and it seemed a pity to sour her fun. Plenty of people had also complimented me on both my appearance, Ginny's, and the quality of her tack – all of which made it hard to be churlish.

Resigning myself to do my best and accept whatever happened with a good grace, I swallowed the drink I was holding and went over to where Henry was bringing the cart through the service doors. Ginny followed, slipping her bit into her mouth as we reached the cart. I felt a new rush of adrenaline as I took hold of one of Ginny's wrists and led her into position. Near us, Todd was putting Vicky in harness, a very basic affair that would leave most of the strain on her arms instead of her hips and shoulders. She was facing away from me, her rear view as impressive as the front, with her high, pert buttocks and elegant legs striking a familiar chord of excitement in me.

'How's the betting?' I heard Todd call to another man nearby.

'Vicky's on three to one,' he answered. 'The favourite's that tall black guy; he's five to four.'

I searched for the man they were talking about, finding him at the very farthest end of the enclosure. He stood perhaps six foot four and was an obvious winner. His skin was a deep brown and appeared to have been oiled, while each muscle stood out in clear definition. He was obviously a body builder and I supposed represented pretty much the ideal masculine figure. Nevertheless, looking at his naked body produced none of the thrill that Vicky had touched off in me.

With Ginny's wrists secured I mounted the cart and joined several others in a test lap of the track. The cart ran well on the concrete floor of the warehouse, Ginny moving with easy strides and certainly among the best of the group. The spectators were beginning to gather, pressing against the barrier and jostling for position further back. Their attention was crude, making me feel the focus of lust for perhaps three hundred men. Had it not been for the fence and the solidly built security men I might have been scared. As it was, the feeling was disconcerting but undercut by a deliciously wicked thrill. It was perhaps like flaunting oneself in front of someone who can do nothing about it; something I'd often wanted to do. Better still was the pleasure of having Ginny to show off – a different, but equally exhibitionist thrill which might similarly be compared to the game of pulling friends' skirts up so that people saw their panties.

Ginny was certainly revelling in the attention, walking with her chin up and her breasts thrust out, showing herself off absolutely shamelessly. There was little doubt that she had the most opulent and sexual figure among all the girls present, and every head turned as we went past. After taking a couple of laps I was feeling fully in control, with the prospect of being exposed and whipped if I lost all but forgotten. The tension of being about to race was building up as well, causing a hard lump in my throat and a trembling feeling in my legs. Knowing that whatever I felt, Ginny must be feeling double, I kept her in motion until the order came to line up for the start.

The race was scheduled for ten laps and there were some fifteen carts competing. This was out of a total of over twenty, and it was clear that the competitors all regarded themselves as potential winners. With five hundred pounds being charged to enter, this was hardly surprising, yet if most of the pony-girls and pony-boys looked worryingly good, the carts and harnesses were less impressive. It was clear that many people either had no idea of basic physics or had purchased equipment designed to look good and nothing more. Several carts were drawn entirely from the pony's wrists, and more than one looked dangerously top heavy. Our own was among the heaviest and more robust, being designed for outdoors, but it was also lower to the ground than most and certainly stronger.

Feeling determined and hopeful I wheeled Ginny into the cluster of carts and ponies gathered behind the start line. We were to set off in a group, there being too many carts to start all abreast, which meant that being at the front carried an obvious advantage. As I was only allowed to call basic orders to Ginny during the race, we had discussed tactics before she put her bit in her mouth and officially became a pony-girl. She was supposed to do her best to pace Vicky and hope that a final sprint would allow us victory. The chance that we would succeed was slim, yet not zero by any means.

Rathwell's team was lined up at the inside of the track, Melody and Harmony now impressively naked, their rich-brown skin reflecting highlights from the warehouse lights. Even had I been told which was which I wouldn't have been able to tell them apart. Both were full breasted and muscular with powerful legs and well-fleshed bottoms. Their hair was beaded in Rathwell's colours of gold and turquoise – a colour scheme continued on their harness and the cart. Rathwell himself was seated, apparently quite relaxed, with the reins in one hand while he used his whip to stroke the naked bottom of either Melody or Harmony.

'One minute,' the PA system announced, causing a stir among the carts.

Ginny nudged up to the line, positioning herself in between Vicky and one of the male ponies. I turned to glance at Todd, nodding in response to his toothy grin. The cart on the other side was driven by a tall, slim man seated much higher than me. His bony face was set in an expression of absolute seriousness. When he didn't acknowledge my nod I turned back to the front, waiting for the off with the tension piling up inside me.

112

The line judge was seated in a high box of the sort used on tennis courts, his starting pistol in his lap. He raised it, calling ten seconds into the microphone, turning his attention to his watch, counting down the seconds.

The pistol sounded and the cart lurched forward, Ginny making a desperate lunge to get ahead of the pack. I smacked the reins hard on her back, yelling at her to move so that we didn't get caught up. The cart to our left bumped against ours, once, twice, forcing Ginny to correct. Vicky was already ahead of us and, unless Ginny managed to pull out, we would be forced to give way or drive into the fence. I yelled, reaching out to shove against their cart. The man merely gave a cold look in return, his pony-boy now pressed close to Ginny, the shafts touching. We had perhaps six inches advantage, no more.

'Give way!' I yelled.

He ignored me, instead pulling his left hand rein to steer his pony-boy into us. I corrected Ginny to the left, only to have him move further in, determined to cut us off.

'Right!' I screamed, pulling on the rein.

As Ginny turned, their cart struck ours hard, as I knew it would. The man's look of cold, aloof dominance changed abruptly to dismay as their lighter cart bounced up, tipped, hung on one wheel for an instant, and then toppled over.

Ginny sprang past as the men's cart rolled, the pony-boy going down suddenly on to his knees. There was a crash and a curse behind us but I paid no attention, instead focusing on Todd and Vicky, now a good ten yards clear of us.

'Good girl!' I called out to Ginny.

We had cleared the pack and were approaching the end of the straight. Other than Vicky, only the tall black pony-boy and another all-girl team were ahead of us. Rathwell's team was on our inside and some dozen yards back, acting as a block to the group of drivers behind. I had been half expecting to be pulled up for fouling, but either what I'd done was considered fair or nobody had noticed that it had been deliberate.

The corner was the next obstacle, a tight turn that would favour smaller, more compact carts. Also low-slung ones, I realised, as the all-girl team in front of us tried to take it too fast and toppled over, the pony-girl staying upright but the driver spilling out. I leant into the curve as Ginny hit it, the cart swaying but staying upright. We had taken it tight, leaving us level with the pony-boy for an instant before he again pulled away down the return straight. Looking to the side I saw the team we had tangled with pulling their cart off to the side. One wheel was almost at right angles to the other, clearly showing that they were no longer in competition. I felt no sympathy, only a slight concern should the two men later choose to make an issue of the crash.

Ginny was trying to follow our plan, but we were slowly losing ground on Vicky. The pony-boy wasn't, however; instead he was coming within a yard of Todd's cart as they reached the far end. She gained on the turn, as did we, the pony-boy's long legs and the consequently long shafts making tight turns impossible. As we made the lap we were comfortably in third, and I allowed myself the luxury of raising my hat to Rathwell as his team passed on the far side of the fence.

We held our position through the next few laps, Ginny gradually losing pace but no more than most others. The third pony-boy was pacing us but some way behind, while a tall red-haired pony-girl and Rathwell's team were also possible challengers. Ahead, the tall black pony-boy had taken the lead, Vicky and Todd pacing him but making no effort to overtake. We lapped our first tail-ender on the sixth circuit, which seemed to give Ginny new energy.

By the seventh, the stamina of Rathwell's two-in-hand had started to tell, coming into fourth place behind us. He tried to overtake on the straight of the eighth but our better cornering kept us ahead, only to have the red-haired girl pull parallel to us after taking the next corner dangerously tight.

'Sprint!' I called to Ginny, using my whip on her for the first time as we started the ninth lap.

The red-haired girl was inside us, and fast, her long legs matching Ginny's pace for pace. The corner was coming up fast, too fast; I leant in, our cart touching theirs. For an instant I had the horrible feeling of losing my balance as we went up on one wheel and then the cart slammed back down, bouncing twice but staying upright. The red-haired girl was inside us, with a yard's lead, then two.

'Come on!' I screamed, once more flicking Ginny's bottom.

On the opposite side I saw that Vicky was running parallel with the pony-boy, desperately trying to get past him. I felt for her even as I screamed for Ginny to run faster. She was tiring, straining to keep our pace but unable to do it. We lost more ground at the corner, rounding it and going into the final lap as Vicky cornered ahead of us. The red-haired girl had the measure of us, and Rathwell was close behind; no more than five yards. The crowds had begun to cheer and clap as we hit the corner with Melody and Harmony almost touching the back of my seat. They pulled out to overtake as we entered the straight, sprinting hard, Rathwell yelling encouragement.

The cheers welled up, mixed with cries of delight and despair. Someone had won, but I didn't know who, nor did I care. Melody and Harmony were parallel with me, then a bit in front.

'Got you!' Rathwell yelled. 'Go girls!'

I brought my whip down hard on Ginny's bottom. She leapt on, gaining a foot and then once more falling back. Rathwell was next to Ginny, yelling at the black girls to pull in and tugging at the reins. The corner was coming up, Rathwell's team moving in ahead of Ginny. They started to turn into the corner, pulling wide.

'Turn!' I screamed, wrenching on the left-hand rein.

Ginny slowed fractionally and turned hard around the pillar, far too sharply. The cart went up, my balance going, Ginny tripping as the cart slewed around, crossing the line sideways even as my shoulder hit the concrete. A bright-blue trainer passed inches from my face and I rolled away, covering my face with my hands.

I lay dazed on the ground, looking up at the bright lights that had been strung along the warehouse girders. My hat was off and my wig askew, my shoulder aching where I had landed. Ginny had stayed upright by some miracle and was looking down at me with concern, unable to do more with her wrists fixed to the cart.

'I'm all right,' I managed, feeling anything but all right as I propped myself up on one arm. 'Did we win?'

'Fourth,' a voice announced from above and behind.

I looked around to see the line judge, still seated in his elevated chair. I smiled at him, my aches and pains forgotten. Fourth meant we'd beaten Rathwell. My smile dropped a little at the next thought. Fourth meant three strokes of the cane delivered to my bare bottom in front of a sizeable audience.

Coming fourth also meant that we were in the prizes, just. Seven hundred and fifty pounds in cash did a lot to compensate for not having done better, despite Henry's disapproval of the whole idea of money prizes. Vicky had won as well, having run a brilliant race that made her the toast of the small gathering of Rathwell's friends who stayed on when the main crowd had cleared. The man she had beaten into second was a professional sportsman and her success was regarded as the high point of what was evidently a long string of victories.

There were about thirty people at Rathwell's private do, mainly from the group who had actually been involved with the pony-carting. Vicky and Todd were there and had latched on to Henry, Ginny and I after the race. The tall redhead and her female driver were also present but, fortunately, not the male couple I had made crash.

I was awaiting my caning with a mixture of trepidation and resolve. Rathwell could strip my bottom and apply the cane to me, but three strokes were all he had and I was determined to take them with as much dignity as I could manage. Rathwell being Rathwell he hadn't simply taken me aside, put me over a chair and given me a quick three. Instead he'd announced to everybody that I was due to be caned and set up a whipping stool right in the middle of the warehouse to keep me in mind of what was coming to me.

Vicky and Todd were sympathetic, but I could see in their eyes that they were looking forward to seeing my bare bottom whacked. Ginny and even Henry were little better, commiserating with me but clearly excited. I was quickly learning that one trouble with presenting a dominant image is that there are plenty of people who'd far rather punish a dominant girl than a submissive girl.

I suppose it makes sense. Having the willing submission of a beautiful, naked girl like Ginny or Vicky is wonderful, but having a fully clad, strong-willed, dominant woman getting shyly down on her knees and reluctantly exposing her bottom for punishment is even better. I'd have loved to have watched one or two of the haughty, dominant women who were there get the same treatment but, unfortunately, it was me who was going to be stripped and beaten for their amusement and not the other way around.

When my time finally came I was trembling hard despite the amount of brandy I had drunk. Rathwell went to stand by the whipping stool and called for quiet, then summoned me by name. As I walked out into the middle of the warehouse every eye was on me. I kept my chin up, walking slowly to stand in front of the whipping stool with my hands folded behind my back, awaiting orders. Rathwell was grinning maliciously and tapping a long, pale-yellow cane against his palm.

'I'm going to enjoy this,' he announced. 'Get over the stool.'

I started to dig under the front of my corset to get at the button of my shorts, but he raised a finger and waggled it as if telling off a naughty dog.

'Tut, tut, tut,' he said. 'My privilege, I think.'

I stopped, instead obeying his first instruction and placing my hips against the padded stool.

'Come on, Amber,' he chided. 'Head down, bottom up, let's not have any of your hoity-toity little airs. Or will I have to have Melody and Harmony spank you first?'

That was a much more appealing idea than being caned by Rathwell. I hesitated before bending over the stool properly. Maybe it was my hesitation, maybe he would have done it anyway, but it was then that Rathwell decided to push his luck.

'Come on, girls,' he called over to the two black girls. 'I think a spanking from you two would teach her a valuable lesson.'

I made to protest, as this was no part of the bargain, then choked back the words as strong arms encircled my waist. The sensation was just too good, and I could feel my resistance slipping away as they handled me. They both took hold of me, one putting her hands between my legs and groping for the button of my shorts. It popped open and I felt my zip come down, then the shorts were being tugged off my bottom. One of them giggled at the sight of my flowery panties. I was lifted, my feet leaving the floor. Their hands had gripped my panties, preparing to strip my bottom.

'Take her knickers down on three,' Rathwell called. 'One . . . Two . . . Three.'

I felt a little tug and my pants were down, my bottom plump and bare in front of everybody. People started clapping and jeering and I found myself blushing furiously even as the girls started to spank me. They did it thoroughly and methodically, taking a cheek each and making sure not an inch of my poor wriggling bottom or thighs was spared. I tried to remain passive and dignified, but the slaps stung and I had soon started to kick and squeal as my bottom warmed and reddened. They stopped as suddenly as they had started, only to take one throbbing bum-cheek each and pull them apart, displaying every detail of my fanny and anus to the people sitting behind me.

This raised more jeers from the crowd, the girls moving back to leave me limp over the whipping stool. I was sobbing with humiliation, my dignity forgotten as Rathwell approached with the cane.

'Not so high and mighty now, are we?' he asked.

I didn't reply, my head swimming with the feeling in my bottom and the knowledge that I'd been spanked in public. He raised the cane and brought it down hard, making me yelp and sending a line of fire across my behind.

'One!' the crowd called, their voices raised in delight at my beating.

The second came quickly, even harder than the first.

'Two!' the crowd yelled happily.

I was whimpering and panting as I waited for the third. He was in no hurry, walking around me, stroking the smarting lines on my bottom, tracing a line down between my cheeks, burrowing between them, touching my anus, then my fanny.

'Bastard!' I managed, but it was a fairly pathetic effort and we both knew it.

He laughed, moved back, and suddenly brought the cane hard around in an arc, landing it plumb across the fattest part of my bottom.

'Three!' the crowd called even as I kicked and yelled.

I lay over the horse, feeling the familiar ecstasy of having been skilfully beaten and humiliated. Rathwell moved in front of me, pulling his fly down to produce a skinny pink cock. For all my revulsion for him I found I had to do it, and my mouth was opening automatically as he took me by the hair. I gaped wider, making no resistance as he fed me his penis, rubbing it in my mouth until my lips closed around his shaft and I began to suck.

The crowd was silent, watching in awe as I all too willingly sucked Morris Rathwell's cock. It stiffened fast, swelling as I licked and sucked at it. I was intensely aware of my naked bottom, especially the hot cane lines. Rathwell had bared it and whipped me; he had had me spanked by two pony-girls while the crowd jeered and catcalled at the state I was in. Now I was sucking on his hard little prick, tasting his cock as he held me by the hair and fucked my mouth. He jerked into me and suddenly my mouth was full of salty, slimy come. It dribbled down my chin and smeared on my cheeks and nose as he pulled out and wiped it on my face.

All I could do was groan in submissive bliss, sticking my tongue out to show everyone my mouthful. I heard one or two exclamations, presumably at the sheer filthiness of what I was doing. Then hands were helping me off the stool, guiding me down on to the floor. It was one of the black girls, taking me by the hair as her master had done, indicating the dense mat of black curls in between her legs as I sank into a kneeling position.

'This is Melody, girl, and you're going to take me all the way,' she said.

She moved forward and pushed my face into her, sighing as my tongue found her clitty. I couldn't see anything, but I knew it was Harmony when fingers touched me between the legs, one finding my anus, another my vagina. I squeaked as a finger was inserted roughly into my bottom-hole, only to have my face pushed back into Melody's fanny.

Harmony started to finger me, quite rough so that I could hear the wet noises of her fingers moving in my vagina. That wasn't all, and I realised that she was playing with herself as she worked her fingers in my two holes. It was more than I could resist not to put my fingers to my own fanny, masturbating shamelessly without a care for who saw or what they thought. I was near orgasm when Melody came in my face, then coming as Harmony's fingers started to really work inside me as she too began to come. I screamed, felt the muscles of both vagina and anus clamp on to Harmony's intruding fingers, grabbed Melody around her bottom so that I could pull her back against my face, and hit a long, drawn-out peak that left me weak-kneed and gasping on the warehouse floor. I was vaguely aware of clapping as I sank down on my side, then another arm was around me – Ginny's.

Six

I spent most of the week after Morris Rathwell's event either sulking in my room or wandering around the farm thinking. The pony-cart race and its aftermath had taught me something about myself that I wasn't really sure I wanted to learn. When I'd first been spanked by Henry I had become so excited that by the end of the day and my third punishment I would have even let him try and put his cock up my bottom. I was attracted to Henry, though. Not physically, but by his combination of openness and maturity. He was big and powerful, too, which added a delicious feeling of genuine physical helplessness to the experience of being put across his knee. Physically I hadn't even been attracted by the pony-boy who'd come second in the race, and I certainly wasn't attracted by Morris Rathwell. I didn't like him either, but it was that very fact that had made having to submit to his will such a turn on. Even the spanking from Melody and Harmony had been under his orders and, after he'd used the cane on me, I'd been quite unable to resist taking his cock in my mouth. The uncomfortable fact is that not only does being spanked make me want to do as I'm told, but I also enjoy it more if I feel I'm being taken advantage of.

The only good thing about it was that Rathwell hadn't realised the extent to which I'd been willing. By the end of it he could have taken my virginity and I'd have been as willing and eager as I undoubtedly was in his imagination. I knew how he imagined me because he'd told me afterwards. Being an egotistical bastard, he saw me as desperately attracted to him but too proud to admit it. He was sure that I'd always relished the thought of sex with him and that the humiliating part had been to service his pony-girls. That simply wasn't true. I'd have gladly played with the girls at any time, but once I'd been caned I'd have sucked any cock offered to me, and the more repulsive its owner the more I'd have enjoyed it. Unfortunately the eagerness of my response to punishment made it hard to refute his boasts.

The whole thing left me seething with humiliation and the desire for revenge. If Rathwell had caned me briefly and without fuss, honour would have been satisfied. After all, when I'd made the bet my assumption had been that three or four quick cane strokes would be no big deal. He'd taken advantage of me but, of course, what I'd really misjudged was my own ability to keep cool. I'd always thought of myself as cool and poised, but now I knew that once I submit, I go to jelly, and that was really mortifying.

Ginny had gone back home on the Monday after the pony-carting meet. This also depressed me. It wasn't until the middle of August that I was really back to my old self. Henry had been completely cool about doing without his evening suck for two weeks, and I made up for it anyway by being his maid and pony-girl for the entire weekend a fortnight after Rathwell's race. He put me in nipple clamps – metal things like miniature book presses – which was exciting, and finished off on Sunday by putting a candle in my bottom-hole and having me kneel on the table while he ate by its light. He then caned me and let me suck him. I took ages over it to make up for lost opportunities, licking and stroking until he finally took me by the hair and brought himself off in my face.

After that I told him I wanted revenge of some sort on Rathwell. He advised against it, pointing out that Rathwell was likely to accept any challenge I made and then concoct some Machiavellian scheme that would leave me getting punished again. He also pointed out that as I was now challenging I would undoubtedly be made to accept a tougher deal than before.

'He'll put up a high stake to tempt you, and then win by bending the rules,' Henry insisted. 'I've seen him do it before. There was a girl called Sara in the club once, a pretty little thing with almost white hair and freckles. She thought she could outwit him but she ended up letting him bugger her. You wouldn't want that would you?'

'No,' I admitted, but it made no difference. I still wanted my revenge.

There was another meet at the very beginning of September, which we were going to and I had decided to challenge Rathwell there. The problem was how? Over the next two weeks I spent a lot of time pondering Henry's old albums and picking his brains. We also tried plenty of pony-girl games and other sexual diversions. He introduced me to having my bottom and breasts tickled with stinging nettles, which helps to give a great orgasm but then throbs all night. I enjoyed the birch more, especially being sent out to pick a bundle for my own punishment and then being caught unexpectedly in the scullery and thrashed with my jeans and pants pulled unceremoniously down over my hips.

I learnt a lot during that August, and came to accept things that before would have been unthinkable. Not that my basic character changed, just my ideas of what was and was not acceptable. I can't really deny that Henry corrupted me, at least in the conventional sense, but there was never a more willing pupil.

What finally gave me an idea of how to beat Rathwell was something that Henry wouldn't do. This was a game called pursuit-capture-punishment, which had many variations but essentially involved releasing a wild pony-girl into the woods and retrieving her, in bondage and well spanked. Henry's group had generally played it with one girl and several hunters, the prize being the captured pony-girl's submission. Henry declared himself too old and fat for it, pointing out that I would be able to elude him all day without difficulty. Rathwell was pushing fifty and, while he obviously kept himself in shape, it was my guess that his opinion of his own fitness greatly exceeded the reality. Also, when he had played the game at Henry's he had never been particularly good, being too tall and nothing like agile enough to catch a nimble girl. By contrast I had plenty of stamina and was sure I could catch Melody or Harmony. Although I could have played the part myself or got Ginny back over, neither of us had the characteristics that made the perfect wild pony-girl. Henry stated that the best runners were always small, lissom girls who combined brains with an indifference to mud and scratches. The description fitted one person I knew exactly: Susan Wren.

The next problem was getting Rathwell to accept the challenge. The knack seemed to be to make him think he could win and that it was me he'd be chasing.

His September meet was in an old aircraft hanger in Essex. Ginny came with us and managed to win her class in the pony-girl show Rathwell had arranged. This was mainly because she looked good enough to eat, but partly because of the smart turnout Henry and I had achieved and the quality of my tack. Not only did Vicky Belstone remind me that I had promised to make her some, but several other club members expressed an interest. By the end of the meet I was seriously considering taking pony-girl harness manufacture up as a sideline to whatever craft I set up in.

It was at the after-meet party that I finally got a chance to talk properly to Rathwell. He had been showing me attention and making his normal remarks about my body and sexual ability, but there had always been too many other people around to make my challenge. I had managed a measure of revenge by persuading Harmony that it was only fair to let me spank her. She was doubtful at first, saying that she really ought to ask Rathwell's permission. I ran a fingernail down the back of her neck and a minute later she was across my knee in one of the toilets with her beautiful dark-chocolate bottom stuck up while I spanked her. Rathwell was less than pleased when he found that Harmony's bottom had been smacked without his permission, his reason being that we hadn't let him watch. That got him in just the mood I wanted him in and, when he had finished demanding that both Harmony and I take canings from him and Melody, I made my challenge.

'A pursuit-capture-punishment at old Henry's place?' he said. 'Nice idea, nice idea, but I want some serious stakes this time, no puppy stuff.'

'What about the unqualified submission of the loser to the winner?' I suggested. 'Barring penetration and subject to stop words.'

'Come on,' he laughed. 'I wasn't born yesterday. That would mean you could tie my balls to the cart if you wanted but I couldn't shag you, and that's what I want.'

I winced but had to concede his point, a ban on penetration was definitely an advantage to me. He was evidently less off balance than I'd hoped, as the next comment proved.

'You know you really want me to fuck you, Amber darling,' he continued, 'so that's part of my stake.'

'Hang on,' I responded, trying to regain control of the discussion. 'My virginity's really not on offer.'

'We'll see about that, but what about your button, then? I bet that's tight.'

It took me an instant to register what he was saying and I then realised he was suggesting buggering me. Anal penetration had always held a sort of depraved fascination for me. I didn't mind a finger so much and I'd made Ginny kiss my anus often enough, but the idea of Morris Rathwell's cock in my rectum left me speechless.

'Dirty bastard!' Ginny put in, and both Melody and Harmony gave him disapproving looks.

'I think not, Morris,' Henry remarked.

'Well, you've got to try,' Rathwell responded, completely unabashed by everyone's disapproval. 'You've got to make a decent bet of it, sweetie. Where's the fun unless you've really got something to lose?'

'And win,' I reminded him. 'If you want to put up heavy stakes for me, you'd better be able to match them. I don't think you can.'

'Wait a minute, girl,' Rathwell answered, clearly stung by my comment. 'No one, but no one says, that Morris Rathwell can't match their stake. If you think your fanny's so bloody precious I'll put up three acres of prime land against it, freehold. That's fifteen grand, of anybody's money.'

'Morris!' Harmony gasped.

He was basically valuing my virginity against three acres of land, an idea that obviously appalled Harmony but didn't seem that awful to me. I hesitated, and then realised that there was something Rathwell had forgotten.

'I'll take it,' I answered boldly. 'The three acres against intercourse with me.'

'Amber!' Ginny exclaimed.

'Amber, are you sure about this?' Henry added.

'Don't do it, girl,' Harmony put in.

'Hey, the girl wants it, can't you see?' Rathwell replied, with his face set in the most lascivious expression I had ever seen. 'You're on, sweetie, so you had better make yourself ready for Morris's big red happy stick.'

'Tiny pink happy stick would be more accurate,' I answered, and turned on my heel, hearing a snicker behind me; Melody's I think.

Henry and Ginny were pretty surprised by the bet I had accepted, but I had been unable to resist. If there was one thing I wanted more than anything else it was a piece of land of my own on which to set up my business. Renting was all very well, but ownership of land would give me a solid base from which to defy my father. Then there was the point that Rathwell had missed in the heat of the moment. He didn't just want to fuck me, he wanted my virginity. He had a thing about it, and had often asked intimate questions to find out if I was still innocent on the numerous occasions he had tried to corner me at my parents' house. I was a virgin when I made the bet, but that didn't mean I would be one when the day came to risk submitting to him – not that I intended to lose.

I suppose it would have been easy to ask Henry to fuck

me, and I'm sure he'd have been gentle and careful. I'd seen Ginny's vagina stretched around his cock, though, and, to be honest, was a little scared of the sheer size of it. Next to Henry's, Rathwell's cock was like a chipolata next to a salami and I knew I would have no more difficulty taking it than I did the handle of my hairbrush. That wasn't the point. I was prepared to risk getting fucked by Rathwell, but determined not to give him the satisfaction of having taken my virginity. If I won, he would never have to know but, if I lost, I would tell him afterwards.

It also occurred to me that letting one of the farm boys seduce me would be easy. Several had shown interest and would have been on top of me and humping away in the hay almost before I'd made my acceptance clear. The problem was that doing so would cause complications in that they'd then expect to be around me all the time. What I needed was an older, understanding man who didn't have a penis that would have looked more in proportion on a donkey.

The result of being so fussy was that by the second week in September I was still a virgin and beginning to suspect myself of putting it off. I had, however, managed to get in contact with Susan and arrange to visit her in Oxford. Her letter had been pretty direct, pointing out that we had unfinished business and telling me to bring my school uniform. On the way up I couldn't stop thinking about the implications of this and, by the time I got to her college, I was ready to throw her on the bed, spank her and have her on the spot.

Finding a note stuck to her door telling me she had gone punting came as a bit of a downer. I was supposed to meet her at somewhere called Rainbow Bridge, which I finally managed to identify, and found her lying back in a punt with a man seated at the opposite end. Vowing that I would take the inconvenience of lugging my case halfway across Oxford out on her bottom, I hailed them across the river.

Susan sat up and I immediately realised that something very dubious was going on. She was dressed in her school uniform, right up to the tie, which I was sure wasn't normal dress for undergraduates. She waved cheerfully and indicated that I should cross the bridge to them. The bridge was an arch of concrete looping high over the river and from the top of it I could see right down into their punt, making me doubly certain that she was up to something. At Bridestowe our skirts had been a demure knee-length affair and girls, such as Ginny, who tried to wear them any shorter quickly got ticked off. Susan's skirt was of the pleated dull-green tartan it had always been but had been altered so drastically that in her sitting position I could see the front of her panties. So could the man who was punting with her.

He was of medium height and indeterminate age, with sandy hair and glasses that produced an intensely intellectual look. Although slim, a slight paunch hinted at too much good living, while muscular arms protruding from rolled-up sleeves suggested participation in more sedentary sports.

'Hi, Amber,' Susan greeted me. 'This is my tutor, Dr Rudge. Francis to us. Francis, this is Amber, whom I told you about.'

'Delighted.' Dr Rudge greeted me, taking my hand to help me down into the punt.

There was a definite twinkle in his eye and I wondered just how much Susan had told him. Feeling a little embarrassed and once more vowing to take it out on Susan's bottom, I made myself comfortable beside her and quickly fell back into a conversation as easy as those we had had at school. She looked as mischievous and impish as ever, perhaps more so with her skin tanned from her time in the Caribbean and her hair cut into a short, boyish style. The sun had brought her freckles out, and she actually looked more like the popular image of a public-school girl than she had when she really was one.

Dr Rudge turned the punt up river, away from the spires and towers of the university. At first we passed several other punts, also houses and schools on the bank. Then we passed under a bridge and were gliding between open fields with the willows that lined either bank shading most of the river. It was a hot day, and blissfully easy just lying back in the punt and sliding noiselessly along. They had loaded a hamper with goodies and we took lunch in the shade of a willow, washing down oysters and cold ham with champagne and then a pink wine similar to the one Henry favoured.

As we ate Susan explained how she had quickly become involved with her tutor. His combination of intellect and lack of inhibition had appealed to her and, despite her initial intention of coming out as a lesbian, she had soon found herself as his girlfriend. It didn't surprise me particularly. Dr Rudge had effectively taken the place in her life which I, and also Ginny, had occupied while she was at school. He was older than her and in a position of authority; both characteristics I knew she liked. Also, while somewhat quiet, there was a strength and confidence about him that I could see would be strongly appealing to her.

When we had finished we relaxed for a while and then started up river again, coming into even more lovely country with poplar plantations and little woods on the banks. It was very beautiful and very calming. The river was so clear that we could see the sandy bottom three feet or so below us. In many places there were small islands, some of the trees even joining over our heads to enhance the beauty of the river. I was trailing a finger in the water, half-drunk and totally at ease in the warm sunshine. Nobody had spoken for while, all three of us content to enjoy the drowsy late summer afternoon in silence. Susan had her head on my shoulder and was playing with my hair, an intimacy which Dr Rudge took completely in his stride.

'Amber,' she said, very quietly and with a catch in her voice that I remembered from a certain viaduct in Devon. 'If your uniform's in your case why don't you get into it?'

'And then?' I asked, pretty sure what was coming.

'Spank me,' she answered, so timidly that it put an instant lump of desire in my throat.

I'd spent a lot of time over the previous three months

thinking about what I'd do with Susan when we finally had the chance. If she wanted it in front of her tutor, then that was fine by me. I also remembered how she liked it.

'Steer the punt back behind that little island please, Francis,' I instructed.

'My pleasure,' he replied, with evident relish.

The island provided a short section of water overhung with willows and blackthorn, and was peaceful and isolated enough for me to spank Susan without fear of interference. I rummaged in my case as the punt turned slowly back, finding my uniform and passing it to Susan item by item.

Once in the shelter of the island I climbed on to the bank and changed, the feeling of getting into a uniform once so familiar now producing an odd sensation of doing something improper. Dr Rudge turned his back politely as I stripped and passed my clothes to Susan. She made no secret of her attention to my body, watching me undress with such open admiration that when I was naked it was more than I could resist not put my hands on my hips and ask her if she liked what she saw.

She blushed prettily and nodded, handing me a pair of school-style white panties and asking if I would leave my bra off. I'd been intending to wear rather a nice lacy one for her, but complied with her wish although I knew that the light top would leave my breasts easily distinguishable to Dr Rudge. In my mind he came in the same category as Henry – a pleasant man I could trust. His relationship with Susan also put him in the category of being somebody I had no concern showing off in front of.

As I finished dressing I found that I could well appreciate the fantasy that Susan had created. When we had been about to punish her on the viaduct she had said that she wished it had happened for real at school. Whether she would have actually enjoyed it if it had I wasn't sure, but the idea of spanking her myself had been one of my favourite fantasies and her being in her uniform was very much a part of that. Now we could indulge ourselves without fear of recrimination. Dr Rudge could watch and, when Susan's bottom was red and hot, I could invite him to take advantage of her turned-on state and then watch myself. Only when I was adjusting my socks did Susan drop the bombshell on me.

'I told Francis about your little difficulty,' she said shyly, 'and he'd be happy to volunteer if you like.'

'I'd be honoured, in fact,' he added.

'About Rathwell . . .' I began.

'Yes,' Susan answered.

I found myself blushing furiously and, for a moment, was lost for a response. However, the best course of action was suddenly obvious. If they could be open about me with each other, then there was no reason to hold myself back.

'Well, you've certainly earnt your spanking, you little brat,' I said, grabbing Susan and pulling her towards me.

She stumbled and sat down hard on the muddy bank, soiling her skirt and squeaking as I took her by the ear. A low willow branch provided me with an impromptu spanking seat and I had quickly hauled the protesting Susan across my lap. Her skirt was smeared with mud, with a good slice of her panties showing beneath it, clean and white. I lifted her skirt, ignoring her kicks and half-delighted, half-alarmed squeals. Her pants were stretched taut, bulging with cheeky teenage bottom; ideal for spanking purposes. I tugged them down, feeling her start to tremble as her pert little rear came into view.

I settled her panties around her thighs and started to spank, holding her tight around the waist and making sure that no section of her bottom escaped its share of slaps, just as Henry always did when I was in the same ignominious position over his knee. Susan made no attempt at retaining her dignity or modesty, squealing and kicking for all she was worth. Dr Rudge stood coolly admiring his young girlfriend getting beaten.

Her buttocks were soon nicely red and her squeals had started to give way to moans. I carried on, revelling in the pleasure of giving a spanking that I had so often fantasised over. Occasionally I would glance over to Dr Rudge, finding him completely absorbed in the scene in front of him. For all my excitement I was unsure about letting him take my virginity. After all, however intimate he was with Susan, I'd only met him that afternoon. She had told him that I needed it, though, which made me feel vulnerable and almost panicky, especially as deep down I knew that I was unlikely to get a better opportunity. I put new effort into the task of warming Susan's bottom, taking out my anxiety on her as well as extracting a leisurely revenge and readying myself for sex.

I was going to have a cock put in me, and the thought terrified me. One thing was certain, though: if I was to surrender myself I wanted them both completely open and intimate with me. When I had seen the ecstasy of orgasm on their faces, then they could have me unreservedly.

Susan had begun to sob; a sure sign that she was warm and ready to receive the sexual service that it's so good to get after a thorough spanking. I dipped a finger in to check, finding her wet and swollen. She sighed as my finger slid inside her, wriggling her bottom eagerly for more. I pulled the finger out and put it to her mouth, making her taste her own excitement.

'Ready for it, aren't we, slut?' I asked her, planting another hard smack on her bottom. 'I'd better show it to Francis, hadn't I?'

I took hold of her thighs and pulled them open until her panties were stretched tightly between her knees. Her fanny was gaping and pink between them, the entrance smeared with white juice. She moaned softly, lifting her bottom for me. I shifted my hands, spreading her cheeks wide, admiring the little brown dimple of her anus. It was pulsing a little, as if in expectation of something sliding up it. It was far more than I could resist. I dipped my finger back inside her to lubricate it, then touched her anus, easing the little hole open and probing inside. She gave a little gasp of shock and pleasure as my finger went deep into her bottom.

'Have you buggered her yet?' I asked Dr Rudge, who had given up trying to look casual and was stroking his penis through his trousers.

132

'Amber!' Susan squeaked in alarm.

'I . . . er . . .' he began and stopped.

'Maybe I should,' I teased Susan. 'With the wine bottle. That might teach you a lesson for offering me on a plate to your tutor!'

'I thought you wanted to!' Susan protested.

'I do,' I answered, 'and I might well allow Francis to be the one. Now, tell me, has he buggered you?'

'Yes,' she admitted very quietly.

Just the way she said it excited me, as did the thought of pretty little Susan surrendering her anus to her boyfriend. I wondered if he'd do it in front of me, because she was certainly ready, her anus opening as I moved my finger in and out, fleshy and wet.

'Were you in your school uniform?' I asked.

'Yes,' Susan whispered.

'I'd love to see that,' I said to Dr Rudge. 'Would you show me?'

Susan moaned but made no effort to get up. Inside she was warm and damp, making me wish I had a cock to fill her with. Dr Rudge was somewhat at a loss for what to do, but his instincts weren't. The outline of his penis was clear under his trousers; a ridge that hinted at a full erection. I began to finger Susan faster, making her breath come hard as she started little kicking motions against the ground.

'Let me see you,' I breathed, glancing down towards his cock.

He undid his trousers and let them drop, taking everything else with them to go naked from the waist down. As he straightened, his cock reared up from between the two sides of his shirt. It was reddish pink and heavily veined, the skin so thin and taut that it looked as if it was in danger of bursting. A darker ring of flesh circled the shaft below the swollen, shiny head. It was the cock that was going to fill my vagina – a thought that made me swallow.

He stepped out of the punt, taking hold of his erection and pulling at it as he came forward. He was smaller than Henry, but then Henry had never tried to fuck me, even though he'd been in my hand or mouth more times than I could remember. The dominant, in-control feeling I'd built up while spanking Susan began to fade as I watched him masturbate himself in readiness for our wet, vulnerable holes. He was close, his erection within my reach. Then he tapped the head of his cock on the back of my hand. It seemed to me an aggressive, commanding gesture, as if to suggest that we ought to be paying court to his cock instead of playing together. I suddenly felt incredibly dirty and submissive and eager to see him take his pleasure with Susan before I got down on my knees in the mud so that he could have me as well.

I pulled my finger slowly out of Susan's anus. Despite myself I found my mouth opening for it. Unable to resist the urge to be really dirty I put the finger that had been up Susan's bottom into my mouth, looking straight into Dr Rudge's eyes as I sucked on it. He swallowed and his tongue darted out to wet his lips.

'Oh, Amber,' Susan moaned.

She was looking back, her pretty, freckled face a mask of unrestrained passion. She'd seen what I'd done with my finger.

'Guide it into me, please,' she said weakly. 'Right into my bottom, please, Amber, please, sir.'

I reached out and gingerly took his cock in my hand. It felt hard and rubbery, bloated with blood from the pleasure of watching me spank Susan and finger her anus. His hand went to his pocket, producing a little silver packet. I took it, raising my knee to keep Susan in place over my lap. Francis held his cock out by the base, stretching the skin even more. I put the condom to the head and rolled it slowly down, encasing his cock in translucent rubber. Somehow the condom made his cock look even more threatening, encased in rubber armour that removed the last reason for not putting it into Susan's anus and, later, my vagina.

Susan sighed deeply and raised her bottom, ready and open. I took hold of her cheeks and spread them, stretching her moist bottom-hole. He bent his knees, then put the head of his cock against her anus, making it contract briefly and then open as she relaxed herself to accommodate him. I adjusted my grip, using my fingers to keep Susan's cheeks open and take Francis's erection in my hand. The head of his cock began to go in, Susan gasping as her anus stretched, then giving a sharp cry as her ring was forced wide and the stem of his cock slipped inside her.

She started to whimper, panting and sobbing as he began to work his cock slowly back and forth in her bumhole, nudging a little deeper with each push. Inch by inch it went inside until it was wedged fully up her bottom with his pubic hair touching the open crease of her spread cheeks.

'That's so good,' she sighed.

She was looking back at me, mouth open and face flushed. Her blouse had fallen open while I was spanking her, leaving her tiny breasts showing. Her school skirt was hanging down her back, muddy and dishevelled. Her pants were down around her knees, white and innocent – a shocking contrast to the penis protruding from her bottom-hole and Francis's slow, measured pushes as he buggered her. Her buttocks were red from spanking, the skin goose pimpled, the cheeks up and open to let him into her.

I slid my hand under Susan's belly, finding the coarse hair of Francis's balls and then her fanny. The tone of her moaning changed as my fingers delved in between the lips of her pussy, finding it soaked with her juice, the clitoris a hard button at the top of her soft inner lips. I began to rub, running the tips of my four fingers back and forth over her clitty. Her breathing – already deep and fast – became more urgent still. Her body felt tense under my arm, the muscles straining with reaction to what was happening to her. Her legs were as wide as her panties would allow them to go, her bottom pushed up to meet Francis's belly as he pushed himself deep into the tight opening between her cheeks. She groaned, her fingers clutching at the wet grass beneath her head, her hips starting to buck.

'Yes Francis, harder, deeper,' she called as she started to climax.

He took her by the hips and pulled her hard against himself, forcing his erection to the very hilt in her anus. She grunted – a crude, animal noise from deep in her throat. The movement of her hips became frantic, as if desperate to get yet more sensation from the hand against her fanny and the cock in her anal passage. Twice more she grunted, with every muscle in her body tense, started squealing like a rutting pig and bucking frantically, then gave a last little cry and subsided across my legs, breathless and exhausted.

Francis began to pull back, holding the root of his cock as he withdrew. I was impressed by his control for not just carrying on and coming up her bottom. I was also very aware that the rigid length of erection now being pulled from my friend's anus was shortly going to be in me.

'Slowly, Francis, slowly,' Susan cautioned. 'Ow, my bottom-hole, it feels so sore.'

'It'll soon be better,' he said soothingly, the first time he had spoken since he volunteered to fuck me. 'Are you ready, Amber?'

I had begun to shake. Not the gentle shivering of anticipation of a beating or submitting to someone, but a strong trembling that made my jaw quiver.

'Yes,' I said, trying to sound brave but feeling anything but. 'Would you hold me, Susan?'

'Of course,' she answered as she rose from my lap. 'How are you going to go?'

'In the punt,' I said. 'I think that would make a nice memory.'

'The same as me,' Susan said.

Francis was busy putting on a new condom, a process that left his cock only half stiff inside the new rubber sheath.

'I don't want to be awkward,' I said, 'but I'd rather it went in bare for a bit first. I should be safe anyway at the moment, but you can put one on if you want to come in me.'

'Fine,' he said, 'but perhaps you could both help a little.'

'Sure,' I offered. 'I don't mind sucking your cock.'

'That would be nice,' he replied, 'but perhaps if you could both bend over and show me your bottoms?'

I couldn't help but giggle at his request, which took a lot of the tension out of the situation. There he was, a respectable college tutor, and what he wanted to see was two schoolgirls bending over to show off their bums.

'Fine,' I said. 'Whatever turns you on.'

I put my arm around Susan and we bent over together, pulling our backs in and keeping our knees together to stick our bottoms out as sexily as possible. As I took hold of the hem of my skirt we both turned to watch over our shoulders. His cock was already stiffening in his hand, the head jerking up and down as he pulled at it. I started to lift my skirt, doing it slowly and watching his face. His eyes were fixed on our bottoms, drinking in the sight of the tartan school skirts being lifted to reveal tight white panties. With my skirt up I put my thumbs into the waistband of my panties and began to ease them down. I really thought he was going to come as two schoolgirl bottoms were laid bare for him, one pert and tight, the other full, even a little chubby. I took my panties down around my thighs to make sure he got a good view of my bare bottom. Susan was the same, sticking it out with a cheeky grin on her face. He stopped, I'm sure only an instant before he came.

'Thank you,' he breathed.

His erection was now sticking up like a flagpole, almost vertical and so swollen that the skin was shiny even on the shaft. He pulled his shirt up over his head to stand naked in front of us with his turgid penis sticking up, ready for my virgin fanny. I pulled my panties up again, although it was pointless to do so.

I started to feel vulnerable again, but determined not to delay things. Susan had climbed down into the punt and was tugging my sleeve, gently but insistently. I followed the pressure, climbing in and lying back on the long cushions that covered the bottom of the punt. There was a lump in my throat again as I parted my thighs, Susan cradling my head in her arms as I readied myself to be entered.

Her fingers went to my blouse, popping the buttons open one by one until she could open it and bare my breasts. She began to stroke my nipples as Francis climbed into the punt, naked and in a state of arousal that was not to be denied. I put my hands under my bottom, groping for my panties and pulling them down around my thighs.

In doing so I had removed the last barrier between my vagina and his cock, an action that seemed terribly important. I'd always seen my panties as a barrier between myself and what men wanted to do to me; now they were gone. I was surrendering myself, rolling my legs up and opening my thighs until my useless panties were stretched tight between them.

He went down on his knees, his erection rearing up in front of me. His hand went to it, pushing it down, aiming it at my defenceless vagina, touching me, moistening his cock in the wet flesh of my vulva, putting it to the opening, stretching me, filling me, deflowering me as it slid inside. There was a sharp twinge at the mouth of my fanny as his cock nudged the opening, and then it was up me, all of it, filling my vagina.

I sighed deeply as he took hold of my legs and began to fuck me. The sensation of his cock shaft moving in and out through the mouth of my vagina was bliss. Not quite enough to make me come, but still bliss. I relaxed into Susan's arms and closed my eyes. She was stroking my breasts, whispering to me and soothing me as he moved back and forth inside me. I could hardly believe I'd done it. I'd actually let a man into me; let him use my vagina for his pleasure while I was rolled up with my pants around my thighs. I'd shown off for him, flirting and being really dirty to turn him on, then submitting to entry.

How he resisted coming inside me I'll never know. After what we'd done with him and in front of him it must have taken extraordinary control. Nevertheless, he rowed me slowly for a good ten minutes, occasionally giving a flurry of faster strokes that had me moaning and clutching at my legs, which I was now holding up for him. It seemed to go on and on, leaving me dizzy with pleasure. After a while Susan pulled up her blouse and gave me a nipple to suck, then put her hand between my legs and began to rub at my clitty.

Almost as soon as her finger touched me I started to feel the onset of orgasm. I never could come from just the feeling of a full vagina, whether it's a man's cock, a hairbrush handle, a courgette or anything else that's inside me. Having my clitty rubbed is a very different matter, especially when my mouth is around a small, hard nipple, my legs are being held while I'm fucked, and the girl who's masturbating me is also playing with my breasts. I let go of my legs and pulled Susan to me as I started to come, sucking hard on her nipple, then kissing her as she moved her mouth on to mine. My sex started to pulse around Francis's cock, my back arched in ecstasy, and I was gasping my passion into Susan's open mouth. Even as my climax exploded I felt Francis pull out, and an instant later, something wet and warm splashed on my naked breasts and belly. He'd come on me; a realisation which sent a second climax through me with Susan still rubbing hard at my clit.

I lay there for a long time after we had come, snogging with Susan until I had really had my fill. When she finally pulled away she moved down my body to lick the come off my breasts and stomach – an exquisitely submissive gesture that Francis watched with a proud and proprietorial eye.

After cleaning up and making ourselves decent we simply untied the punt and drifted down river with the current, Francis only making the occasional adjustment to our course with a paddle rather than the pole. At first we were drowsy, Susan lying in my arms with her head snuggled on to my chest. By the time we got to Rainbow Bridge we had started to meet other punts and rowing boats and Francis was forced to stand up and steer properly with the pole.

I started to explain the full details of the Rathwell situation, Susan willingly volunteering for the job of wild pony-girl and Francis offering his services as a referee. I was sure Henry would welcome him, yet doubted that Rathwell would accept him as impartial. I invited him to come in any case, both because Susan wanted him to and because the more support I had the better.

Now that their cheeky plot to get me to surrender my virginity to Francis had succeeded, he was a great deal more voluble. He was fascinated by the idea of pony-girls and sympathetic to my position with my father, remarking that in his experience parents whose expectations differed from those of their offspring were the rule rather than the exception.

The light was already beginning to fade by the time we reached the moorings which their college shared with several other city centre colleges. I hadn't realised that we'd been so long, and was astonished to find that we'd been playing together for well over an hour. It had seemed like a few minutes yet, on reflection, I'd had Susan across my knee for maybe as much as ten minutes and that had only been the start.

We ate in the hall of Susan's college, after which Francis had to attend a meeting. I thanked him and warmly kissed him goodbye, giving his cock a gentle squeeze in between our bodies. He left us at the bottom of the staircase in which Susan had her room. It was in an old part of the college, made of stone worn smooth by time and with a strong atmosphere of dignity and learning. Her room was much the same, high in the building with a view over the roofs of other, lower structures. I spent a long moment looking out of the window, half envious of Susan, half happy for her. Soft arms encircled my waist, her head coming to rest against my back with a wisp of hair tickling my neck.

I turned, kissing her, holding her to me, scrabbling urgently at her blouse. Without a word we sank on to the bed and began to make love, exploring each other with complete intimacy. She had covered her uniform with a light coat, which was the first thing to go. After that we stripped each other slowly, kissing the more sensitive areas as they came bare. I was quickly naked and peeling Susan's pants off even as I straddled her face and settled my fanny on to her mouth. Her own sex was directly in front of my face, warm and richly scented with her musk. I buried my face in it, my tongue searching out her clitoris even as hers found mine.

We came together, our sex then becoming less hasty and more deliberate. I had her kiss and lick between my bottom-cheeks, pushing her tongue into my anus as I knelt on all fours. The sensation was exquisite, leading her to want the same from me. I could hardly refuse, especially when she presented me with her bottom and brazenly demanded a lick. She was on her bed, kneeling with her thighs well apart and her bottom stuck up. Her fanny was open and wet, glistening with our mixed juices. Above it her anus made a wrinkled knot of darker flesh, tempting my tongue in what would for me be a gesture of abject submission.

I hesitated – my lips an inch from her bumhole – braced myself and kissed it, drawing a giggle and a sigh from Susan. It felt glorious to be licking her and I was soon burrowing my tongue into the little hole, as dirty and abandoned as she had been with me. She came again like that, with my tongue in her anus while she played with herself.

After that we paused, sharing a bottle of wine in bed and then once more beginning to tease and caress each other. As the night progressed I increasingly took the dominant role. Susan wanted another over-the-knee spanking and put on her uniform to take it. I dressed too, and when I had warmed her bottom I made her kiss my feet and beg for more. A ruler and then a hairbrush left her bottom smarting and pink and her on a natural high of pure submission. Giggling with wine and sex, we became gradually dirtier, using the hairbrush handle first in her vagina then her bottom. I stripped her but stayed dressed myself, adding to my feeling of dominance. We experimented with bondage games, me tying Susan's hands behind her back and tormenting her breasts and fanny. When I needed a pee I did it all over her in the small shower attached to her room, directing my stream first over her breasts and then actually into her mouth as she knelt naked in front of me.

Some time in the early hours of the morning I had her tied face down on the bed. She was nude, her upturned bottom as red as a tomato, the hairbrush protruding from between her cheeks where it was wedged up her anus. I could see her sex-lips from the rear, swollen and pink, now shaved and slick with the skin cream we had been using as a lubricant. She was breathing fast, her excitement rising again from my treatment of her.

'I'm going to wet the bed, Amber,' she said suddenly.

For a moment I thought she wanted to be untied but, before I could do anything about it, a trickle of pee had started to run from her fanny. It built quickly to a stream, pooling on the bed between her thighs and soaking into the blankets. She was panting and sobbing as she did it, obviously in ecstasy. I watched her pee gush out, my own excitement rising as she soiled her bed. The sight was more than I could resist and I buried my face in between her thighs, putting my face to her still dribbling fanny, tasting her pee, swallowing some, then lifting my head and letting it run out of my mouth on to her bottom and back.

I untied her and we made love again, licking and stroking each other frantically in the sodden bed, totally unrestrained in each other's arms until we had both come again and finally collapsed into exhausted sleep.

Seven

Inevitably Susan and I were a little embarrassed by just how carried away we had got with each other when we awoke that morning in Oxford. Our shame soon turned to giggles as we did our best to cover up our misbehaviour. The rest of the day was spent sightseeing with her and Francis, and only that night did we once more make love together. I returned to Hertfordshire the next morning feeling extremely happy with myself. I had satisfied the passion for Susan which had been building up in me for months, years, really. I was no longer a virgin, and I had lost my virginity in a situation that was both delightfully eccentric and memorable. Better by far than surrendering myself to some clumsy farm boy in a barn or outhouse. I was also confident in my ability to beat Rathwell and claim my piece of land.

Henry was delighted by my experience and demanded a blow-by-blow account of my weekend. I gave it all except the most intimate moments with Susan, watching him get gradually more excited as I described our sex play. When I had finished there was nothing for it but for me to get into my uniform once more and allow him to spank me. Once my bottom was warm and I was in my usual submissive state, it just didn't seem fair to deny him my vagina any more. Bending over his favourite armchair, I let him enter me from the rear, my bottom warm under the weight of his belly as he worked his oversized cock slowly into me. It hurt a little but felt wonderful once it was inside me and I was soon playing with myself while he took his time with me and finally came over my bottom.

The next day we contacted Rathwell and set a date for the pursuit-capture-punishment when Susan and Francis would be able to come down. It was to be the last weekend in September; something of a risk as outdoor pony-girl play is definitely not a cold weather sport.

As it happened, the weather on the Saturday before the race was exceptionally mild but also wet. It had rained hard all night and was still drizzling when Susan and Francis arrived. Henry and Francis got on well over lunch, but were too inhibited by each other's presence for us to indulge in the gentle afternoon sex play I had been hoping for and which had become normal between Henry and I. This was a shame as I'd been hoping to coax Susan into having sex with Henry.

Their reluctance didn't extend to watching Susan and I practise for pursuit-capture-punishment, however, and when the clouds finally broke in the middle of the afternoon Henry took deck chairs outside and set them up for the two of them. Rules demanded that the wild pony-girl be completely naked except for her shoes, while it was felt to be good etiquette for the hunter to be fully and traditionally dressed. I had jodhpurs and boots from school, and Henry had insisted on buying me a pink jacket. I dressed and put my hair up with a red ribbon, which completed an outfit that both he and Francis complimented me on. I also had a coil of soft rope and a riding whip: one for tying Susan; one for her bottom when I caught her.

Susan was already in the yard, having only had to take her clothes off and get into socks and trainers. This wasn't to say she hadn't made an effort with her look. The socks came up above her knees and were patterned with broad red and black bands. This really highlighted the rest of her nudity and had my pulse racing as soon as I saw her. Next to Henry she looked more tiny than ever – a fragile, naked nymph with her pert breasts pushed out as she stretched in the warm, moist air. She had kept her fanny shaved, and I could see her sex lips peeping out from between her thighs.

She was in an active mood, and full of energy as she

warmed up. While we were changing she had confided in me that the thought of being naked in front of Henry made her feel a little nervous but extremely submissive. Going nude for the larger crowd on the following day was a more daunting prospect, as was running from Morris Rathwell.

On Henry's signal she sped off up the big field, her heels kicking up little plumes of water with each pace. I waited, Henry eyeing his stopwatch as Susan vanished around the end of the rectangular spinney. Beyond it I knew she had two main choices: turn back and conceal herself or move to the top of the field in its shadow. The woods at the edges were out of bounds, but not the beech hedge on the ridge, nor the enclave at its middle.

'You're off, Amber,' Henry said. 'I'll sound the horn if your hour runs out.'

I set off up the field at a slow run, keen not to exhaust myself. I made for the gap between the spinneys, knowing that Susan must cross my field of vision if she wanted to get to the left-hand half of the big field. She didn't, and once I had reached the ridge and checked the enclave I started to move back down, certain that she was trapped in the rectangular spinney.

Only she wasn't, or at least not that I could find. The rules precluded climbing trees or burying herself in leaves and, although the spinney was pretty dense, it was also narrow. I reached the end feeling puzzled and wondering where I had made a mistake. She wasn't in the spinney, I was pretty sure of that, which meant she had eluded me and could be anywhere.

I changed tactics, running to the top of the field and along the hedge, searching in it as I went. I failed to find her and so once more made for the spinneys, this time running through the round spinney in a random pattern. Again nothing came of it and I emerged into the field feeling seriously frustrated.

So it went, until I was certain that she'd cheated in some way and this made me feel badly thwarted. Eventually the horn sounded and I had to return to Henry and Francis, completely defeated. As I reached them I heard a cheerful laugh behind me and turned to see Susan emerging from the rectangular spinney. I waited with my hands on my hips while she skipped down the field, laughing and twice turning cartwheels until she reached me and gave me a kiss before going to Francis.

I accepted a badly needed cup of tea from Henry and listened to Susan explaining how she had stayed just deep enough in the spinneys to watch me, anticipated my search pattern and always kept one step ahead. She had eluded me the first time by dashing across to the round spinney in the few seconds it had taken me to check the enclave. Twice after that we had been on opposite sides of large trees but, once I had started to get worked up, avoiding me had become increasingly easy.

'She's far too good for Morris,' Henry remarked, when Susan had finished her explanation. 'I think we should take precautions, though. Greasing her might be an idea.'

'Like a pig?' I asked, delighted by the idea.

'Yes, please,' Susan laughed.

'Butter always proved best in my view,' Henry continued, 'although lard has its advocates.'

'Why not a proper body oil,' I suggested. 'Something that smells nice.'

'It soaks in too quickly,' Henry replied. 'A pound of butter is the thing, and also cheaper.'

'Vaseline is a better lubricant,' Francis put in. 'I find butter melts too fast.'

'Have you greased a girl before?' I inquired.

'Not entirely,' he answered. 'And not for such exotic purposes but, as you know, I have my preferences.'

Susan blushed and giggled.

'Let's test it this evening,' I suggested, seizing a chance to get round the men's reservations by arranging something specific. 'We can play with candles and things.'

The idea was accepted enthusiastically and, after another cup of tea, I made a second attempt to catch Susan. This time I was successful but only after a long chase across the big field to the sound of the men's laughter as we slipped and slid on the wet ground. When I finally had hold of

146

Susan's arm I pushed her down, sat on her back and gave her two strokes with my riding whip to comply with the rule that a captured pony-girl must be brought in visibly spanked. I then lashed her wrists behind her back, slung her across my shoulder and brought her in triumphantly. The time was forty-two minutes and, if she'd been greased, I doubt I'd have managed to get hold of her at all, so I was pretty confident that we could beat Rathwell.

It had started to drizzle again during our second practice run, so we went inside to discuss tactics while Henry began the preparation of an evening meal even more elaborate than usual. Susan was full of clever ideas – as was Francis – and by the time Henry appeared to ask me to lay the table I was certain that the competition would be a walkover for me. I had found it exciting as well, and so had Susan, although it would have been better if I'd caught her in good time and been able to take her up to the enclave for a more leisurely and intimate punishment.

My efforts to get Henry and Francis to be completely open in each other's company were moderately successful, with the testing of various lubricants on our arms. We eventually decided on a mixture of butter and Vaseline, by which time Susan was sitting on the scullery floor with her dress rolled down to her waist and liberally smeared with goo. Both men were enjoying watching, so I grabbed Susan and, after a brief and messy struggle, managed to straddle her back. I made a great show of pulling her dress up. Her panties were white, lacy and obviously quite expensive, which made it even more satisfying to pull the back open and smear a liberal handful of the muck down them. She giggled as I rubbed it into her bottom, then squealed as I put a hand down between her cheeks to lubricate her bottom-hole. My finger went in easily and I played with her anus until she began to moan and push her bottom up, only then stopping abruptly and pulling her thoroughly soiled panties tight up between her cheeks so that the yellowish mess squelched out of the sides.

The show had been too much for Henry and, when I looked up, he had his cock in his hand, stiff and ready for me. I crawled over, leaving Susan in a puddle of greasy mess. Kneeling in front of Henry I opened my blouse and pulled my bra up, folding his erection between my tits. He sighed deeply and began to push it up and down, fucking my boobs until his great cock looked fit to burst. I then pulled back. Susan was still on the floor, but kneeling by Francis and stroking his crotch through his trousers. I held my breasts out to him, offering him the same pleasure I had given Henry. As I had guessed it was more than he could resist, and he made no protest as Susan started to undo his fly.

That broke down the final barrier and his erection was soon nestled between my tits while Susan sucked greedily on Henry's cock. Both men came in our mouths, leaving Susan and I to share a sticky, salty kiss and retire to the bathroom to wash and come under each other's tongues.

I actually slept in Henry's bed that night, though mainly for comfort as Susan and Francis were together. We slept with me sat in his lap, quite innocently until I was awakened at some point in the early hours by a hand gently pulling my nightie up. I let him explore, lifting my nightie and putting his hand down the back of my pants. I obliged by lifting my thigh so that he could get to my fanny. He opened me slowly with a finger, waiting until I was wet and moaning for him to take me. We fucked slowly with the gusset of my panties pulled to the side and my bottom stuck out into his lap. He stayed in me for ages without either of us coming and, at last, we rolled apart and masturbated together while we talked about what we'd like to do to Susan and Ginny.

It had been raining hard outside when Henry woke me for sex, but the morning was a blaze of sunshine. Unfortunately the yard was three inches deep in a disgusting pale brown slurry and the big field was a morass with pools of water standing in the hollows. I stood looking out of the window for a long time, watching the clouds scud across the sky. The weather looked fresh and distinctly autumnal. So it proved, although Susan made no objection as long as she had a blanket when she wasn't running.

Rathwell turned up in the middle of the morning, driving his ostentatious gold Rolls Royce as always and acting his usual, disagreeable self. Both Melody and Harmony were with him, behaving with their usual combination of vanity and friendliness. They were quite heavily dressed and seemed to find the weather unpleasant, which added to my confidence. Rathwell didn't, acting as cock-sure and self-satisfied as ever, with remarks about what he thought was my inevitable defloweration. Melody was as bad when it came to teasing me, although Harmony was more sympathetic than anything.

I had dressed in my riding outfit, which was immaculate, Susan having sweetly volunteered to polish my boots and brush my jacket immediately after breakfast. Rathwell matched me almost garment for garment, only spoiling the effect with trainers instead of riding boots and sporting a flashy cravat in turquoise and gold silk. Having determined by tossing a coin that it would be Melody who ran for Rathwell, she opened the boot of the car and went into the house with a bag. Rathwell then drew two objects out, one of which alarmed me immediately and the other which I found unsettling despite not knowing what he intended to do with it. It was a yoke. The first item was a bolas made of three solid rubber balls attached to lengths of soft rope which joined in a central knot.

'Is that legal?' I asked Henry, who was standing by me.

'The bolas?' he answered. 'I fear I know of nothing that outlaws it. Indeed I can't really even say it's against the spirit of the game.'

'Nothing in the rules,' Rathwell put in. 'Nothing in the rules, and old Henry wrote them, so he should know. Nice idea eh, Henry? Who's your wild one, then? Tell me it's that tall blonde with the massive knockers.'

'I'm afraid Ginny's not here today,' I told him. 'Another friend, Susan, will be running for me.'

'Good-looking is she? Nice body?'

'She's very pretty,' I answered coolly, 'but judge for yourself.'

Susan had come out of the scullery and was walking

towards us alongside Francis. She had a blanket over her shoulders which hid her body but, with each step, she showed her red and black thigh-length socks and a little leg. Her hair was in bunches and tied with red and black ribbons, which alone was enough to set my pulse fluttering. Rathwell whistled lewdly.

'How many more dirty little cuties do you know?' he demanded.

'Oh, one or two,' I lied as, in fact, other than girls who Rathwell knew as well, Susan and Ginny were my only two erotic playmates. 'This is Susan Wren and her boyfriend, Dr Francis Rudge.'

'Nice to meet you, Sue, Doc Rudge,' Rathwell replied.

I saw Francis wince and Susan stuck her tongue out at Rathwell in a gesture that was calculated to earn her an even more tender bottom if he ever actually caught her.

'What's that for?' I asked, overcome with curiosity as to why he had brought a yoke.

'It's a yoke, Amber,' Henry said with a sigh.

'I know,' I answered, 'but it's for a real horse. It's not pony-girl kit. Is it?'

'Not exactly,' Rathwell said, favouring me with a lewd grin, 'although, as old Henry will tell you, they can be used for ploughing competitions. You'd be good at that, with those sturdy thighs and shoulders, not to mention your big, muscular bottom.'

'But we're not doing that today, are we?' I queried.

'No, no, just look on it as decoration for now,' he answered.

He clearly had no intention of telling me what it was for, so I let the subject drop instead of allowing him to get to me. Henry seemed to know what Rathwell intended but preferred to keep me in blissful ignorance. Instead of pressing the point I asked Rathwell if he would accept the toss of a coin to determine who ran first.

'Sure,' he answered. 'I suppose I can trust old Henry to be a fair ref, I remember him ruling against Jean often enough.'

'Myself, Francis and Harmony can mediate any

disputes,' Henry declared, 'but we need Melody before I go over the rules.'

'I'm here,' Melody announced from the scullery door.

Like Susan she was covered, but only with a short leather jacket that left most of her long, dark legs showing. She had her blue trainers on and bright-yellow ankle socks, also yellow and pale-blue spray colour in her hair. This had to be a mistake as it would show up like a beacon in the spinneys.

'You look pretty,' Susan said as Melody walked up beside her.

Melody smiled and tousled Susan's hair, a gesture that gave me a quite irrational pang of jealousy.

'Your attention, please.' Henry declared. 'The rules are as always. Susan and Melody, pay attention. You may run anywhere within the boundaries of the big field and the two spinneys you can see up the slope. The hedge at the top is fair ground but the woods to either side are not. Each hunter will have an hour to catch their pony, rope her, punish her and bring her back. Hunters may not carry timepieces. Bottoms may be smacked in any way the hunter pleases, but there must be some colour to the pony-girl's rear cheeks when she is returned. After an hour any pony-girl remaining uncaptured is considered to have escaped. Stop words are as usual, but should only be used in dire need. You are dressed beautifully, Amber. You, Morris, although I suppose your dress is not actually against the rules, really should consider the sartorial implications of combining training shoes with riding gear. Are you sure you wouldn't like to borrow a pair of my boots?'

'Thank you but no,' Rathwell replied. 'Now, if you could find a coin, I'd like to get started. I'm eager to introduce little Amber's virgin twat to the old happy stick.'

'Very well,' Henry answered, 'although I doubt that you will gain that privilege. You may call.'

He put his hand into his pocket and pulled out a fifty pence piece, which he flipped high and caught dextrously before it could land in the mud.

'Heads,' Rathwell called.

'Tails,' Henry declared, looking at the coin in his hand and then showing it to Rathwell. 'Amber may choose.'

'Susan runs first,' I stated without hesitation, reasoning that it would be better for me to know what time I had to beat, if any.

'One other thing,' Henry put in. 'I feel it would be fair for Melody to have a chance to familiarise herself with the ground. Amber?'

'That's reasonable,' I admitted, although slightly irked by Henry's obsession with fair play.

'Excellent,' Henry declared cheerfully. 'Let's have our stirrup cup then.'

He disappeared into the kitchen and returned with tots of hot rum punch which we drank at a gulp. Melody then jogged away up the field, leaving a clear trail through the morning dew. This was an unexpected problem. When we had practised, the grass had been wet but dull, leaving no trails to speak of. Now the entire meadow was carpeted with a multitude of tiny dew drops, each reflecting its scintilla of light and each ready to be shattered by someone's foot. The hunters would now have a far easier task, especially the one going first. Annoyingly, it was just too late to choose to have Melody run first. Resigning myself to a tougher run, I walked over to where Harmony was standing talking with Francis.

'You'd better get Susan greased,' I said to Francis.

'You're right,' he said.

'Ready for it?' Harmony asked, her voice sympathetic.

'Don't worry about me,' I assured her. 'I don't intend to lose, but I can handle it if I do.'

'You've got spirit,' she answered. 'Look, I'll give you a hint. If you want to turn Melody on so she doesn't fight too hard, just get her on the ground and pee on her.'

'Really?' I asked, not at all sure if Harmony's advice could be trusted.

'Believe me, girl. Do that and she'll be putty in you hands,' Harmony assured me.

Or a raving, spitting hell-cat, I thought to myself,

intrigued by the idea but very cautious. After the way Melody had teased me it would also be a pleasure, and I quickly decided that it had to be done, but only once she was securely tied and helpless.

'What are you up to?' I heard Rathwell's voice from behind me.

'Never heard of a greased piglet?' Francis answered, continuing to slap handfuls of our revolting lubricant on to Susan's now naked body.

'Nothing in the rules says a wild pony-girl can't be greased,' Henry said, wagging his finger at Rathwell. 'No more than they mention bolases.'

'I . . .' Rathwell began and thought better of it, instead waving at Melody where she was visible walking along the ridge.

By the time Melody returned Susan was fully greased, nude and glistening in the bright sunlight, her tanned skin and freckles highlighted by her oily coating. Rathwell took a coil of rope from Henry and tucked it into his belt.

'Make it easy and I'll just spank your little tush,' he said to Susan. 'Give me a hard time and I'll take the whip to you.'

'Hey!' I protested automatically.

'Don't worry, Amber, I'd quite like a taste of the whip,' Susan answered cheekily. 'Not that the poor old boy'll catch me anyway, so you'll have to do it instead.'

I laughed at the immediate flush of annoyance on Rathwell's face. Susan had hit a soft spot and riled him, which with luck would make him a less efficient hunter.

'We'll start on the half-hour,' Henry interrupted. 'In just two minutes.'

Susan began to run on the spot, watching Henry until he gave the signal and then taking off up the field. She ran fast considering how wet the ground was, and quickly disappeared around the end of the rectangular spinney.

'This shouldn't take too long, I think,' Rathwell remarked in what was supposed to be a bored tone as he walked slowly over to stand at the edge of the field.

For all his nonchalance I could tell he was nervous. A

vein in one of his hands stood out, pulsing occasionally, while the long, bony fingers were trembling ever so slightly.

'You're off, Morris,' Henry announced.

Rathwell started forward, moving at an easy lope. I could tell he was fit for his age, yet could hardly see him out-running or out-thinking Susan, and so turned back to Henry with only a moderate flutter of apprehension in my stomach.

'What do you think?' I asked.

'The dew is a problem,' Henry answered. 'Yet I have faith in both Susan and yourself.'

'Morris is going to get you, girl,' a voice spoke from over my shoulder.

It was Melody, who had come up to stand close beside me. She had also put her hand on my bottom, cupping my cheeks right in the middle and prodding meaningfully at my pussy with a finger.

'Virgin,' she continued, and there was definite lust in her voice. 'Say, if I had a strap-on, I'd fuck you myself.'

'If you've got one on you, you can,' I offered, 'but your master wouldn't be best pleased with you now, would he?'

'It'd be well worth a whipping,' she answered, then leant closer to whisper in my ear, 'especially as when I'd had your pussy I'd push my big, black hard-on right up your posh little behind.'

I gulped and felt the colour rise to my cheeks, imagining Melody mounted on me and putting a strap-on dildo to my anus. Not that I'd ever seen such a thing, but it was something I'd imagined often enough even before I knew such things were actually made. She was trying to get to me and succeeding although, as I was due to take a riding whip to her bottom, it seemed a foolish move. Unless, of course, her intention was not to discomfort me but ensure that once I caught her she got properly dealt with.

'Throw the competition and you can do exactly that,' I whispered back. 'I mean it, up my bottom, and you can beat me, too.'

Melody stepped back and looked me right in the eye. Her emotions were hard to read, but I'd certainly shaken

154

her. She raised her eyebrows and stepped away, walking over to talk to Harmony. I gave them both a wicked grin and stuck my bottom out a little, getting raised eyebrows from Melody and an appraising look from Harmony.

Up the field Rathwell had vanished into the rectangular spinney, evidently having seen no tracks on the far side. Susan emerged from the other end, crouched low and moving towards Rathwell. She was taking a risk, yet had every chance of eluding him. He would also be unable to use his bolas in the spinneys.

By the time he emerged from the end of the rectangular spinney, she was in the circular one. He stood and looked around, checking for trails and finding none. It was all I could do not to laugh as he scratched his head in puzzlement. Susan appeared again, backtracking her footprints between the two spinneys and making a mess of the dew so that it was impossible to determine which way she had gone. Rathwell entered the rectangular spinney again and vanished from our sight.

For a long time we saw nothing, then Susan suddenly burst from the circular spinney, running at full speed with Rathwell close behind. He was trying to get his bolas going, but the effort slowed him and Susan was getting away. It whirled over his head, making an eerie whistling noise. He ran on, then threw, the bolas aimed straight for her. Susan stopped, turned, waited and then threw herself flat, the bolas passing harmlessly over her. Rathwell started after her, only for Susan to jump up, grab the fallen bolas and sprint away across the field. I couldn't resist clapping as her laughter floated back to us, light and girlish. She was dancing across the meadow without a hint of fatigue, laughing and taunting Rathwell, then swinging the bolas high into an oak, where it caught.

'I should have included you two in the bet,' I called to the black girls, 'as my sex-slaves for a week.'

'Any time,' Harmony called back, earning a smack on her leg from Melody.

Henry's stopwatch showed twenty-six minutes, and Rathwell showed no signs of even coming close to Susan.

Over the next half-hour they chased and dodged around the field, Rathwell becoming increasingly cross and Susan increasingly cheeky. Finally she overdid it, actually touching his jacket before darting away. He shot a foot out, tripping her, and the next instant was kneeling across her and pulling her wrists together in the small of her back. She kicked futilely, still laughing as her arms were lashed. Glancing nervously towards us, he gave her half-a-dozen hard strokes on her upturned bottom. She continued laughing in between squeaks as he whipped her and afterwards, kicking and squirming to make life difficult for him. Finally he managed to get her across his shoulder and started towards us at a slow jog.

I had to admit she looked entrancing, balanced on his shoulder with her wrists lashed together and her sex-lips peeping out from between her thighs, six red lines criss-crossing her rounded, girlish bottom. He was a very different matter: red-faced, covered in mud and grease, his clothes soaked and one pocket of his smart jacket torn almost completely away.

'Fifty-eight minutes and thirty-seven seconds,' Henry intoned as Rathwell crossed the line. 'Cutting it a bit fine there, Morris.'

Rathwell said nothing for once, instead lowering Susan into the mud and going to lean against the wall of one of the stables, puffing and blowing. Melody hurried over to him with a tumbler of rum punch, Harmony sauntering behind.

'Let the old boy get his breath back and I'm ready,' I told Henry and Francis, making sure my remark was loud enough for Rathwell to hear. 'Well done, Susan, nice run.'

Rathwell shot me a dirty look as Francis bent down to untie Susan.

'That was great,' Susan sighed. 'Really good fun. A proper beating would have been nice, though, with a warm-up spanking first and then perhaps being made to count the strokes out loud.'

'I didn't have the time,' Rathwell growled, and then turned back to what was becoming an intense conversation with Melody and Harmony.

I looked at them, finding Melody nodding seriously and Harmony looking uncertain. Whatever it was obviously boded no good for me, yet it was impossible to see how I could fail unless they broke the rules, which would mean immediate victory for me. Finally they broke up, Melody sauntering towards me with a look of insolent self-assurance on her face. She shrugged off her jacket as she came, tossing it to Henry. Underneath she was naked, big dark-skinned breasts stuck out, the nipples darker still and stiff. Her belly was firm and muscular, her pussy hidden in a nest of thick, crinkled hair, sprayed yellow and blue like the hair on her head.

'That's sweet,' I admitted, determining to take my time with her if I caught her quickly.

Something about her powerful, dark body and insolent manner brought out the submissive in me, especially after her taunts about what she wanted to do to me. I was the one with the whip and rope, though, and for now was determined to gain her submission.

'I'm ready for you, girl,' she said, putting her hands on her hips and throwing me a typically impertinent look.

'We'll go in three and a bit minutes,' Henry announced.

Melody looked round, nodding confidently to Rathwell, who returned a knowing leer. I took the rope from Francis, winding it into a hank. Susan came up to me, smiling and bright eyed despite being scratched in several places and completely coated with a mixture of mud, leaves and grease.

'Good luck, Amber,' she said quietly.

'Thanks,' I answered, tousling her hair as Henry signalled Melody to go.

My adrenaline rose quickly as I watched Melody run lightly up the big field. Instead of using Susan's route, she made straight for the gap between the spinneys. Rather than turn into one, she continued on, finally disappearing from view beyond the rectangular spinney when she was a good halfway to the ridge. I wondered if she was attempting some sort of complicated double back, as otherwise she would have only the ridge hedge to use for cover.

'You're off, Amber,' Henry announced.

I started forward, following Melody's trail. It ran clear between the spinneys and on to the ridge, with no sign of her having returned. Up-slope from me it disappeared into the enclave, which was presumably where she was. I followed, puzzled by her tactics and ready for her to break from the hedge once I got into the enclave. She didn't, but was standing waiting for me in the shelter of the high beech hedges. She stood with her arms folded and her head cocked to the side.

'Right, girl,' she said as I stepped into the enclave. 'Now I'm going to teach you a lesson. First I'm going to tie your hands with your own rope, then I'm going to take down those fancy jodhpurs and your panties too. Maybe I'll strip you bare. After that I'm going to take a long time over that sassy white behind until it's just as red as a London bus and I'm ready to come. Then you can suck my titties, kiss me right down between my cheeks, and lick pussy until the horn goes. Right?'

I didn't answer, realising that this was their trick. It wasn't against the rules either. A wild pony-girl is expected to put up a fight and, if she wins, that's hard luck on the hunter. Normally, of course, the girl craves nothing more than to be caught and made to submit to the hunter. Now I found myself wishing that the more openly submissive Harmony had won the toss.

Melody was smiling and walking towards me with every sign of confidence. I hesitated, threw my whip down and feinted a dash for the field, then charged her. I hit her full on and we went down into the puddle that had formed in the centre of the enclave. She squealed and grabbed at my wrist, trying to get her weight on top of me. The pressure came on to my arm, forcing me back inch by inch. She was incredibly strong, her face showing a grin of triumph and delight as I began to give way. My own feelings began to betray me, the mental need for her to dominate me rising as her physical strength overcame me.

'Better to give in easy, girl,' Melody said through gritted teeth, 'or I'll take you back tied and your little girlfriend will see you.'

It was the wrong thing to say, making me think of Susan, naked and trembling in my arms, begging for punishment. The image fired new determination and I started to push back. It was hopeless, but for a moment she was off balance. I twisted and rolled, finding myself behind her and managing to plant a hard smack on her meaty bottom. For a moment she was distracted, enabling me to crawl away, only for her hand to catch on to my jodhpurs and pull them down over my bottom. I kicked out, contacting something soft. Melody squeaked and wrenched herself away. I sat up to find her jumping to her feet. She spun around to face me. I stayed low, waiting for her in a squat.

'Harmony says you'll be easy to handle once you've been peed on,' I said, determined to give her a dose of her own medicine.

She leapt at me like a wild cat, knocking me back and hissing wordlessly as she clawed at me. I went down under her, grabbing at her wrists to stop her scratching me. For a moment her naked breasts were in my face, then her legs were straddling my waist, pinning me to the ground.

'No way!' she shouted, flustered far beyond what I had expected. 'You're going to get that, not me!'

I twisted again, throwing her off me to land hard in the mud. She grabbed at my blouse, tearing it open, her nails catching one of my breasts and leaving a long, scarlet scratch. That really made me see red. She was grappling me, trying to roll me on to my front. I resisted, taking her weight on my arms and trying to force her back. For a moment there was deadlock. Melody's face was contorted with the strain and her passion, her eyes burning with determination. She grunted, wrenching furiously at me but only gaining an inch. Once more there was deadlock then, slowly, painfully, she began to give. Her expression changed from determination to alarm as I bent her arm back, my teeth gritted together with the effort. She gave a grunt of consternation as I began to twist her arm, then a furious sob as I applied an arm lock and triumphantly straddled her back.

I was filthy with mud and my blouse had been torn completely open, also my bra, leaving both breasts uncovered and soiled. My jodhpurs were half-down, my panties sodden and torn across the seat. My skin was scratched and wet, yet none of it mattered. By good luck the rope was within reach and I made quick work of lashing Melody's wrists and attaching them to her waist, then lashing her ankles to leave her completely helpless. I stood up, panting and exhausted yet utterly triumphant.

It was hard to judge how long we had been fighting, but nothing like an hour. I had plenty of time to enjoy my beautiful captive. I pulled up my jodhpurs but decided to leave my blouse open for the moment. The next job was to colour her bottom up, which was less than easy as her skin was the colour of dark chocolate anyway.

'Spanking time for you, Melody,' I told her. 'Then your favourite treat.'

She squirmed in her bonds but said nothing, instead turning her head to look up to me. Her eyes were big and moist, her mouth a little open. I laughed and went to fetch my riding whip. She gave a little sob when she saw me pick it up, and I made a deliberate show of smacking it against my palm as I approached her.

'Red as a London bus, is it?' I teased her as I laid the tip of the whip gently on her naked bottom. 'Well, let's see what colour yours goes shall we?'

The answer was a sort of glossy purple, as I discovered after warming her bottom by hand and then giving her a dozen moderately hard cuts with the whip. She hadn't said a word, but had begun to breathe deeply and evenly once I'd spanked her and had responded to the whipping with little gasps and moans. She'd also struggled a bit at first but, by the end, was lying full length, completely subdued. I sat on her thighs and started to explore her bottom, meeting no resistance as I pulled her cheeks open to inspect between her legs.

Her pussy lips were so dark as to be almost black, her bumhole the same colour. Both entrances showed bright pink centres, her pussy moist with her juice, her bumhole swollen and a little open.

'If I had that strap-on thing . . .' I said.

'Please,' she sighed.

'Sorry . . .' I began, 'but then again.'

My riding whip was one I had borrowed from Henry, with the handle topped with a big tiger's eye. Melody's pussy looked open and inviting but, knowing what she'd intended for me, I decided that it was the other hole that deserved to be filled. I spread her thighs with my hand, burrowing a finger into her pussy and drawing it out moist with her juice. She made no resistance, instead pushing her bottom up to make it easier for me. I sucked my finger, tasting her and adding my spit to her juice. She gave a little squeak and clenched her bum-cheeks when my finger touched her anus and she realised my intention, but then sighed and relaxed as I slid my finger into the tight hole. I spent a little while working her open and then pulled my finger out, replacing it with the head of my whip. The tiger's eye was as wide as a good-sized cock – certainly more so than Rathwell's – and Melody squeaked prettily as it popped up her bottom. I began to bugger her with it, pushing the whip in and out and then pulling it out completely only to enter her again. She was quickly moaning and gasping, but I finally pulled it out, conscious of the time.

'Put it in again, Amber,' she pleaded.

I complied, inserting the tiger's eye in her bottom not once, but three times more and then leaving it in place. She was writhing her hips in a lewd, abandoned motion to make the whip handle move in her anal passage; a sight that had me wishing I could take the time to really enjoy her submission. Telling myself to get on with it I stood up and rolled her over on to her back. As I did so her knees came apart, offering me her open, wet pussy, the whip handle protruding from her anus beneath. She drew her ankles as far towards herself as the lashing would allow, then looked up at me hopefully.

'Make me come, Amber, please?' she said, her voice showing how badly in need she was.

'Maybe, if you're quick,' I answered even as I pulled one boot off.

161

'What are you doing?' she asked. 'Just lick me. I'll be there in no time.'

'I think you know what you need first,' I answered, pulling my jodhpurs and panties off and laying them on my boots.

'No, Amber, not that,' Melody squeaked. 'That's special, just for Harmony.'

'You know the stop word,' I said, stepping across her body to stand, legs apart, over her chest.

'Oh God,' Melody sighed, shutting her eyes and opening her mouth.

Well if that wasn't an open invitation I'd never seen one. My bladder was quite full, certainly full enough to do what had to be done. Still, I had to squeeze and concentrate before I could do it on Melody. She opened her eyes to find out what was happening just as the stream erupted from me, catching her full on her chest and splashing over her lovely big breasts. She shut her eyes quickly, arching her body and opening her mouth as far as she could. I leant back, my stream of pee splashing against her neck, then her face and into her open mouth. It filled up her mouth and ran out of the sides, trickling down her cheeks and into her hair. I was laughing, revelling in the pleasure of peeing on the girl who had threatened to do the same, and worse, to me. Melody closed her mouth and swallowed, groaning as she again opened it to be filled. I stopped, holding back the last of my pee.

'You tramp!' I remarked, a little shocked by the sheer wantonness of her response.

'Do it in my mouth again, Amber,' she begged, 'then make me come.'

I sank to my knees, putting my fanny directly over her mouth and then letting go. Melody's mouth filled up until my pee was running out of the sides. Her breath was coming hard, pushing her tits against my bottom. I moved down her body, kissing her neck and breasts, tasting the sharp, tart flavour of my pee and the salt of her sweat. My fanny was still running, dribbling pee on to her belly and over her pubic mound. I kissed her belly button, putting

162

my tongue into the pool that had filled it, then her hair and finally her pussy, finding her clit and starting to lick. She tasted strong, musky and female, mixed with the taste of my own pee. I put my fingers back between my legs and started to masturbate, all thoughts of getting back to the yard lost in the heat of the moment.

Melody groaned, pushing her hips into my face as she started to come. I knew she'd swallowed when she started to call my name. The thought of her drinking my pee had me dizzy with pleasure and my finger was flicking hard on my clitoris. I stopped licking as Melody's orgasm subsided, scrambling round until my bottom was over her face. Her tongue quickly found my clitty, licking hard, then moving to my vagina as I sat up straight on her face.

'Lick my bottom,' I demanded.

Melody didn't hesitate, her tongue probing my anus even as I got my fingers back to my clit. It felt wonderful, riding my captive's face as she licked my anus – the one act I found more servile and dirty than any other and what I fantasised over more than anything else. Even better, if I hadn't successfully subdued her, it would have been my tongue that was probing her anus instead. As it was, her bumhole was stretched around the handle of my whip, a gesture of dominance more exquisite even than the tying of her hands and ankles or peeing over her beautiful dark-chocolate skin and into her open mouth.

I came, screaming so loudly that they must have heard us in the yard. My cheeks were spread wide over her face, her tongue deep inside me. My pleasure lasted a long time, building to an exquisite climax as I savoured the results of my conquest, making my back arch and my mouth open so wide that my jaw ached. I was incredibly sensitive, feeling Melody's tongue wriggle in my anus, aware of the exact position of my middle finger on my clitoris, feeling simultaneously the warm sunshine, the wet grass, the caked mud on my nipples and the taste of girl strong in my mouth.

Finally it was over and I let myself slide off Melody, leaving her gasping on the grass. For a moment I lay on the grass, then the need to get back struck home. Not that it was a big problem. I had no idea of the time, but it seemed impossible that we had been fighting and playing for anything like an hour. Still, it seemed better to be safe than sorry, and so I got to my feet and started to put my clothes back on.

'Will you walk?' I asked Melody, expecting her to agree and hoping that she would.

'No way, girl. You've got to carry me,' she answered cheekily.

'Be fair,' I said. 'I made you come, didn't I?'

'Yeah,' she laughed, 'and then stuck your butt in my face to get your own kicks. Morris says you're stuck-up, which is why he's so keen to take your cherry, but I reckon you're a dirty bitch.'

'Only for girls,' I answered, 'and men if I'm . . . no, never mind. Look, are you going to walk or not?'

'Sorry, Amber, you've got to do it the hard way, just like Morris did,' she said lightly. 'Still, you're strong, you should manage. It's not many girls can get the better of me.'

'I don't doubt it,' I said. 'Come on, be nice, I'll submit to you later, any way you like.'

'That's tempting,' she answered, 'but I've got to say no. See, there's a big thank you in this for Harmony and I if we win. Besides, you look so high and mighty in your mistress gear, the truth is, I'm just dying to watch Morris fuck you.'

Pausing only to extract my whip, I began to try and pick her up, thinking how lucky I was that I'd remembered in time that she was Rathwell's girlfriend. I'd been going to say that I enjoyed sex with men as long as they were dominant and preferably beat my bottom first. A piece of information that I very definitely did not want Rathwell to have.

Picking Melody up proved almost impossible. For a start I was tired. She wouldn't help at all, instead writhing like an eel every time I got a grip on her. Finally there was the mud and water, which made everything that much harder. In the end I had to drag her by the feet, an exhausting process in itself. By the time I came to within sight of the yard I was in an even worse state than I had been after subduing Melody. I'd fallen over twice and was plastered in mud, the last button had come off my blouse and my boots were full of water. In the yard Susan was waving and gave me an encouraging thumbs-up sign, calling something I didn't catch. Henry, Francis and Rathwell were all seated, Harmony standing behind them.

I renewed my efforts to drag Melody, uncertain about my time. It seemed only minutes since we'd started, but I'd really lost all track of time. Susan's actions seemed encouraging, but they were forbidden to actually call out the time to me. Melody's struggles became more desperate, clutching at grass tufts with her hands, wriggling like a fish whenever I tried to lift her, and generally making life difficult for me. It seemed pointless to argue with her, so I just stuck to my task.

Later they told me that it took me nearly half-an-hour to drag Melody down that field, fighting every inch of the way. Susan's signals – at first confident – became urgent and then frantic, but it was when I saw that Harmony was down on her knees in front of Rathwell and had his cock in her mouth that I really began to panic. She was obviously getting him ready, and I knew exactly whose pussy that skinny little erection was destined for.

I stopped looking at them, turning my back and putting every effort into dragging the reluctant Melody. She was nearly as exhausted as me, and had given up struggling, but still made a dead weight that needed to be dragged foot by foot over the grass. Finally I made the yard, every muscle in my body aching, dizzy with fatigue, and barely able to get Melody over the line. Even as I collapsed into the mud, Henry was reaching for the horn.

'Amber!' Susan exclaimed, desperation and pity in her voice.

'We'll call that fifty-nine and fifty seconds,' Henry said despondently. 'Sorry, Amber.'

I really didn't care that much. Rathwell was standing to

the rear of the others, his jodhpurs down to his thighs and his cock poking out between the halves of his shirt. In his hand he held the yoke. Harmony was nursing his erection with her hand and looking at me with an expression I found hard to fathom.

'Crawl over here,' he ordered.

'Won't you even let her clean up!' Susan objected.

'Yes, give the poor girl a chance!' Francis added.

I raised my hand to silence them, keen to submit with what little grace and dignity I had left and not make an unseemly fuss. All eyes were on me as I crawled slowly over to Rathwell, the mud squelching up between my fingers and around my legs. My blouse was wide open, my bra a sodden ruin that lefts my boobs swinging naked beneath me. He grinned and pointed to his trainers, both nearly as muddy as my own boots. I put my head down and kissed his feet, obedient, submissive and accepting. Everyone was silent as I knelt up and passively allowed Harmony to guide his erection into my mouth. I sucked, tasting his cock and the mud from his shoes, making no protest when he took hold of my hair and began to fuck my mouth with slow, even strokes.

'Back on all fours,' he instructed, trying to be stern and hard but too excited to really pull it off. 'Put your face in the mud.'

I got down obediently, putting my face into the warm brown slurry as he had directed. Lifting enough to let myself breathe, I waited with my eyes closed. Rathwell's hands came under me, fondling my breasts possessively until he had had his fill. Something hard touched my waist and I realised that it was the yoke. My feelings of submission increased still more as he put it on me, fitting it around my waist and pulling it back. It fitted snugly to my hips, the padding stopping it from being uncomfortable. That was what it was for, then – to improve his purchase as he took me from the rear. Also to humiliate me, of course, in which it was successful, the first real pang of shame coming to me as he pulled it into place against my hips. I was unable to restrain a sigh as his hands gripped my jodhpurs and pulled them down. My torn panties were all that was left to cover me, but as I braced myself for the final exposure, he simply ripped the back away, giving immediate access to my pussy.

'Spread,' he rasped as he lifted my jacket tails.

I parted my thighs as far as my lowered jodhpurs would allow. I felt the sun on my bare skin and knew he could see everything: fanny, bumhole, the lot.

'Cute,' I heard him say and then felt his cock probing my hole.

I let out a whimper as it went in, drawing a satisfied laugh from him as he took hold of the yoke and slid himself up. I put my face and boobs back in the mud as he started to fuck me, utterly defeated and humiliated, accepting Rathwell's cock inside me in a submissive ecstasy stronger even than when Henry had first used me as a pony-girl. It wasn't just what was being done to me but, the fact that it was Morris Rathwell who had me yoked with my jodhpurs down and my pants torn aside; Morris Rathwell who had told me to kiss his feet and put my face in the mud; Morris Rathwell who was making my tits swing in the slime of the yard, and Morris Rathwell whose cock was sliding in and out of my creamy, willing vagina. I put my hand back and started to masturbate, knowing that everyone could see and feeling even better for it. He was pumping hard, slamming against my bottom with each push and making me gasp into my face-full of muck. Suddenly he pulled out and my bottom was sprayed with come, then his shaft was between my bum-cheeks, sliding up and down in his own sperm as he emptied himself between my open cheeks and over my anus. I was near orgasm myself and had also started to cry with the sheer overwhelming emotion of everything. He moved back, leaving me to masturbate, flaunting myself in front of him. My crying was the one thing I was determined he wouldn't see, even as I knelt with my bum in the air and his come smeared into my anus and dribbling on to my fanny. He laughed; a harsh, cackling sound. I knew it was because I was masturbating myself with his semen in front of everybody; because I was totally unable to restrain my excitement after he had fucked me, and because it confirmed his conviction that I genuinely fancied him as a man.

I came then, when he laughed at me. At first it felt as if it was going to be enough to make me faint; a contraction of my muscles that had me gritting my teeth around a mouthful of slime. It was as if a great bubble was about to burst in my head, an agonising feeling that had me tearing at my clit with my fingertips. I peaked, but the deep sense of humiliation that had driven my whole need for orgasm was simply too much. My knees went weak and I slumped down in the filth.

Eight

Henry was furious with Rathwell and pretty well threw him off the farm. I wasn't really so bothered, just totally exhausted and sore almost everywhere. Sure I had lost, but it had been one hell of a day, and Rathwell's face when I told him that I hadn't actually been a virgin after all was something to behold. It had obviously been as big a deal to him as I had thought because his attitude of crowing triumph turned to pique on the spot.

The other thing that made me feel better was the attention I got afterwards. Everybody was solicitous towards me. Melody and Harmony cuddled and hugged me as if I had just joined some exclusive and very intimate club which, from their point of view, perhaps I had. Henry insisted on opening a bottle of ancient Armagnac, a typically Henry-like gesture which I nevertheless appreciated. Francis fussed round me like an old mother hen, fetching this and offering that. Susan was best though; she cuddled me and bathed me and told me I'd really turned her on and then cuddled me some more. I went to bed long before the others and woke up late on Monday morning, by which time my outlook on events had changed considerably.

Pleasure-wise, it was great, and I couldn't help bringing myself off over it. I let my mind wander over what had happened and came over the thought of being put in the yoke which, for some reason, was especially humiliating. As before, the real trouble was my own response and the way Rathwell would see it. I knew that the less appealing the man – and the more shameful the circumstances – the more I'd have enjoyed it. Rathwell saw it as me getting over some sort of barrier to allow me to show how much I fancied him. Also, I knew he'd be unbearably self-satisfied. He'd tell his friends how I'd grovelled and obeyed him, how clever he'd been with his tactics, and how I'd made myself come at the end . . .

I wanted revenge. I desperately needed to win and make him suffer the same sort of indignity I had, and enjoy it. As I lay there brooding and thinking of the feel of his cock inside me and the yoke pressing against my hips I became more and more determined to challenge him again. A weak voice inside me kept raising objections, such as that if I did he'd undoubtedly demand to put that same skinny cock up my bottom. There was also a degree of self recrimination. If I'd had the sense not to get carried away with Melody, I'd have won easily. If Susan hadn't started playing the fool at the end of her hour then Rathwell wouldn't have finished. If only I'd considered the rules of pursuit-capture-punishment properly. In the end, though, it wasn't that I'd lost so much as that Rathwell had won – twice. I needed revenge – badly.

When I went downstairs and announced my intention I got a mixed reception. Henry choked on his coffee and asked if I was sure I was thinking straight. Francis cautioned me to prudence. Susan supported me, viewing it as a game in which I really won either way.

It was the first time Henry had been even a little cross with me, which I didn't like at all but, being stubborn, I kept arguing. Francis simultaneously tried to mediate and to talk sense into me, failing on both counts. Susan kept fairly quiet, but occasionally put in a word in support of my case. Eventually Henry admitted that if I was determined then it was up to me and said I was welcome to use the equipment but not to expect him to help set the challenge up. Only then did he tell me that Rathwell had boasted that he would accept any challenge I could think of and win. That really set the seal on it and, as soon as Susan and Francis had left, I retired to my room to think, ignoring Henry's suggestion that I was merely sulking.

170

I got on my bed and lay on my front with a notebook and a pencil. First I had to come to terms with some ego-deflating truths. I had a tendency to let my own passion betray me, I wasn't more cunning or intelligent than Morris Rathwell, and I was far less experienced than him or indeed Melody and Harmony. I then made a list of Rathwell's faults – or at least the relevant ones – which included arrogance, drinking rum by the bucket, the assumption that money was always the solution, and finding me attractive. The next list covered the qualities of himself and his team for pony-carting. The girls were fast, strong, had stamina, were exhibitionistic and anything but shy. Rathwell was experienced and inspired their loyalty, which I found hard to understand. On the other hand, Melody and Harmony were good – but not the best – and both had a soft spot for me, although in Melody's case this was not necessarily to my advantage. Rathwell was fit for his age but no more, weighed too much for a good pony-cart driver, and tended to be too showy for his own good.

The answer then had to be to get together a team better than the black girls and choose a sport that would give me every advantage. The team was the first problem. It would have to be superlative and come as a surprise to Rathwell, which wasn't easy. Ginny was as good as Melody and Harmony, but no better, and over any distance they'd undoubtedly win. I only knew one pony-girl who could definitely out-run them: Vicky Belstone. Actually there were two people I knew who were good enough, but the other wasn't a pony-girl – or at least not yet. She was Miss Ellen Campbell.

I got up from the bed with a wicked grin.

There was no point in seeking Miss Campbell out until I had a challenge accepted by Rathwell. Henry pointed out that visiting him at home was like walking straight into a trap but, as I obviously enjoyed being utterly humiliated by him, then it wasn't such a bad idea. I told Henry not to be grumpy but decided to visit Rathwell at his office instead, which would prevent him from doing anything sneaky like getting the girls to spank me and then taking advantage of me.

His office was in the city. It was an old building, narrow and four stories high, yet looking tiny in between the modern blocks on either side. It was one of those odd bits of London where everything got bombed except one building, or so my father had explained. I had rung ahead and arrived shortly after two o'clock in the hope that Rathwell would have had an alcoholic lunch and be easy to goad into a poor bet. The receptionist greeted me with a friendly smile and told me to wait in Rathwell's outer office while he finished talking to some colleague with whom he had had lunch. I climbed the stairs and pushed open the door with his name on it, finding a large airy office with a secretary busy typing at a desk. She looked up as I came in. She was a coloured girl, pretty and very smart, the perfect businessman's secretary. Also the perfect businessman's pony-girl. It was Harmony.

'Hi, Amber,' she greeted me with. 'Come to get even with Morris?'

'Yes,' I admitted.

'We didn't think you'd be able to stay away,' she replied. 'Look, come over here.'

I crossed the room quickly, aware of the conspiratorial tone in Harmony's voice.

'You've picked a good time to put a challenge in,' she whispered as I sank down on my haunches next to her chair. 'Morris has got this deal going through with some guy who owns a load of wasteland down in the East End. He signed before they went off for lunch and Morris is well pleased with himself as he's going to make a packet on the deal. He's well keen on you, too, even more so because you tricked him . . .'

'Tricked him?' I queried.

'Pretended you were a virgin,' she explained. 'He's got this thing about virginity, and he's got one major thing for you. He really thought he'd done it, and got you as his slave into the bargain, the way you went with the yoke and all. Then you up and go straight back to Henry and tell him you'd let that guy Francis shag you and old Henry and all! Morris was steaming! See, he thought that after you'd subbed to him and come for him and everything, then you'd want to come and be his slave-girl . . .'

'The arrogant pig!' I interrupted.

'Well, Morris has his faults, but he looks after his girls. So anyway, he's steaming and he wants you so bad he told Henry he'd take any challenge you named. What he wants now is to sex your bottom, and if you don't like that you'd better quit now, 'cause whatever else he goes for, that'll be part of the bet.'

'Thanks,' I answered, feeling more than a little alarmed.

Being buggered by Morris Rathwell would be painful and humiliating. That I could take. Spending the rest of my life knowing he'd done it was something else entirely. Harmony had been as sweet as pie ever since I'd spanked her in the toilets at the second pony-girl meet. Certainly she'd always been more sympathetic to me than Melody, which made me wonder.

'Harmony,' I asked tentatively, 'would you throw a race for me?'

'No way, girl,' she laughed, her accent slipping further from typically secretarial to the odd mixture of London and American she and Melody normally used. 'You want your pussy kissed, I'm always here, but cheating on Morris is out.'

'Just a thought,' I answered, feeling a mild but delightful flush at her suggestion of licking me.

'Oh, yeah, but didn't you just push Melody's button,' she continued. 'She wants you nearly as bad as Morris. As her pet.'

I hadn't realised before that Rathwell didn't simply want my sexual submission; he, Melody – and probably Harmony – wanted me as the fourth member of their household. I would be the junior member, too, licking, sucking, probably scrubbing the floor with half-a-dozen whip stripes on my bare bum . . .

It just wasn't going to happen. I might enjoy a good

spanking, suck men's cocks or be a pony-girl, but when and if I moved in with a lover it would be a girl and I'd be the dominant one. Still, Rathwell seemed to think that if he turned me on enough I would be begging for the privilege. That was something I might be able to use to my advantage.

'So, if you're his secretary, what's Melody?' I asked, curious to know how the set-up worked.

'His wife,' Harmony answered.

A sharp click of the door to the inner office alerted me and I stood up, asking Harmony a polite question about her job, as a man in a loud check suit emerged from Rathwell's office. Rathwell followed him, ignoring me completely until he had shown the man out and then turning to me.

'Well, well, if it isn't little Amber,' he drawled. 'Come back for more, have we?'

'Perhaps,' I answered cautiously. 'You said to Henry that you'd take me on over any course and in any style I chose?'

'And beat you,' Rathwell added. 'Come into the office. We'll talk. Harmony, tell any callers I'm in a meeting.'

'Yes, Mr Rathwell, sir,' Harmony answered, her voice betraying just a hint of impertinence.

'So what's the deal?' Rathwell asked as he sank into the big leather chair behind his desk. 'Take a seat. Bacardi? Whisky? Cognac?'

I accepted a glass of brandy, of which he poured about half the bottle into an enormous balloon glass.

'A race over distance, at Henry's,' I said, sipping the brandy and finding it far inferior to what Henry served. 'I'll tell you the details on the day.'

'I can see you're trying to work it to your advantage,' he answered, 'but I don't care as long as the bet's right. I'll have the competition details three days before though, that's straight. So, I've had your twat, what've you got to put up?'

'What do you want from me?' I asked, trying to look cool and in control.

'What don't I want from you?' Rathwell answered,

blowing his cheeks out. 'Look Amber, I'll be straight. I'm a good-looking guy, I've got money, I've got power. I want you to be with me. If you want to put it in the form of a bet to save your pride, then that's cool, but you know you want it. Come on, Amber, Henry's a fat old boy who hardly ever even leaves his farm. What's he got that I haven't?'

'A decent-sized cock,' I answered, unable to resist the dig. Rathwell coloured nicely and I went on quickly. 'Look, Morris, you don't really understand me at all. I'm not Henry's girlfriend. OK, we've been to bed –'

'And you give him all the blow-jobs he wants,' Rathwell interrupted, and it was my turn to colour up. 'No eighteen-year-old learnt to suck like you without some expert tuition. He fucks you, you suck him, you're his pony-girl ... What more does it take to make you his girlfriend?'

'I ... I actually prefer girls,' I stammered.

'Yeah, sure, so Melody tells me, but we both know that's shit. You were at that girls' school too long. Sure it's nice to play with girls, but you need cock like all the others.'

'I ...' I began and hesitated.

As usual when I talked to Rathwell, I was losing my grip on the conversation. He could be so crude and so certain of himself that it was hard to know which outrageous statement to argue against first. Not that it mattered; he obviously believed his own opinions regardless of what I said to the contrary.

'See,' he continued, 'you know it, so the bet's this: when I win I want to fuck your backside in front of everyone, so they all see it go in and can watch how much you love it. Then you come and live with us. OK?'

'No,' I managed, my temper coming to my rescue in the face of his unbelievable arrogance. 'It is not OK, and anyway, who says you're going to win?'

'Come on, girl, you know you want it,' he chortled. 'Still, a bet's a bet, and I don't want to make you feel undervalued, so I'll put up the field I promised, plus the old forge that it belongs to. That's got to be worth maybe two, two-fifty ...'

He stopped, making a sign to show how little the sum of a quarter of a million pounds meant to him. There was a lump in my throat and I could feel the tears starting in my eyes. He was effectively buying me; as if I could be traded for goods like a slave. Yet the offer was far, far better than anything I could have hoped for and was exactly what I most wanted, as if he was dangling my dream in front of me. Unfortunately what he was demanding of me was too much and my pride and honour were too strong to simply accept and then back out if I lost. I could feel a tear on one cheek, but part of me remained detached and rational, wondering if I couldn't play on the very arrogance that was making me cry.

'Look maybe,' I started, 'but what if I say I'll be your house-slave for a week? Then –'

'A trial period,' he broke in. 'Yes, that's fair, if that's what it takes to satisfy your pride. When the week's up you'll have found your true self and you can move in properly. So it's a bum-shag and I get you on terms against two-fifty in property. You've got the better deal, but I won't argue because that's the kind of guy I am – generous to a fault.'

'I didn't say anything about my bottom!' I objected.

'That's not negotiable, Amber,' he answered, his voice harder than before. 'Add a few tit-bits to your side if you like as I'm going to win anyway, but the bum-shag stays on the table.'

I'd done it, although the bet was still terrifying. The tears were running down my cheeks but inside I felt suddenly aggressive and determined to bring Rathwell down to size.

'Two things,' I said. 'A public whipping for the loser and no protesting the competition rules I set.'

'Fine,' he answered blandly 'Yes, as long as the course is fair. As for the whipping, I don't go submissive.'

'It's not negotiable,' I imitated him.

He paused, suddenly looking as insecure as I felt about taking his cock up my bottom. I realised I'd really got to him, and in a way I hadn't expected. I'd thought he'd take it easily and had suggested it partly because I knew that being buggered by him would be much more bearable after my bottom had been warmed. As it was, the thought of risking a whipping from me seemed to worry him more than giving away a great chunk of real estate. Maybe it did. He was rich and would probably manage to fiddle the money back from his taxes. His pride was irreplaceable.

'It's not negotiable, Morris,' I repeated.

'OK, but believe me you'll pay for that suggestion,' he finally answered.

'Good. Let's shake on it,' I said.

'I'll get Harmony to put it in writing,' he replied, suddenly businesslike. 'Will you accept her as witness?'

'Yes,' I told him, taking his hand and shaking it.

'Great,' he said. 'Now how about a blow-job to seal the deal while she types it up?'

Rathwell didn't get his blow-job, or at least not from me. For all his humiliating sexual suggestions and dominant manner I just wasn't in a submissive or turned-on mood. As I left he called Harmony in and I heard the key turn in the lock, so I imagine that she was sucking away by the time I stormed out of the building and turned towards Moorgate and the railway that ran back to Henry's.

My mind was swimming. On the one hand I had the chance of gaining exactly what I most wanted, and winning would enable me to defy my father with impunity. On the other hand what I was risking was truly alarming. Logically, I kept trying to tell myself, I had the better end of the deal. A whipping, Rathwell's skinny little cock up my bum and then a week as his house-slave wasn't such a big deal at all. Emotionally it was one hell of a big deal and I sat on the train staring out at suburban London, the thought of what he planned to do to me going round and round in my head.

As I approached the station I got more and more worked up about it. I'd seen Susan take Francis in her bottom; seen her anus stretched taut around his intruding cock; heard her grunt and pant like an animal as he worked it in and out; felt her buck and writhe as she came with an erection filling her anal passage . . .

177

I had to masturbate. It was more than I could resist. I cut across the fields on my way back from the station, found a quiet place at the edge of Henry's land, took my panties off under my skirt and pulled it up to get at my pussy. It was a wonderful orgasm, but I was in tears as I came and, as I walked on, one thought kept coming back to me: I had to win.

Two days later my plans were taking shape. I had evolved an idea that I was sure would give me every advantage I could fairly take. It relied heavily on Rathwell's assumption that I would never be able to outdo him in the pony-carting stakes, and so I borrowed the Land Rover and set off for Bridestowe Ladies' College and Miss Ellen Campbell.

The last traces of light were fading over Cornwall when I parked. To one side of me was the majestic sweep of Dartmoor; to the other the lower land falling to the river Tamar in a succession of hills and valleys. In the nearest valley a cluster of lights stood out from the gathering night – Bridestowe Ladies' College. Just looking at it infected me with a nostalgia so strong that I had to wipe my eyes. When I'd been there my most earnest desire had been to get out. Now I was out it seemed to me a haven – safe and secure from the pressures of the outside world.

I had decided against simply breezing in and visiting Miss Campbell's cottage. For one thing it would raise eyebrows as I had officially been expelled for assaulting her. Also, every girl except the new fourth form knew me and it would be impossible to pass unrecognised. I'd been popular and, according to Ginny and Susan, had become something of a legend after my expulsion. The popular myth among the girls was that Miss Campbell and I had argued over her refusal to allow juniors to canter or gallop when riding on the moor. This had been carefully propagated by Susan and was enough to make any girl a hero. The truth was very different and was not something I wanted to have to discuss.

Instead I took a leisurely dinner at The Bear, indulging

myself in Cornish oysters and langouste simply because I'd never been able to afford to before. This was washed down by Dutch courage in the form of a bottle of Tokay and an Armagnac, both tastes for which I had to thank Henry. The next section was even more nostalgic – getting into the school grounds without being seen. There were several routes, but the best for my purposes was to go down into the village and walk along the stream to the point where it ran behind Miss Campbell's cottage. I'd been fifteen when I'd last done it, and it was a lot harder and less exciting than I remembered. For all that I reached the cottage at a few minutes after eleven, finding the kitchen light on.

I walked up the bank from the stream, grinning to myself and imagining her face when she saw me. I could see the faint outline of a figure through the kitchen curtain. She was washing up and singing softly to herself. I moved closer, indulging a voyeuristic thrill as I came to the side of the cottage and peered through a gap in the curtains, lifting my hand to rap on the window.

I stopped dead. I had been expecting the lithe, dark-haired figure of the woman who had been so keen to seduce me. Instead the woman doing the washing up was extremely slender, had skin like alabaster only heavily freckled, and a tumble of red curls falling to her bottom; her bare bottom.

My first thought was that Miss Campbell had changed her accommodation, but that only lasted a fraction of a second. I knew those red curls and I knew that tiny, round bottom and those long, coltish legs. It was a girl, Caroline Gibson, who had been in the hockey team with me. If she was doing Miss Campbell's washing up, and dressed in nothing but a frilly pinafore, it could only mean one thing. Miss Campbell might have failed to get me as her lover, but she'd succeeded this time.

The first emotion to hit me was jealousy, which was completely unfair. The second was lust and a craving to have another peek at Carrie, especially to see if her pretty bottom had felt the sting of Miss Campbell's quirt. I put my eye to the crack again, finding her as before. She hadn't been punished, or at least there was no evidence of it. Her naked bottom was as smooth and pristine as one could possibly want, red curls hanging over the upper surfaces of her cheeks, a few freckles highlighting her sweet curves. Her hair was touching her skin in one place just above the little hollow where the crease of her bottom began. This obviously tickled, because every now and then she would give her bum a little shake, making her cheeks wiggle.

It's strange, because I must have shared showers with Carrie dozens of times and never particularly wanted to jump on her. Watching her was a very different matter, and my hand was quickly down in the V of my crotch, massaging my pussy through my jeans. As I watched she dropped a tea spoon and bent to retrieve it, showing me the tight, pouted lips of her pussy and the tiny pink spot of her anus. I swallowed, rubbing harder between my legs and willing her to drop something else. Instead she turned to reach for a drying-up cloth and I had to move quickly back.

The question, of course, was what to do. Having Carrie there made things more complicated, but I hadn't driven two hundred miles to back out at the first sign of a hitch in my plans. Feeling deliciously wicked, I again peered in and then knocked on the kitchen door. Carrie scampered away in a flurry of hair and pinny that sent a chuckle to my lips. For a minute there was absolute silence and then I heard the sound of heels clicking across the floor inside. The door opened, revealing Miss Campbell looking both puzzled and annoyed, her expression quickly turning to surprise.

'Amber!' she gasped.

'Hi, Ellen,' I managed, determined to establish myself as an equal. 'May I come in?'

'I . . . I suppose you'd better,' she answered. 'Why are you here?'

'It's a long story,' I said as I stepped inside. 'How about asking little Carrie Gibson to make a coffee and I'll explain.'

'Carrie Gibson?' she started and then realised that it was hopeless. 'Yes, well, that's rather personal, but I'm sure you of all people will understand.'

'Absolutely,' I assured her, waiting until the door was closed before calling out. 'You can come out now, Carrie. It's only me, Amber.'

Carrie emerged from the bedroom, now clad in her blouse and panties but blushing absolutely crimson and with her hands folded nervously in front of her. She looked so sweet that it made me want to ease her down across my knee on the spot and spank her lovely little bottom to a glowing pink. I resisted the urge and gave her a kiss and a friendly hug instead.

Of course, as Ellen Campbell's girlfriend Carrie knew the truth about my expulsion and quickly got over her initial embarrassment. Her main question was how I had resisted Ellen, whom she absolutely worshipped and had allowed to tease her into bed without the slightest resistance. She had also been made a prefect, which was what enabled her to stay out of her house so late.

I could see little point in beating about the bush, and so told the entire pony-carting story from the beginning, leaving out only the dirtiest details and the bits were I had been really submissive. They listened in awe – even Ellen – which did wonders for my confidence. Occasionally they would ask questions, which I answered with what I hoped was a casual pretence at considerably more knowledge than I actually had.

'So, that's why I'm here,' I finished. 'I need one super-fit pony-girl to race for me during half-term.'

'Can I come?' Carrie asked, interrupting whatever Ellen had been about to say.

'Sure,' I answered, only to catch a dirty look from Ellen.

Carrie was bubbling over with excitement, and I think that if it hadn't been for her I would have had a lot more difficulty in persuading Ellen to race for me. As it was she raised a few practical objections which were quickly overcome and then went to the window, opening a crack in the curtains and staring thoughtfully out at the college. Carrie was chattering away at a great rate, so I held my hand up to make her be quiet and let Ellen think. I could see Ellen was tempted, but supposed her indecision was prompted by the thought of the risk she would be taking if the story ever got back to the school. As it was, she was thinking about something very different.

She stood back from the window, drew the curtains carefully and walked briskly from the room, never saying a word. Carrie looked at me and shrugged, then I turned as Ellen reappeared in the doorway to her bedroom, carrying the quirt and beckoning me with her finger.

Carrie's mouth opened in a little O of shock, and I don't suppose I looked much more composed myself. The sight of the vicious little implement put a lump in my throat and a tingle between my legs. I could see from Carrie's expression that she knew the quirt was used to discipline unruly seductees. Whether she'd tasted its sting herself, or whether she knew I'd used it on her lover, I didn't know, but it was plain that she found the idea of it being used on me both exciting and shocking.

'May I?' Ellen asked sweetly.

There was only one answer. If I wanted her to be my pony-girl I could hardly refuse her. I nodded and hung my head, excited yet also shamed at the prospect of being punished in front of Carrie.

'Very well,' Ellen purred with all the satisfaction of a cat contemplating a bowl of cream. 'Carrie, help her to shower once she has stripped.'

I began to undress, taking it slowly and passing each item of clothing to Carrie. Ellen watched from the bedroom door with an expression of haughty amusement. Only when I was completely naked did she indicate the direction of the bathroom with the quirt.

'Run along,' she said quietly.

I scampered into the bathroom, stark naked and feeling very vulnerable indeed. Carrie followed, giggling at my naked body. When I had turned the shower on she stripped and came in with me and began to soap me. Ellen followed, standing outside the shower and instructing me to put my hands on my head. I obeyed, but it was too much for me. Carrie's hands were all over me and slippery with soap, not just washing me but exploring my body. I stood it for as long as I could but when she started to soap my breasts I couldn't take it any more and grabbed her, pulling her to me with my hands on her bum. She squeaked but her mouth opened under mine and we were quickly kissing and touching each other without restraint. I heard Ellen laugh from outside the shower curtain – a wicked, musical sound that told me my bottom would very shortly be smarting under her quirt.

'Come out before you two get carried away,' she ordered.

I pulled away from Carrie reluctantly, but knowing who was in charge. We dried each other, again paying more than a fair share of attention to our most sensitive areas.

'I suppose, Amber, I should have you wash me,' Ellen continued after watching us for a while. 'You were my favourite for a long time and being rejected by you really hurt. Now . . .'

'I'm sorry,' I answered, interrupting her because she did sound genuinely hurt and I felt the need to justify myself. 'You just didn't play it very well and, in truth, I've always wanted to be the one in charge.'

'So I discovered,' she went on, 'but if you want me now, and are prepared to be my plaything, then I'll come to Hertfordshire and be your pony-girl.'

'Thanks,' I answered.

'Good,' she said, the softness in her voice gone as fast as it had appeared. 'Then you'd better get into Caroline's uniform. When you're dry, of course.'

Carrie giggled and my cheeks went red. I'd done it for Francis and Susan without a qualm. Doing it for Ellen was somehow more personal – no, nothing could be more personal than the experience Susan, Francis and I had shared – but with Ellen the uniform branded me as specifically submissive. It was also far too small and made Carrie giggle, which was really humiliating. The panties were stretched tight across my bottom and cut into the flesh of my hips. The bra was a joke but Ellen made me go without instead of allowing me to use my own. The blouse was almost as bad because, although I could get it across my shoulders and even do it up, the buttons over my chest were stretched to breaking point. The skirt was a better fit, but it was really the mental effect of the whole outfit that began to bring out my submissive side. When I'd pulled the overtight panties up and Carrie had laughed at me, I'd felt the urge to put her across my knee. By the time I was finished I was more tempted to crawl across hers.

I was ready, waiting for orders and expecting to be made to adopt some suitable position. Instead Ellen took hold of me by the ear and dragged me over her lap on the bed without bothering about the ritual I was used to as preceding a girl's punishment. She twisted my arm up my back and pulled up my skirt, baring me in a brisk, workman-like fashion. I had started to squeal as soon as she caught my ear, and continued as my straining panties were pulled down and she started to spank me. She did it hard and I was bawling and kicking in no time to the sound of the resonant smacks on my bottom and Carrie's laughter.

'This is what I call a brat spanking,' she told me as I started to sob, 'and it's what you've always deserved.'

My bottom was hot and sore, and the lovely contrite feeling that comes only from having been well spanked was starting to come. I had to admit I deserved it, and said so, apologising again and again for being cheeky, sulky, rude, disobedient and anything else I could think of that Ellen might possibly ever have found fault with me for. Carrie thought it was hilarious and was laughing her head off at the state I was getting in. There was a mirror to the side and I could see what I looked like, bent over Ellen's knee in school uniform with my pants around my thighs and my chubby bottom pink and bouncing under her stern slaps. There were tears streaming from my eyes and my face cheeks were as red as those of my bottom. The blouse had burst and my boobs were showing, bare and wobbling in time to my spanking.

When she finally shoved me off her lap and on to the floor I was completely contrite and crawled to her feet to kiss her shoes. I made no effort to pull up my knickers or rearrange my skirt, instead sticking my hot, bare bottom in the air and begging Ellen for the quirt to be used on me. It was, mercilessly, first Ellen and then Carrie, flicking and teasing my bottom, thighs and even my fanny with the cruel, snake-tongued end. It stung every bit as much as I had imagined. The ones on my fanny were incredible and, when they flicked against my clitty, it was like a burst of fire each time. I realised I was coming only as it started to happen and began to beg to have my fanny whipped more. Carrie had the quirt and showed no surprise at my request, instead starting to use it directly on my clit with little, firm flicks, each of which stung crazily and each of which brought me closer to orgasm.

My head was trapped between Ellen's ankles, my whole rear a burning, throbbing mass of exquisite pain, my head dizzy with both the effect of my whipping and the overwhelming feeling of utter, abject submission to her. I came again and again, drumming my feet on the floor and begging Carrie for more until it just became all too much and I screamed out loud.

That put a fairly abrupt stop to our play, as it seemed certain that somebody would have heard. Nothing happened, though, and after ten minutes we once more began to relax. To my alarm it turned out that just because I'd come didn't mean that Ellen had had her fill of me. After all, she hadn't come and, as she was mistress, that was what mattered. My bottom was a mass of fire and my fanny more than a little sore. My feelings for Carrie – which had started out as pretty much pure lust – had also come to include a strong element of vengeance because, throughout my punishment, she hadn't once stopped laughing at me. So when Ellen told me to strip and get back on my knees I obeyed and then hung my head and asked very politely if I could deal with Carrie.

Carrie laughed and told me not to be cheeky, only to have her words turn to ashes in her mouth as Ellen calmly gave me the necessary permission. I didn't waste any time, hauling her across my knee, twisting my arm into her long red hair and setting to on her neat little bum with a will. I had appreciated the effect of what Ellen called a brat spanking and wanted to give Carrie the same treatment. The only trouble was, that where it had had me bawling and kicking, she just laughed, and the harder I spanked her the more she laughed. Her bottom was unreasonably firm, too, and my palm had quickly begun to sting, while she showed no signs of proper contrition or apology whatsoever. Finally I gave up, leaving Carrie's apple-like bottom completely red but also with my own hand smarting.

'Right,' I panted, determined to get some more suitable response out of her. 'Get on your knees.'

'Yes, Miss Amber,' she replied mockingly.

I stood over her, twisting my hand into her hair. I was nude and her face was inches from my fanny. I pulled her head into me, an action which finally got a squeak out of her.

'Lick me,' I ordered.

She hesitated and then her tongue poked out and she began to lap at my clitty, slowly and uncertainly. I let her do it for a while and then pulled her head back. She looked up at me, eyes big and moist but defiant. It seemed odd to me that she took a spanking so well but found fanny licking so humiliating. Still, everyone's different and it boded well for my next intention. I turned, rubbing her face against my bottom, and this time she really squeaked.

'Kiss it,' I ordered.

Her lips touched my skin, gentle against my sore bottom, sending a delicious thrill of dominance through me.

'Between my cheeks, Carrie,' I told her, keeping her face pulled into my bottom and sticking it out as well.

She pulled back and I could hear her breathing hard.

'Oh, Amber, do I have to?' she begged.

'If you want to at heart, you must do it,' I replied.

She gave a little whimper but made no effort to resist as I pulled her face between my bum-cheeks. Then she kissed my anus, gently, delicately but definitely, giving me my favoured gesture of submission.

'Again please, Carrie,' I sighed.

This time she put her tongue out and dabbed the tip against my bumhole, then started to lick ever so gently. I was moaning in seconds, only to be brought out of my trance by Ellen.

'Is that your favourite thing, Amber?' she asked.

The instant she said it I knew that she'd make me do it to her. It was the tone of amusement in her voice, mixed with desire to have me do to her the very thing that pleased me most. There was no point in denying it, either, especially after all the times I'd come over doing exactly that. Now I was going to have to and, even better, in front of a girl who I'd just made give me the same treatment. I nodded and let go of Carrie's hair.

'On your knees, Amber,' Ellen said gently.

Carrie gave my anus a final, lingering kiss and pulled away, leaving me to get into the same position she had been in. Ellen stood up and paced slowly towards me, commanding and elegant in her crimson silk dress and heels. I swallowed hard as she turned. This was it – a submission more abject and more meaningful to me than anything else. I might have sucked Henry's cock and swallowed his come. I might have grovelled at Rathwell's feet and meekly offered my pussy to his cock. However, as a gesture of submission, none of that came close to kissing another woman's anus – kissing it willingly in my role as plaything – as I knelt naked with her bottom pushed into my face.

Ellen hitched her dress up, revealing sheer black stockings encasing her long, muscular legs, a suspender belt with the straps taut against her flesh, and lacy black panties full of soft, womanly bottom. I watched entranced as she slipped her panties down around her thighs and pushed her hips back to offer me her bottom to kiss. That was what made it so emotionally strong – the fact that it was offered and I had to do it of my own accord. Being beaten or letting a man come in my mouth is something that's done to me; now I had to perform the act myself. Neither act is so deliciously rude, either. Even allowing a cock up one's bottom is less rude, less dirty, less humiliating than kissing an anus. That's why I liked girls to do it to me, and ultimately why it was what I so often came over having to do myself.

I moved forward, putting my hands on Ellen's beautiful bottom and opening her cheeks. I could see some of the rear of her pussy, moist and pink, squeezed between her closed thighs. Above it her anus was a neat dimple in a nest of black fur, the wrinkles of brown flesh meeting in a dark valley. I puckered my lips and then hesitated, unwilling to do what I had made Ginny, Susan, Melody and Carrie do to me. I'd done it for Susan, but that had been in play. This was different. Susan had done it for me first, Ellen hadn't, and doing for it Ellen was going to be submission, abject and absolute.

'Come on, Amber, kiss,' Ellen said, sounding gentle but firm.

'Kissy, kissy, Amber, right on her bumhole,' Carrie teased.

I swallowed, shut my eyes and leant forward. My lips touched her, the ring of her bumhole firm against my lips. I'd done it. Carrie gave a little giggle and a squeak of disgust. I felt my tears start and gave in completely, starting to lick. Ellen sighed as my tongue touched her anus, Carrie giggling in delight as she watched me. I took hold of Ellen's hips and pulled her to me, licking and pushing my tongue into her. She moved back and together we sank slowly to the floor until she was seated on my face. Her bottom was spread over me, making it hard to breathe. Her knickers were stretched across my neck, her legs wide over my torso. All I could see was the soft swell of her bottom and the deep red silk of her dress as she sat up straight and put her finger to her fanny, just as I had done to Ginny, Susan and Melody.

'Me too, please,' Carrie squeaked, climbing off the bed to come round in front.

She settled down on top of me, her warm body pressed against mine and our chins touching as she put her face into Ellen's fanny. Ellen sighed as Carrie's tongue found her clitty, rubbing her bottom in my face. My lips were wide, my tongue pushed into Ellen's anus, juice and spittle running down my chin from Ellen's fanny. I wanted to get at my own sex, to bring myself off with Ellen sat on my face and my tongue up her bottom. Carrie's position made it impossible; her pubic mound pressed against my own served to torment me even more.

Ellen came very quietly, but I felt her thighs clench around my head and her anus pulse and tighten on my tongue tip and knew she had reached her climax. She gave a little grunting noise deep in her throat and then it was over and she was dismounting my face.

'Stay,' I gasped, even as I took Carrie's hair in my hand and tried to pull her down on to my fanny.

Ellen gave me an amused look and then my vision was blotted out again as she once more lowered her bottom on to my face. My tongue found her bumhole, burrowing in willingly as Carrie's tongue began to tickle my sex-lips.

I came again, only to have Carrie insist on the same treatment I had given Ellen. I made no objection. I was feeling completely wanton and wonderfully relaxed; more than happy to lick another bottom. She sat over my face first, holding her cheeks open to give me a good look at the tight, pale pink anus that I was to lick, then lowered herself on to me and masturbated while I did it.

It was close to dawn when we finally got to sleep, all three of us in the same bed with Ellen in the middle and our heads nestled on to her chest. My last thought before sleep was one of immense satisfaction, yet I suspect that Ellen was more satisfied still.

Nine

After coming back from Devon in a thoroughly satisfied mood I spent the next few days designing and making pony-girl tack. A trip into London secured me some beautiful textured black leather – thick and strong yet supple. I also bought a couple of skins of a wonderfully soft crimson pig hide and a great bag of nickel-plated accessories. The art of good pony-girl tack seemed to me to be to distribute the weight of the load as evenly as possible across the body while retaining a look that was both sexually and aesthetically appealing. I made Henry try each new design on me as I finished it, only the restraining presence of Brenda and other people who worked for him stopping me from driving him completely up the wall. Not that he minded driving me around the estate; it was my constant demands for detailed reports on the look and feel of the harness that began to wear on his patience. He finally spanked me and made me go to bed in full harness with my hands fastened behind my back, then caned me in the morning when I asked if he'd mind testing a new quick-release catch I wanted to use.

When I was finally satisfied with my design I made three complete sets of adjustable, quick-release tack in black with soft crimson lining, steel fittings and crimson accessories. It looked superb and even Henry had to admit that my time had been well spent. My next target for my team was Vicky Belstone and, when I rang her to suggest meeting up, she responded with delight. I didn't tell her about the harness, instead packing one and presenting her with it when I arrived at the Camden Town flat which she shared with Todd. It was a Saturday and they were both lolling around the flat, Vicky in a track-suit, Todd in just a bathrobe.

She was pleased, to say the least, especially when I refused to accept payment for my work. After admiring it for a few seconds she stripped naked with a total disregard for the supposed embarrassment of nudity, which reminded me of Ginny. Todd and I helped her into the harness, Vicky giving delighted squeaks and coos, Todd equally impressed but pointing out that the tack was in Henry's racing colours while his own were black and yellow.

'Ah, well, there's a reason for that,' I said tentatively. 'I was wondering if Vicky would consider racing for me?'

'I'm yours,' Vicky replied without hesitation.

'Hang on, hang on,' Todd interrupted. 'Who's supposed to be the master around here?'

'You are, darling,' Vicky answered him sweetly, 'but that doesn't mean Amber can't race me if I want, does it? Don't worry, I promise not to run off with her.'

I could tell that while Vicky might be the submissive partner in their sexual relationship, their day-to-day lives were conducted as equals. I wasn't sure why Todd was unhappy with me racing Vicky, unless he was jealous for some reason. As it was, the reason was very different. They argued for a while, Vicky backing Todd into a corner until he finally admitted the truth.

'It's just that Morris rang the other day to say that nobody was to volunteer to race for Amber, on pain of being thrown out of the club. Look, I don't mind you two playing. In fact I'd like to watch or even drive you, Amber, if you're up for it, but I don't want to get kicked out of the club.'

'Start your own,' I suggested. 'Henry and I will join, and Ginny Linslade, maybe my friends Susan and Francis as well. You can use the farm. We'll have a great time. Forget Rathwell. You don't need him. You can drive me any time you like, too.'

'Thanks, Amber, that's sweet of you. We do need him, you know,' Todd sighed. 'He's got all the contacts, there's always some property on his books to use, he puts up great prizes . . . everything, really. I don't want to risk it. What's going on anyway?'

'Basically I've got another bet on with him,' I said. 'You know when I got caned and . . . well, you saw. That was because I lost a bet to him.'

'We know,' Vicky remarked. 'Every time we see him he reminds us about it. We know about you losing the pursuit-capture-punishment at Henry's farm, too. He says he yoked you and you were begging for it by the end. Lying bastard.'

'It's at least half-true,' I admitted. 'He yoked me anyway, and I got a bit carried away. I always seem to when I go sub. I can't really help it. Once I've been spanked I'm up for more or less anything.'

'Me too,' Vicky admitted. 'That's what I like best, as it goes. That and the thrill of winning as a pony-girl. What's the bet this time then?'

'Tough,' I said. 'He wants me as his live-in slave-girl, Melody's and Harmony's too. I've agreed to a week, but he's so arrogant he's sure I'll want to stay on. If he wins he'll also cane me and then . . . then put it up my bottom in front of everyone.'

'Typical Rathwell,' Vicky interrupted. 'What if you win?'

'I get a piece of land and an old forge building, which I really want. I also get to cane him.'

'You get to cane him?'

'Yes. I insisted because he insisted on keeping the buggery bit in. He didn't like it, though.'

'No, he wouldn't. He won't go sub to anyone, not even in fun. I smacked his arse with a whip once, just gently. He went nuts. If you're going to cane him, I want to see it.'

'If I win,' I reminded her. 'I need you on my team to be sure I do. Please, Vicky?'

'I want to do it,' she replied. 'I've got to do it!'

'Vicky!' Todd objected.

'Show some guts, Todd,' Vicky answered him.

'But . . .'

'Sod his club. I don't think he would have the guts to throw us out anyway.'

'Oh yes he would.'

'Well, he can then. It's worth seeing him get caned, and he's an arrogant pig anyway. I'd rather play with Amber and Henry. Ginny Linslade too. Think of Ginny Linslade's tits, Todd; big and round, like melons –'

'Yeah, well,' Todd replied, looking a bit uncomfortable.

'He loves big boobs,' Vicky addressed me. 'Mine aren't enough. He likes yours, but he was really drooling over Ginny's.'

'Yours are nice,' I put in, admiring her bare, firm breasts, each a nice handful if nothing like the size of Ginny's or even my own.

'Thanks,' she answered. 'You can touch if you like.'

I reached out and cupped one of her tits in my hand, feeling the firm, resilient flesh and watching the nipple pop out as my thumb brushed it.

'Will you two stop mucking about,' Todd interrupted. 'What are we going to do?'

'I'm going to race for Amber,' Vicky replied decisively. 'Rathwell can bugger himself, or at least he could if his cock wasn't so short. You, my darling, are taking Amber and I pony-carting. Now.'

She meant it, too. It was already afternoon and, by the time we had got everything together and driven out into the country, the light had started to fade. The day was warm for October, but dry and not sunny enough for many people to be about. This was just as well, because Vicky was determined to go carting somewhere that meant we would definitely get seen. She wanted us to be nude, too, but Todd and I eventually persuaded her to compromise on bras and panties in order to avoid getting arrested.

The idea of risking being seen added something to it for me, and also for Vicky. Todd was more nervous, but I gathered it wasn't their first time by any means. Vicky had been telling me stories of previous occasions as we drove there, mostly involving surprised walkers, bird watchers, dirty old men and so forth. Once, a particularly outraged gamekeeper had chased her and she'd managed to outrun him, pony-cart and all, a feat of which she was especially proud.

I wasn't really prepared, and we had to jury rig their cart to make it work as a two-in-hand. Despite this, once Todd had us both fully harnessed in a lonely spot on heathland somewhere to the south-west of London, we looked and felt deliciously naughty, if not turned out as well as we might have been. It was a place they knew well, and he exercised us for half-an-hour without seeing a soul. His courage increased with time, as, I suspect, did his excitement, and after a while he halted us and unsnipped our bras. The feeling of naughtiness increased as I felt the extra weight of my bare breasts and the cool evening breeze perked my nipples up.

It felt even better topless, running down the quiet, sandy paths with my breasts bouncing bare in front of me and my panties pulled up tight between my bottom-cheeks. The sight of Vicky to my side was enchanting too, and my inability to touch her exquisitely frustrating. Todd drove us silently, guiding us with the reins and gentle flicks of his whip to our bottoms. His signalling system was a little different from Henry's, but I soon got the hang of it.

I was becoming thoroughly turned-on, and beginning to wish someone would see us when I caught a knowing glance and a wink from Vicky. I wasn't sure what she meant until she took an unsignalled turning and sped up.

'Vicky?' Todd said, uncertain and with just a touch of severity.

I felt the pull of the reins against my bit and started to slow, only to find Vicky speeding up.

'Vicky,' Todd repeated, now definitely stern.

I heard the smack of his whip on her bottom; a meaty sound caused by the broad leather snap he favoured. Vicky again increased her pace, forcing me to increase mine until we were going flat out and the cart was bouncing on the ruts in the sand track.

'Vicky! Halt!' Todd ordered.

We paid no attention, turning again on to a broader, smoother path.

'Vicky, no,' Todd ordered hopelessly. 'Vicky, you're topless and so's Amber. Vicky!'

We ignored him completely, Vicky turning on to another track and towards lights that I could see through a bank of trees in the gathering gloom. I was beginning to feel a bit concerned about her intentions, but couldn't really stop.

'Victoria!' Todd yelled as we came in among the trees.

It was too late, not that Vicky made any attempt to stop. The trees were no more than a fringe of pines shielding the heathland from a main road. Worse, the track opened directly on to the forecourt of a service station.

I had a brief glimpse of astonished faces as we shot past the petrol pumps. There was a car wash to one side, the main building to the other. We ran between, slowed, turned and doubled back. A car was just coming in, the driver's face a mask of amazement as we ran towards him. He stopped, Vicky and I turning in front of him to angle for the track and the heathland. Someone shouted, another whistled, and Todd's whip smacked hard against my bottom as we hit the sand of the track.

'Sprint!' he ordered.

There was genuine alarm in his voice and I responded to the whip, leaping forward, trying to match Vicky's pace, taking the full strain of the cart. We were going flat out, tearing down the track as fast as we could run. I heard the sound of a horn behind us and another shout, then lights flooded over us and I realised that somebody had turned a car on to the track.

'Shit!' I heard Todd exclaim. 'Run, you two!'

I was already going flat out and, in any case, run as we might we couldn't hope to go faster than a car. Pictures of my arrest for indecent exposure started to flood my mind, my father's face on discovering that his precious daughter had been arrested for playing pony-girls in public, and topless at that.

195

'Right! Hard right!' he yelled.

I saw what he meant, a narrow track leading between stands of bracken and gorse that opened just ahead. We turned hard, the gorse scratching my leg, then a hidden stump knocking my calf. I stumbled, righted myself and ran on. The lights swerved and an instant later there was a crash behind us.

'Oh fuck!' Todd said. 'Make for the car, fast!'

We ran all the way, a good half-mile of rough track by the end of which my thigh muscles were burning in protest. We stopped by the car and started to sort ourselves out, desperately pulling our tack off as Todd worked on the nuts and catches of the cart. Seconds after it was packed another car pulled into the remote place we had chosen. Fortunately, this car contained a couple more intent on each other than wondering why two half-naked girls were scrambling into their clothes in the middle of the car park.

Only when we were well away did Vicky start laughing. I was still panting and trying to get my breath back, but she was hardly bothered by our run, which gave me a new respect for her stamina.

'Victoria,' Todd said quietly from the front. 'You are in big trouble.'

'How was I to know that some nutter would give chase?' she laughed. 'Anyway, we got away, didn't we?'

'That's not the point!' he exclaimed. 'You bolted and ran through a service station!'

'Naughty, aren't we?' Vicky replied, her voice full of excitement.

'Yes,' Todd answered, seriously, but without any real annoyance.

'Punish us then,' Vicky demanded. 'Take us into the woods and put our faces in the dirt. Whip us and then fuck us both.'

'Don't tempt me,' Todd responded.

'I need it, Todd,' Vicky continued, still giggly but with real urgency in her voice. 'Take us to that car park where the dirty old men like to watch and fuck me in front of them. Amber too.'

'Hey!' I protested half-heartedly.

'Be careful or I might just do that,' Todd answered her. 'But for now I've got a better idea. We're going home, and when we get there you're going to get your special punishment.'

'In front of Amber?' Vicky asked.

'Yes, in front of Amber,' he answered.

She just sighed and lay back in the seat, sliding her hand down the front of her tracksuit bottoms.

'And you can cut that out,' Todd ordered.

'Yes, master,' Vicky replied breathlessly.

'What are you going to do to her?' I asked, intrigued by the idea of watching Vicky punished in whatever strange and novel way they had devised.

'You'll see,' Todd assured me.

Vicky just groaned. By the time we got near their flat she was fidgeting in anticipation and kept looking back at me with an expression that told me she was very keen on my being there to watch or even join in. As we turned into their road she had her hand down her panties again and was talking to me, fast and nervously, about how much she wanted me to drive her. I was ready to have her as soon as we were through the door, only for Todd to suddenly slam the brakes on and pull in sharply behind a box van.

'What's the matter?' Vicky demanded.

'That,' Todd said, nodding forward.

Vicky turned, but I had already seen what had alarmed Todd. Outside their flat a gold Rolls Royce was parked at an angle. Morris Rathwell was getting out of it.

'Shit!' Vicky exclaimed.

'What shall we do?' Todd demanded.

'I don't want him to know you're racing for me!' I insisted.

'Nor do I,' Todd added.

'Just brazen it out, then,' I suggested. 'I'll go.'

'Sure, but that's why he's here, isn't it?' Vicky responded. 'To sign me up to run for him.'

'You're probably right,' I admitted.

'I know I am,' Vicky insisted. 'He's a sneaky bastard. If

he knows you're going to make it a distance race he won't just use Melody and Harmony. He'll use a four-in-hand to get real stamina, and maybe make mid-route pony-girl changes. He'll want me and Trisha because he doesn't take you too seriously.'

'Who's Trisha?' I demanded. 'And what do you mean he doesn't take me too seriously?'

'Trisha's the tall girl with the red hair who came in third the first time you raced,' she answered. 'She's good, but if Rathwell was really worried about you having a chance of winning he'd hire a couple of male athletes.'

I didn't reply, my cheeks burning with shame and fury at the discovery of how little Rathwell thought of my challenge. Sure he was going to try and make sure he outdid my team, but he obviously regarded it as a straightforward task. He was at their door, his finger jabbing at the bell.

'Let's wait until he goes,' Vicky said.

'He'll just come back tomorrow,' Todd objected.

'Tell him you've twisted your ankle,' I suggested.

'Oh, yeah, and that'll really drop us in it when she turns up next week as your pony,' Todd pointed out.

'Why not just turn him down?' I asked.

Vicky made a small noise that implied my suggestion wasn't as easy to do as it sounded.

'Morris can be very persuasive,' Todd said, 'especially when Vicky wins so much in prizes at his meets.'

'I'm sorry,' I said, feeling suddenly depressed. 'It's not fair of me to make you risk things. I thought he'd be more sporting about it.'

'Huh,' Vicky snorted. 'Morris Rathwell? Sporting? He's a control freak, and he's never happy unless he's manipulating people. You're very sweet, Amber, but you're a bit naïve.'

'I know,' I admitted.

'Look, we'd better get on with it,' Todd put in. 'Let's go for the twisted ankle bit and worry about the details later. Amber, you stay here.'

I ducked down, watching through the bottom of the

window as Todd and Vicky walked over to where Rathwell was still pressing their bell as if it was inconceivable that they might be out on a Saturday night. Vicky leant on Todd's shoulder, limping convincingly. I saw Rathwell turn at Todd's greeting and a discussion quickly started. After a while they went into the flat and I was left alone in the car.

My depression became deeper as I waited. I'd been really flying after our pony-carting run, and being seen and then chased had given me a real buzz. Then there had been the prospect of watching Vicky get punished and maybe taking the same myself if it was something that appealed to me. Now I was huddled in the back of a car while Rathwell tried to persuade Vicky to race against me. She gained a lot from Rathwell's club, and I really had no right to ask her to risk losing it. The most I could hope was for her not to run at all, and then the best I could do would be to put Ellen and Ginny up against Melody, Harmony and maybe Trisha as well. We'd lose.

Finally Rathwell emerged, walking to his car with a self-satisfied grin on his face. As soon as he had gone Vicky came running over to me.

'It's worse than we thought,' she explained. 'When I told him about my leg he said it was OK because he could hire an athlete and he's already got Trisha signed up. He also wants Todd to drive for him. He reckons you must have invented a competition that will make the best of your natural advantages over him, like weight –'

'That's exactly what I've done,' I admitted, interrupting Vicky's flow.

'You have to be cleverer than that to catch him napping,' she answered. 'He reckons you'll go for stamina more than speed and go for something involving hills to make the best of your weight advantage.'

'Hell,' I swore, feeling more depressed than ever.

Rathwell had more or less second guessed my entire strategy. Things were getting out of hand, desperate even.

'Come up, and we'll talk it over,' Vicky suggested.

I agreed, glad of their company and any ideas they might

have. Unfortunately, for all their support, they simply didn't have as much to lose as I did and, after we had drunk a couple of beers, Vicky started to get back into the naughty mood that Rathwell had interrupted.

'I think I should be punished now,' she told Todd after a break in the conversation. 'That'll cheer Amber up.'

I smiled weakly, not really feeling up to it but not wanting to spoil their fun.

'Fair enough,' Todd answered. 'You certainly deserve it.'

They went into the bedroom, leaving me to my drink my beer and listen to Vicky's giggles from the far side of the door. Despite my fit of the blues I became more and more intrigued, finally getting up to try and peep through the keyhole when the door opened. Todd appeared first, holding a lead in his hand. On the end of the lead was Vicky, naked on all fours with a dog collar around her neck to which Todd's lead was attached. She had a blue rubber ball in her mouth and, as she advanced into the room, I saw that she also had a tail. This was furry and the same near-black colour as her hair, and was glued to the small of her back in some manner. It also stuck up almost vertically, doing nothing to hide the view of her pussy and bumhole. I saw this when she turned and deliberately waggled her tail at me.

'Meet my puppy-girl,' Todd announced proudly. 'She's called Fluffy, and she can do a few tricks.'

I couldn't help smiling as Vicky – or rather Fluffy – came over to me and dropped the ball at my feet, looking up into my eyes and wagging her tail. She looked really sweet and it was a fun image, yet I appreciated how humiliating it would be for her. Todd let her off the leash to play and I threw the ball for her, laughing as she retrieved it with all the unrestrained enthusiasm of a real puppy.

Todd went into the kitchen and I continued to play with her, throwing the ball, making her beg and then starting to stroke and pet her when she began to rub her face insistently against my leg. Only when Todd reappeared did

I realise just how humiliating the role could be. He was holding a dog bowl with Fluffy printed on the side and filled with what looked like a mixture of bread and tinned tuna. Or at least that's what I hoped it was. She ate it with gusto, on all fours, with her pretty face buried in the plastic dog bowl. When she had finished she licked the bowl clean, then crawled over to Todd and let him feed her dog biscuits – real dog biscuits – out of his hand.

Watching her was really turning me on, partly because of her glorious nudity and the uninhibited way she was showing off, but mostly at the thought of the utter humiliation of eating out of a dog bowl on the floor. This was better still when Todd passed me a couple of dog biscuits and she nuzzled them out of my hand, her soft lips brushing my palm in her eagerness to be fed. I couldn't help laughing either, which must have made it even stronger for her. When she turned to go back to Todd I could see that her pussy was creamy. She put her face into his lap and started nuzzling his crotch, her naked bottom thrust right out at me. There was something blatantly rude and unrestrained about the way her rear view showed and her indifference to the fact.

'I could put her in her kennel and you and I could make love if you like?' Todd asked. 'She'd really get off on that.'

'Thanks, but that's not really my thing,' I said, immediately feeling a bit bad about denying myself to him.

'Oh, right, sorry,' he responded. 'I thought . . .'

'No, no,' I said hastily. 'It's nothing personal. I prefer girls. I like men too, sort of. I know Rathwell fucked me . . .'

'But it was the humiliation you got off on,' he said.

'Yeah,' I admitted.

'Don't worry,' he answered. 'Vicky's the same in some ways. She loves being humiliated by me, but when we make love it's as equals. Isn't it, Fluffy?'

She wagged her tail vigorously, again nuzzling his crotch. I felt really mean, especially as if he'd ordered our bums in the air while we were out carting I'd have allowed him to fuck me without hesitation. The way he'd put it just seemed too intimate, though, and not the way I wanted it at all. My reluctance was obviously going to spoil the scene.

'Oh, I'm being a real bitch,' I said. 'Why not just spank me like the snotty little brat I am? Then you can fuck me.'

'You're sure?' he asked. 'That's how you like it?'

'I'm sure,' I answered.

'Tied up?' he queried.

'If you like,' I replied.

He almost ran from the room, returning a moment later with a great armful of rope and a short board. He put Fluffy on her leash and tied it to a table, then turned back to me. I was told to strip and kneel with my arms behind my back, which allowed him to tie me so that the board was along my back and the ropes made a web around me with loops and knots. It was extremely complicated and left me completely helpless. He had roped up my breasts, winding a double coil around each one so that they stuck out really rudely. They also felt hard and my nipples wouldn't go down, which made me constantly aware of them. My arms were crossed over the board, which meant that I couldn't get at anything or protect myself at all. My ankles were tied together but my knees were lashed with a rope that went over my back, leaving my thighs spread wide and my bottom up high.

When he was finished, Todd had a leisurely grope of my bottom and took a wooden paddle to me. The slaps started gently, making my bum wobble and bounce. It was soon warm and throbbing as he became firmer. My feelings of humiliation built up as he beat me for no better reason than because he enjoyed it and, by the time he had given my poor red bottom a last dozen hard smacks full across my cheeks, I was as pliable and submissive as ever. I expected him to mount me or put his cock in my mouth, but he did neither, instead going to sit down and letting his puppy-girl off her leash.

She crawled straight over and started licking me, concentrating on my face at first but then going to my neck and flanks. This tickled and quickly had me squirming and begging her to lick my pussy. But she wouldn't, instead teasing my thighs and bottom-cheeks, even licking my anus and pussy but never giving me what I wanted. It was driving me to distraction and I was soon begging for an orgasm, only to be called a slut by Todd and for Fluffy to come round to my face and kiss me, filling my mouth with the taste of my own pussy.

Finally Todd called her off and came around to my head. He'd been playing with himself over the sight of her licking me. His trousers were open with a thick, stubby erection sticking out from the fly and his balls bulging over the top of his jockey shorts. He took me by the hair and put it to my mouth, ordering me to kiss the tip. I obeyed and then opened wide for him to slide his penis into my mouth. He did it, pulling my hair until his erection was pushed in to the hilt and then telling me to suck on my own. My mouth was wide around his shaft and I began to bob my head up and down as soon as he let go of my hair. It felt great to have a new cock to suck. It was rude and submissive, and made better by having been tied and beaten first. Todd's cock was thick and had a large, meaty head, which added to the rudeness of sucking it. Physically, cock size isn't as big a deal as its made out, especially when your pussy's wet and open. Mentally it is important, though, and the sight of a big, fat erection really adds to my pleasure in submitting to a man.

I was hoping he'd come in my mouth and then wipe his cock in my face, which was one of the things I'd come to like even though – or perhaps because – Rathwell had been the first to do it to me. He didn't, though, instead pulling out and mounting me instead. I must have been soaking, because his cock slid in without difficulty and he was riding my upturned bottom in seconds with my pussy gaping around his erection. Each time he went into me he caught my sore bottom and made my body push against the ropes. This was great at first but quickly became too painful and I was forced to call yellow. Todd dismounted, laughing at the state he'd put me in and then starting to untie the ropes.

Over the next couple of hours I got a fair idea of what

203

it would feel like to be the Rathwell's sex-slave. Vicky came out of puppy-girl role and they dominated me together, most of which consisted of them using my mouth for their pleasure. First I was stationed in the kitchen doorway, kneeling and with my hands tied behind my back. Each time Todd passed he'd slip his cock into my mouth for a while, while Vicky would press my face to her pussy and make me lick her. That carried on while they prepared food, which I had to eat out of Vicky's dog bowl, down on the floor while they sat at table.

After dinner Vicky caned me for some imagined error, leaving six hot lines across my already tender bottom. Doing this to me was too much for her self-restraint, and she took me into the bedroom afterwards, sitting on the edge of the bed and opening her thighs for me to lick her all the way to orgasm. Todd watched, stroking his erection and then mounting me again while I licked at his girlfriend's pussy. I was in heaven with his cock inside me and my face in Vicky's pussy, but they again denied me my orgasm. Vicky came in my face, Todd restraining himself with difficulty.

I discovered why when they served apple pie and ice-cream ten minutes later. Mine was put in the dog bowl and I was told to wait until they had finished. Todd then got down on the floor and ordered me to suck him erect again. I obeyed willingly, hoping he'd treat me to a mouthful while Vicky made me come. Instead he made me suck until he was at bursting point and then came all over my dessert. I ate it with my face in the dog bowl, tasting his come mingled with the sweet flavours of apple and vanilla, my sense of humiliation building to an unbearable peak. Inevitably I started to cry before I'd finished and had to assure Vicky that this was normal for me to stop her taking me out of role.

Instead she nodded understandingly and made me lick up the last smear from the bowl before untying my hands and telling me I could masturbate. I did, on the floor in front of them with my legs spread shamelessly wide. Vicky came to help in the end and, when I'd come, we lay cuddled in each other's arms for a long time before getting up for a much-needed wash.

I stayed the night with Vicky and Todd and drove back in the morning. They had distracted me briefly from my problems with Rathwell, but it didn't make them go away. He seemed to be out-thinking me whatever I did, and had already managed to severely curtail my plans. I had to submit the race plan to him by Wednesday, which left me three clear days to finalise things.

Ginny rang after lunch to find out the details for the next Saturday and we had a long conversation which cheered me up but solved nothing. Susan called later and was a good deal more helpful. Her advice was to set the rules in some way that made Rathwell think he had an advantage that was actually a disadvantage. She also suggested getting over the team problem by creating a pony-girl corral from which we would pick our teams. This in turn gave us an idea that left me smiling broadly when I at last put the phone down.

'Getting anywhere?' Henry enquired as I entered the study.

'Maybe,' I answered, crossing the room and sitting down on his lap.

'Are you going to tell me?' he said, moving in the seat so that his hand was on my bottom and I had easy access to his crotch.

'Yes. See what you think,' I replied, my fingers starting on his fly buttons in what had become a familiar routine.

I explained Susan's ideas, working Henry's cock and balls out of his fly as we talked. He was fully erect by the time I finished, his hand kneading my bottom gently as I tugged at his cock.

'You know Vicky and Todd and I went carting on Blackheath yesterday,' I reminded him.

'You said,' he replied.

'And how you used to occasionally take Jean out in the woods. By the way, do you want to come in my hand or another way?'

'Anyway you like, my dear. Yes, she used to love the thrill of risking being seen. As you discovered, it can be genuinely risky.'

'What about the cross-countrys you used to run?'

'It's fine if the pony-girls are in bikinis and masked, but it was impossible to satisfy everyone. Jean always wanted to be nude while some of the others were too shy or had the sort of job that made it too risky.'

'Did she ever do it nude?'

'A few times, mainly in Wales. Twice near here, but rumours started to get round so we stopped before anyone found out that the farm was involved. Even now they talk about it in the village occasionally, but everyone reckons it was people out from London. You can blame anything on townies around here and it'll be believed.'

I stopped talking to concentrate on Henry's cock, sucking for a bit and then taking his balls in my mouth and using my hand again. I enjoyed it, especially when he came and it splashed in my face, but my heart wasn't really in it. Instead I was thinking on what Susan had said and a plan was gradually forming in my mind. By the time I had finished showering it was all worked out. It didn't absolutely guarantee my winning the bet, but I felt pretty confident that it would be enough. What Henry would do to my bottom afterwards was an entirely different matter.

Ten

On the Saturday morning I was up at dawn, ostensibly to oil the cart and check the harness, but in practice because I was far too excited to sleep. This was it: the day that would see me as Morris Rathwell's sex-slave or as a landowner in my own right. I had faxed him the race plan on Wednesday, cheekily sending it to his office. I had expected at least some protest, but it came back by return with his signature scrawled casually across it.

I'd also managed to find the time to visit Trisha, taking her for a drink on the Thursday lunchtime. I'd last seen her as a pony-girl, naked but for green ribbons and her harness. She had been driven by a tiny woman with a shaved head, tattoos and piercings, which had made me assume that they were an open lesbian couple and fairly outrageous. Nothing could have been further from the truth. Her driver, Ginger, was a lesbian – or a butch dyke as Trisha described her – but, while they raced as a team and Trisha occasionally subbed to her, they were not partners. Trisha, indeed, was a barrister and a fairly high-powered one at that. She had met Rathwell while acting for him, been his girlfriend for a while and stayed involved with pony-carting when they split up. She still had a soft spot for him but had found him just too arrogant to live with. When I gave her the details of the bet she said she thought I had the better deal by far. I had found myself a bit awed by her at first, until her natural submissiveness started to come out in response to my own character. After that we got on really well. In fact, had we not been in a

Bloomsbury wine bar I'm sure we'd have ended up having sex – and with me in charge – but I'd had to content myself with a frustrating journey home by train and once again playing with myself in the woods.

The rest of the week had been spent making things for the day, including full tack for a three-in-hand and my secret weapon to destroy part of Rathwell's tactics. Now I was ready – or at least as ready as I ever would be – with every detail worked out to perfection. Other than the stomach-churning prospect of losing, my only concern was that I was not driving myself. Given that Susan was so much lighter than anyone else, including Todd, we had decided that she should drive, giving whatever team I got a considerable advantage.

Ginny had arrived on the Friday night but was still asleep after a fairly riotous evening with Henry and myself. Everyone else was due in the morning. There would be six pony-girls in all, plus Rathwell, Henry and myself, Francis, Susan, Todd and little Carrie. That made thirteen in all, and it would be the biggest meet on Henry's land for a long time. The weather was cloudy and cool, but dry. Not perfect pony-carting weather, but good enough.

Henry and I breakfasted and then got Ginny up by the simple method of tipping her out of bed. Ellen and Carrie arrived shortly afterwards, with Vicky and Todd joining us a few minutes later. I was unable to resist looking out of the window every few minutes, constantly expecting the appearance of Rathwell's gold Rolls Royce. Instead a seven-ton truck arrived, bumping to a stop in the middle of Henry's carriageway. The driver was a swarthy young man, which made me think that somebody had chosen a singularly inappropriate moment to make a delivery until I saw Melody sitting beside him.

It was a typical Rathwell gesture, undoubtedly meant to shake me as much as show off. All of us went outside, lining up by the truck as Melody and the man jumped down and came around to the tailgate.

'Hi,' she called cheerfully. 'Hi, Amber, little one. This is Stefan, who'll be racing with us today.'

The man nodded to us, smiling as Henry completed the round of introduction. He was tall, muscular and quite obviously no genuine pony-boy. I heard the sound of another car and turned to see Rathwell arriving. Next to him was Harmony and, in the seat behind, another man – this one blond, fair-skinned and, if anything, more physically impressive than Stefan.

Rathwell favoured me with a confident leer and introduced their companion as Sven. I smiled back, refusing to show my emotions. I'd suspected he'd bring paid athletes in, choose one as his lead if he won the toss, and hope I didn't risk picking the other in the corral. He had, but thanks to Susan's brain I was ready for him, the only problem being that if things went Rathwell's way we would now be racing four-in-hands, which made a complete mockery of my perfect three-in-hand tack system.

Stefan and Sven shot the bolts on the truck doors, lowering the ramp to reveal the interior. I looked inside and received another jolt to my confidence. Set up in the interior, gleaming in turquoise paint and golden anodised aluminium, was a brand new and obviously well-designed pony-cart. The seat was low and elegant, slung between high mountain-bike wheels of some twice the diameter of those on Henry's cart. The frame looked light yet strong, the shafts curving forward to meet a bar designed for a four-in-hand. Gold leather harness hung from this, my sole consolation being that it looked skimpier than my own harness design.

They rolled the magnificent cart out and Melody and Harmony trotted it round to the stable yard. I followed, feeling increasingly nervous as I watched how easily and smoothly it ran. I was paying so little attention to anything else that I squeaked and jumped when somebody pinched my bottom. I turned to find Rathwell himself behind me, smirking confidently.

'Well, Amber darling,' he said, 'I suppose we'd better make a race of it, for form's sake, but you know you're going to lose, don't you?'

'No,' I said obstinately.

'Proud and wilful, that's my girl,' he continued. 'I'll enjoy your complete submission, Amber, I really will. I'm afraid I don't think much of your competition plan, though. The corral idea's silly. How can we trust each other's ponies? Todd's riding for me by the way, so you can forget tiring my team on Windbreak Hill. I imagine he's a good stone lighter than you, maybe more.'

'Susan's driving for me,' I answered. 'She weighs seven stone two.'

'Ho, ho, playing me at my own game, eh?' he laughed. 'Well, we'll see.'

Henry joined us and Rathwell stopped tormenting me. I had set the corral up to one side of the yard, a square area marked off with old show-jumping fences. People were milling around Rathwell's new cart, pretty well ignoring Henry's despite the gleaming new red-and-black paint-work. I had to admit ours looked pretty crude next to his, yet I knew ours balanced well and could only hope that its greater solidity might help.

The sound of another car announced the arrival of Trisha, leaving only Susan and Francis to come. Half-an-hour later there was still no sign of them, so I decided to get things started and fill them in later. Henry had positioned a stump by the scullery door, and I climbed on to it to make myself higher than the others.

'Ladies and gentlemen!' I called, then waited for the talk to subside. 'There are still two people to come but I think we'd better get on with things. Let me run over the course and the rules and then the ponies can get ready and we'll choose teams. As you all know, I am racing against Mr Morris Rathwell for a not insubstantial bet. We will be running a cross country with checkpoints. The first checkpoint is in Kerry Woods, the second at the edge of Henry's land. Both points are marked on the map. Teams may reach the checkpoints by any route they like, although I have marked an obvious and relatively lonely route on the map. At each checkpoint teams must collect a signature, one pony-girl must be punished in a specific way and clothing must be reduced. At the first checkpoint one pony-girl will have her bottom nettled and all will remove their bikini tops. At the second checkpoint one will be birched and they must all strip. I have marked a route that stays on Henry's land all the way back. There is a steam traction fair in the village, so the countryside should be pretty empty. Is that all clear?'

'Clear enough,' Rathwell spoke up, 'if unnecessarily complicated.'

'Good,' I answered him. 'If the ponies could get into role, then. I take it you've all got bikinis? The tails are in the scullery when you're ready.'

The eight ponies went into the house, dispersing to various rooms under Henry's guidance. I went to the scullery. Ten tails were laid out on the table, six in the colours of the various girls' hair, two black and two blonde. Rathwell followed me inside.

'What's with the tails then?' he asked. 'They look nice, sure, but they're only really good for show. We find they drop off too easily for racing.'

'These won't,' I assured him, holding up the nearest, a honey-gold one designed for Ginny.

He studied it, puzzled for an instant and then understood. This was my masterpiece. The design consisted of a small conical plug on the end of a curving shaft of black rubber around a metal core. The plug was designed to fit into the pony-girl's anus, which would hold it in place and also produce an extra thrill. The actual tail – a hank of artificial hair two feet long – came from the other end, the length of the shaft meaning that it would appear to protrude from the base of the pony-girl's spine.

'The plug goes up the girl's arse, right?' he said. 'Neat, I'll give you that. You can make one for yourself when I've won.'

'I already have,' I answered.

'Can I have mine in, then?' Ginny called, appearing in the doorway stark naked.

'Coming right up,' I said, kissing her and then dipping my finger in the tub of grease I had prepared earlier.

Rathwell watched in fascination as Ginny stuck her

211

bottom out. I pulled her bikini pants aside and inserted a greasy finger into her anus. The tail followed, Ginny giving no more than a little squeak of surprise as her bumhole stretched to let the plug in. I attached the single strand of fishing line that held the tail around her waist, smiling as she admired her tail in the mirror and then ran outside in absolute delight at how she looked. Rathwell was impressed, too, and appeared not to realise that there was a possibe catch in what I was doing. To enjoy having a plug up your bottom you need to be pretty dirty minded. To accept one at all you at least had to feel that it was not utterly unreasonable to have your anus penetrated. As Vicky had explained to me, a lot of men get hung up about that because they feel it makes them somehow gay. I don't pretend to understand why that is, but I was counting on it.

Vicky and Trisha came down next, holding their bikinis and gloriously naked and wet from the shower. Vicky was delighted by her tail – a glossy black one that went perfectly with her hair. I greased her bottom and popped the tail in, sending her out into the yard with a firm smack on her rump. Trisha was a little shyer, and insisted on fingering her own bottom, but was every bit as proud of the striking ginger tail I had made for her as the others had been of theirs. By the time I had got hers in, the others were queuing up. I had crafted Melody and Harmony's as sprays of the beaded plaits they sometimes favoured, in blue and yellow, which delighted them both. Neither objected to my greasy fingers in their bottoms, a process that was beginning to seriously turn me on. Ellen followed them, demurely inserting her own plug but giving me a cheeky wiggle of her bottom as she left. That left Stefan and Sven, who had watched the last three tail insertions with considerable pleasure. Both wore only brief bathing trunks, which now showed impressive bulges at the front.

'Come on then, boys,' I said, holding up one blonde and one dark tail.

'What, us?' Stefan asked.

'Yes, you're running, aren't you?' I demanded. 'Pony-boys have tails too, you know.'

'We're not pony-boys,' Sven answered.

'You are if you're racing,' I said. 'Look, you can grease each other if you don't want my finger up your bottoms.'

'We're not gay,' Stefan interrupted crossly.

'Hang on, hang on,' Rathwell interrupted. 'Where does it say the tails have to hold in up the ponies' arses?'

'It doesn't,' I admitted, 'but it says tails must be worn and these are the tails.'

'Hold them between your cheeks or something,' Rathwell suggested, meeting immediate opposition from both men.

'Oh, and remember it's bikinis too,' I put in after a while. 'I've got a couple that might fit you. Sort of, anyway.'

I walked out into the yard, leaving them to argue. It was impossible not to grin. I had seriously disturbed Rathwell's plans, maybe terminally. The sight of the six pony-girls in the corral was also something to grin about. They were all in bikinis, while I would have preferred them naked, yet there was plenty of beautiful bare girl on display and each of them had matching tails hanging down over their bottoms. Henry was lining them up for a group photo, bottoms pushed out and tails sticking up cheekily. The effect was remarkably natural, or at least convincing, if not exactly natural.

It was perhaps a little cold, but the sun was breaking through the clouds and nobody seemed to mind, presumably because of the air of excitement that was already building strongly among us. Todd and Carrie were chatting together by the side of the corral, she pouting a bit because she wasn't a pony-girl. I crossed to them and joined in the conversation, promising Carrie a red tail but suggesting that she could happily get kitted up even if she wasn't racing and that she could use a blonde tail for the moment. She scampered happily into the house, entering the scullery door just as Rathwell emerged from it.

His face was red and he looked furious, but no more so than the two men coming behind him. I smiled sweetly as he made straight for me, Henry stepping to my side as Rathwell reached us.

'Is something troubling you, Morris?' Henry asked calmly.

'These rules . . .' Rathwell began, then stopped, seeing the expression of bland politeness on Henry's face.

'I believe you said you could beat me over any course and under any rules I chose?' I reminded him.

'And I can,' he snapped. 'With or without these two prudes.'

'I'm no prude,' Stefan declared. 'I said I'd pull the cart, didn't I? I will, too, but not in a girl's bikini and not with one of those things up my arse! You can keep your money!'

Sven nodded agreement behind him.

'The rules are the rules,' I said. 'Still . . .'

'Well, if you're not going to be any help, you can get out of here,' Rathwell snarled at them, interrupting me.

'Gentlemen, please,' Henry put in, raising his palms. 'There is no need for unpleasantness. 'Sven and Stefan may help man the checkpoints, acting as neutral observers. Now I think we should choose teams.'

Both men were keen to stay, which was hardly surprising given how many half-naked girls there were around. Rathwell backed down, regaining his temper and presumably aware that it was unwise to insist on them leaving when they might easily complain about the race. I felt I was winning, especially as we would now be racing three-in-hands and it was his tack structure and not mine that needed adapting.

'We'll toss for first choice, then,' Henry announced. 'The challenged party calls. Morris?'

'Heads,' Morris called as Henry flipped the coin up.

Henry caught the coin and flipped it on to the back of his hand, revealing the Queen's head. Rathwell gave a satisfied chuckle while I drew my breath in. I had been hoping to win, yet the drawback was not as bad as it might have been.

We walked over to the corral, both inspecting the ponies who were lined up and facing us. We both knew Vicky was the best, and I was sure he'd pick her, which was annoying. Trisha and Ellen both looked good, although the

214

red-haired girl had the advantage of experience. Ginny, Melody and Harmony were all good enough and of roughly equal standard.

'Trisha to lead,' Rathwell announced, surprising me until I remembered that he still thought Vicky had twisted her ankle badly the week before.

'Vicky leads my team, then,' I said, catching an amused glance from Rathwell.

He, of course, had no idea that Vicky's injury was phoney, nor that I had pretty well subverted her. He paused before making his next choice, looking at Ellen's sleek, runner's build but then shaking his head doubtfully.

'Melody,' he finally decided.

'Ginny,' I said without hesitation.

Rathwell looked at me in surprise. Ginny had put on a little weight over the summer, and her body was more opulent than ever. She was still trim waisted and lithe, but lacked the muscle of either Harmony or Ellen. He shook his head ruefully and turned back to look at the pony-girls. I could see how his mind was working. Ellen was obviously the better runner, yet he had never met her and knew only that she was a friend of mine. Still, he had a whip and could make sure she ran her best.

'Ellen,' he finally said, his confidence overcoming his caution.

'I'll take Harmony, then,' I said.

We took our teams out of the corral, tied ribbons in our colours to their tails and started to hitch them up. He had fractionally the better team, given that the pace would be dictated by a team's slowest member. He also had the better cart, but was soon struggling to put his pony-girls into an even three-in-hand formation. I had all three girls fully harnessed by the time he had decided how to arrange them, and had the pleasure of being able to drink a cup of tea while he pulled and swore at the straps and traces of his system.

When he had nearly finished I heard a car coming up the drive and stopping at the front of the house. A moment later Francis appeared in the archway, followed by Susan.

My jaw dropped as I saw her. She was the same as ever, tiny, impish, but grinning apologetically and holding up her right arm, which was in plaster.

'Sorry, Amber,' she said as she approached. 'I was cycling down the Cowley Road and a lorry clipped my elbow. That was yesterday evening, and we've been in the hospital all night.'

'Thanks for making it anyway,' I replied, my spirits dropping sharply despite my efforts to put a brave face on things.

Not having Susan to drive for me meant that my efforts to give the advantage to the lighter rider had blown up in my face. Todd weighed less than me, not to mention the extra weight of Henry's cart. I was now firmly at a disadvantage.

'Would you care to throw in the towel, Amber my darling?' Rathwell said unctuously. 'I'll take you on as house-slave anyway.'

'No, I'll drive myself,' I retorted.

Actually I had little choice, short of putting Carrie in the hot seat. She was certainly as light as Todd, being slimmer if a little taller, but had no experience at all. My only chance was to do it myself and hope that my tactics prevailed.

'Well, if everyone's ready I think we should get underway,' Henry announced. 'Who's on the checkpoints?'

After a little discussion we sent Francis and Susan out to run the far checkpoint and Stefan, Sven and Carrie to the near one. Carrie was now in full pony-girl gear and looked delightful, especially with the tail hanging down over her trim bottom. Both Sven and Stefan evidently felt the same and the little flirt was teasing them outrageously as they walked away together.

'Is she a virgin?' I heard a voice at my elbow – Rathwell's.

'No,' I said emphatically, although I had no idea if she was or not. 'At school she used to take the boys from the village on three at a time. Anyway, you're not having her.'

Rathwell merely laughed and went back to his team. I

watched him go and then told my girls to kneel. They sank down as one, bottoms presented to me as I climbed over the shafts and took my seat. Directly in front of me was Vicky, the look of her svelte, muscular haunches renewing my confidence a little. I had put Harmony on the right, in the best position to taste my whip should she prove reluctant to pull her weight. Ginny was on the left, her magnificent bottom spilling out of her impractically small bikini pants.

'Rise,' I ordered.

They rose smoothly. I took the reins and gave the command to walk, tapping Vicky's bottom gently with my whip. I was in full riding gear, which I had chosen on the assumption that I would be waiting in the yard with Henry and Rathwell. The pink jacket felt warm, which reminded me that there was a hip flask in the pocket. I took a pull at it, the Armagnac gilding down my throat to put new resolve into me on the spot.

'Halt,' I said as we reached the edge of the yard.

Todd reined his team in next to me, turning and grinning wolfishly. I had half-hoped he would throw the race for me but, like various other people, he seemed to find the idea of me being buggered and used as Rathwell's sex-slave thoroughly stimulating. If I beat him it would have to be fairly and, as we sat waiting for Henry's signal, I wasn't at all sure I could do it.

He looked cool and in control and I knew he was one of the most experienced drivers of all. Their cart outshone ours like a modern sports car standing next to a sixties-style limousine. Trisha, Melody and Ellen all looked supremely fit and, if their harness lacked the careful design of ours, then it was still far from crude. I took another pull at the flask, telling myself not to be defeatist.

The waiting seemed to last forever, until finally Henry's phone rang. It was Francis, calling on his mobile to report that both checkpoints were in place. Henry called to us as he came back outside, my pulse thumping as he walked towards us.

'On my call,' he announced. 'Go!'

I flicked the whip on Vicky's bottom and snapped the reins. My pony-girls took off fast, as did Todd's team, and we raced up the big field, side by side until their weight advantage began to tell and we started to lose ground. The sight of my team running was beautiful, especially the tails swishing from side to side across their bottoms. I found myself wishing for time to appreciate them, and determined that I would take them out again sometime, win or lose.

We entered the woods at the top, managing to keep them from increasing their lead as we made for the hairpin of the track were Ginny and Henry had once tricked me into making an exhibition of myself by the railway. As it happened a train was passing as we came out of the woods and started across the field, but I no longer cared, intent only on trying to stop my rivals increasing their lead. It was hopeless. They had fifty yards on us at the beginning of the field and perhaps seventy on the far side. Ahead was the gate that led from Henry's land on to a public bridleway. Todd slewed his team to a stop and unfastened it, then slammed it shut the instant his cart was clear. I cursed him as we too had to stop, losing another few yards.

The track was broad and dry, running in a perfectly straight line to a fringe of trees that I knew marked the road. I saw them turn ahead of me and called frantically for more speed, only to reach the road and find they'd disappeared. The first checkpoint was in Kerry Woods, a dense copse on the brow of the hill in front of us: Windbreak Hill. The cart ran smoothly on the tarmac of the road, allowing me to check my map properly before turning them on to a footpath that led up the hill.

'Run!' I begged, ignoring the startled looks of two cyclists who were coming down the track towards us. 'Make way!'

They moved, refusing to meet my eyes even when I thanked them as we barrelled past. I glanced back to find the girl staring at us in slack-jawed amazement: a look that would have done wonders for my streak of exhibitionism in less fraught circumstances.

By the time we got to the top of Windbreak Hill all three pony-girls were panting and running sweat. Even Vicky was showing the strain yet, as we pulled in, we saw Todd pull away. Trisha's bottom was red with nettle rash where her cheeks peeped out around her bikini and all three girls now had bare, bouncing breasts. Susan was holding a great bunch of nettles in one gloved hand, Francis a bottle of water and a stopwatch.

'You're three minutes thirty-five behind,' he announced as we stopped.

'Tickle Ginny,' I instructed, grabbing for Harmony's bikini top and pulling it up over her full, dark breasts.

Ginny squeaked as Susan pushed the bunch of stinging nettles against her bottom, turning it to make sure her cheeks were well covered. I had Vicky's tits bare as Francis pulled Harmony's bit out to water her, and had pulled Ginny's top off before he got to Vicky. I saw how red Ginny's bum was as I remounted the cart. It was speckled and sore looking. I knew how it felt, stinging and then throbbing; a wonderfully erotic sensation and hopefully one to spur a pony-girl on.

'You can go,' Francis said, stepping quickly to the side as Ginny started off.

The next section of run was a long, winding path through woods at the top of the ridge. It was rough going and we never so much as glimpsed Todd's team. I was starting to despair as we reached what I new was roughly the halfway point: a junction with a lane that led down to the village. In the valley below us we could hear the whistles and clanking sounds of the steam rally, with the church spire and the roofs of houses occasionally glimpsed through the trees.

The pony-girls were straining for me, even Harmony, yet I was sure we were losing too much time. They were panting, their bodies wet with sweat and spattered with mud. Dappled sunlight came down through the trees, the undergrowth closing in ahead to create a dim tunnel. Entering it the girls had to duck and bunch up, slowing us further. Soon we were moving at a walk and I was really starting to panic, trying to stop my tears and wishing I'd never been so obstinate and stupid as to challenge Rathwell.

We finally made the village road and crossed it to find the second checkpoint. Carrie and the two men were hidden in among the trees and there was no sign of Todd's team.

'Four minutes twenty-seven behind,' Stefan announced. 'Which girl is to be beaten?'

'Harmony,' I said, intent on keeping Vicky as fresh as possible. 'On your knees, girl.'

Harmony sank to her knees, Vicky and Ginny crouching to let her bring the cart down. I started to work Ginny's bikini pants down as Sven swished his birch against the black girl's bottom. Harmony moaned and put her face in the dirt, an act of abject submission to the tall Dane. As Ginny kicked her pants off I started on Vicky's, tugging them hard down over her hips. For a moment her legs parted and I had a glimpse of the wet, pink centre of her pussy in its nest of fur. I kissed it gently and then stood to speak to her.

'You know what to do now, Vicky,' I whispered. 'Run like you've never run before and don't stop for anything.'

She nodded, her eyes looking full into mine.

'Hang on,' I instructed Sven. Just let me get this one's knickers off.'

He paused and Harmony lifted her bottom obligingly for me to take down her bikini pants. I pulled them off and stuffed them in my pocket, Harmony once more presenting her bottom for the birch. Carrie was watering Vicky as I climbed back into my seat, Stefan standing to the side and watching Harmony being beaten with evident pleasure.

'Come on!' I urged.

'Fuck me, Sven,' Harmony moaned as the birch lashed down across her bottom once more.

'No way!' I said. 'I'm not falling for that one again. Let's go!'

'Come on,' Sven said. 'You've lost anyway, so let's have some fun.'

'Later,' I insisted. 'Rise!'

Harmony obeyed, but Sven's hand was on her bridle and for a horrible moment I wondered if Rathwell hadn't set the whole thing up. If they insisted on getting their kicks with Harmony then I was finished, and she was obviously willing. I struggled for something to say, choking on my words, the tears starting in my eyes.

'I'll play with you,' Carrie chirped up suddenly. 'You can birch me while I suck Stefan. Come on.'

Sven turned without hesitation and I wheeled the cart.

'Thanks, Carrie, I'll remember that,' I called over my shoulder, catching a last glimpse of her going down on her knees in front of Stefan while Sven raised the birch over her trim hindquarters. The blonde tail was sticking up over her bottom, her cheeks were bared for the birch, and her mouth was open for Stefan's cock. I would never have guessed she was such a dirty little tramp, but now I knew I was glad of it.

We turned back on to the road, the cart accelerating on the tarmac. We were some five minutes behind; a hopeless task unless Susan's strategy paid off.

'Run like the wind!' I yelled, smacking Vicky's bottom with my whip. 'No turning!'

They obeyed, three stark-naked pony-girls with their tails bobbing behind them and their boobs bouncing in front, pulling me just as fast as they could go, straight towards Sapsford Village and the annual steam traction rally.

The track leading on to Henry's land passed to our right. My heart gave a leap as I saw the marks of tyres in the mud – unmistakable pony-cart tyres. Susan had been right. A team driven by Todd and consisting of the three more modest pony-girls would never risk sprinting naked through the village, especially when two had the added shame of red, recently punished bottoms. Rathwell had picked his team for sheer power; I'd picked mine for their dirty minds. Todd, Trisha and Ellen had respectable jobs. Melody was a slut, but she was in a minority. My team were very different. Vicky and Ginny were exhibitionists

221

through and through and Harmony was no better than Melody. As for me, at that moment I'd have more than happily driven the team down the middle of Oxford Street, never mind a country village.

The track they had taken led back to Henry's in a long curve, crossing another road and joining the big field halfway up. On the map it was nearly three times the length of the road and pretty rough as well. If we couldn't make up the lost five minutes then it was my pony-girls who deserved to be caned and buggered, not me.

Of course we still had one major obstacle to overcome: the village itself. Planning to drive a miniature cart pulled by three naked pony-girls through a village is one thing. Doing it is another. As we passed the Sapsford sign and the first house we were going flat out, the pony-girls' legs flashing in the light, driven as much by the immediate prospect of public exposure as by my commands and whip. Vicky and Ginny had known my plan, but Harmony hadn't, yet she was making no effort to do anything but go as fast as she could.

We saw our first person as we started into the gentle curve that leads to the green. She was middle-aged, stick thin and staring at us with absolutely ferocious disapproval. It's hard to shake your upbringing, and hers was just the sort of look I was used to getting when found doing something I knew I shouldn't be. As a large number of aunts, au-pairs and teachers had found out over the years, all that look does to me is make me obstinate. Be it given for jumping in a puddle in my best shoes, refusing to attend church, or pony-carting in public, the result is the same.

Not one of my pony-girls slowed, running hard past her and towards the corner that hid us from the green. There was a straggle of people ahead; several men standing around a van, and a couple of elderly women talking by a cottage door. Their heads turned as we approached, staring, laughing nervously, passing a shocked remark.

We were going fast, but that only means ten miles an hour or so. They all got a good look as we passed and my sense of being exposed really started to build. Then we came out on to the green and I realised that all my previous experiences of being exposed were nothing. The green was packed. To our left a great crowd of people were milling around outside the Green Man. To our right the road was solid with parked cars and bustling with yet more people. Ahead the green was studded with antique steam engines and thronged with humanity.

The pony-girls did their best to keep their speed up, but it was hopeless. We had to walk across the green. People stared at us, people laughed at us, people made disapproving comments, people made waggish comments, but they wouldn't get out of our way. I was quickly wishing I'd worn my hat and veil, but then that wouldn't have been fair on the pony-girls. After all, I was dressed. They were naked but for leather straps that did nothing to hide their breasts, fannies and bottoms. I used to be ashamed if my skirt blew up and my panties showed, even if nobody was looking. How much stronger their feelings were as we paraded ourselves so blatantly in front of perhaps five hundred people didn't bear thinking about. It's the disapproval that hurts. All three of them had run naked in front of Rathwell's crowds at pony-carting meets and enjoyed every second of it. Now it was very different.

Of course there was nothing we could do but walk on. I had planned to cross the green at full speed, and had never imagined that it would be so crowded. Running was physically impossible, but we still had to cross and I was soon asking the more awkward bystanders to move. They did, turning, gaping, sometimes finding something to say, but never once interfering with us. I suppose it actually takes a lot of guts to grab a naked girl but, whatever the reason, nobody did and we finally made it to the verge of the crowd, trotting, running, then once more going flat out for the far side.

Only as we reached the opposite corner of the green did I see the police car parked by the Post Office. A small group stood by it, one woman expostulating angrily, a man pointing in our direction. A head peered out of the car's window, turning to look at us.

'Sprint!' I yelled. 'There are police!'

Even as the team surged forward it occurred to me that it had been the very thickness of the crowd that had saved us. We had been invisible from the car until we reached the far side of the green, and now they were having to turn in a press of bystanders who showed no more compunction to move than they had for us.

All of this disappeared as we rounded a corner. It wasn't far to the turn off for the farm, yet the chances of making it seemed slim. Of course, what I couldn't do was put Henry in jeopardy. Better to be arrested than turn into his drive in view of the authorities. With the noise of the steam fair I could hear nothing behind us, then came the sound of a siren and my heart went into my mouth. It lasted only an instant, but I knew what it meant. The drive was visible ahead, but too far; far too far.

'Turn here!' I ordered.

They didn't need to be told. A track led to the right, going somewhere and I didn't care where. We turned, finding a narrow lane leading down between the houses and finishing at a fence. Beyond were woods: Henry's woods.

'Down to the fence!' I called.

Fortunately Vicky ignored me, instead turning hard behind the buildings and stopping behind a van. I heard the sound of a car, approaching, passing, then fading into the distance.

'Now down to the fence,' I demanded.

Vicky tugged left, back towards the road. Instantly I realised she was right. It would be impossible to get through the woods in time to win and, despite everything, we still had a chance. I dismounted and ran up the lane, peering out to find the road deserted. I was about to signal them when the police car appeared in the distance, coming towards us. It was going slowly, the man in the passenger seat peering left and right as they came.

'They're searching,' I hissed. 'Come on!'

They didn't hesitate, running down the lane to the fence and clambering over as I lifted the cart behind them. We ran into the woods, pushing through the undergrowth, the girls heedless of scratches. Twice I glanced back, seeing nothing, the third time glimpsing the car as it passed the lane. It seemed to slow and I froze, waiting for the inevitable.

It went on and a moment later the trees had closed around us and the houses were invisible. We pushed on into more open woodland where I could remount and soon reached a track. I felt elated yet guilty, aware of what I had risked yet unable not to feel pleased with myself. The pony-girls ran on, slower now, and bumping along the rough track with obvious difficulty. Ginny was beginning to flag badly, and Harmony also was obviously on her last legs. Vicky alone seemed to have any energy left.

As we moved through the wood my feeling of elation faded to be replaced by a sick sensation in the pit of my stomach. I was sure we had lost, and that we would come into the big field to find Rathwell's cart drawn up with him standing smugly beside it. I found myself clenching my buttocks at the thought, thinking of his cock prodding at my bottom-hole, opening me, buggering me as I knelt with my pants pulled down and my buttocks spread for him.

The two outside pony-girls slowed, exhausted and sensing my despair. Vicky was forced to drop her pace, and I was about to give the command to walk when I heard a sound to our side up the slope. It was a call, Todd's voice yelling for more speed.

'Run!' I screamed, but only provoked an exhausted stagger from Harmony.

I had one last chance, utilising a design feature of my harness that I had invented for just such an emergency. Ginny was trying hard but was dragging her feet and appeared to have a stitch. Harmony was worse, completely incapable of doing more than walk. Ahead was the light where the track opened into the big field, the stables visible beyond. I heard Todd's voice again, closer and ahead.

'Run, Vicky!' I yelled as my fingers went to the snap locks that held the outer ponies' traces to the cart.

The first came open and Ginny moved forward, the

cart's weight no longer on her. The other snapped and Harmony did the same, the traces trailing in the dirt as Vicky took the full strain. I wrenched at the junction lead and the swingletrees fell away to either side, Ginny falling back, Harmony collapsing to the ground. Vicky moved into a trot, then a run, her sheer power filling me with delight.

We burst into the big field. Todd's cart was visible away to the side and upslope. They had the advantage, but I could see they were as tired as us. Melody was staggering, Trisha limping slightly but still fast. Ellen alone was moving at the steady lope of the experienced long-distance runner, yet I could see the red marks left by the birch on her buttocks and thighs and knew that her bottom would be burning. Todd turned, saw us and yelled for speed.

Vicky surged forward without having to be told. Todd's cart slewed, Melody simply unable to keep pace with the others. A yell went up from the yard and I looked ahead to find Rathwell on his feet, gesticulating frantically to his team. Todd yelled for speed again and gave Melody a sharp crack with the whip.

At that instant I knew we would make it. If Todd had ever been in harness himself he'd have known that the whip is there for play. It may encourage a pony-girl under normal circumstances but, in a desperate sprint, it only hinders. He drove Vicky, too, who usually won and so really didn't know how it felt to be driving an exhausted pony-girl.

Now I had Vicky and, when it came down to it, she was simply the best there was. When I saw Todd he was perhaps ten yards ahead and well up the slope. We were neck and neck with a hundred yards to go; then we had the lead and I was yelling with pure joy. Rathwell was leaping up and down in fury, and Todd was screaming at his team. We closed on each other, aiming straight for Rathwell, my team coming in at a steep angle. Vicky's foot crossed the line, then a wheel, and we were home, turning, brushing Rathwell as he slapped his hand to his forehead, the cart slowing, stopping, even as Trisha crossed the line. Her knees buckled immediately, Melody and Ellen following her to the ground to collapse exhausted before Rathwell. Vicky stayed up, proud and tall, standing directly in front of Henry's chair.

Henry nodded to me and rose, taking Vicky's bridle as I dropped the reins. Todd was dismounting. I nodded to him as he extended his hand. I took it, shaking it and returning his smile. Trisha smiled at me, Ellen managing a weak grin. Melody looked at me and shook her head, puffing hard as she rested on all fours, regret written clearly on her face.

Eleven

I flexed the cane. Despite every effort to maintain a stern, aloof dominance appropriate to my role as mistress, I was grinning from ear to ear. It was impossible not to. In front of me Morris Rathwell was tied securely to a wooden frame in the shape of an X. Morris Rathwell, the purely dominant, never-whipped king of pony-carting, was now without a stitch. Morris Rathwell, master of Melody, Harmony and almost me, now stood with his muscular buttocks twitching in anticipation of the cane.

He had been furious at first, but he knew his whole reputation rested on always keeping his word. After all, if he backed out on me, then what sweet virgin would ever again risk herself in a bet? There were just too many witnesses although, to be fair, he never so much as suggested altering the terms.

After a long period of rest and cleaning up, he had signed over the deeds to what was now my land, with Henry and Trisha acting as witnesses. After that it was me, not him, who had delayed his punishment. I was dead sure that if he'd won he would have wrung every instant of pleasure from my submission and I was now determined to do the same. First I'd insisted on all six pony-girls getting back into full harness for a group photo. Then I'd had Melody, Trisha and Ellen kneel to be photographed with their bottoms up and their faces in the dust of the yard. Trisha and Ellen already had smarting red bottoms, and my whip soon gave Melody her share of punishment. Henry took photos front and rear, the latter with my team lifting the girls' tails so that their fannies showed, and also the plugs in their bottoms. I'd then lined them all up – including Carrie and Susan – and been photographed in my full kit, standing proudly at the end of a line of eight bare-bottomed girls, Susan alone not bearing the marks of punishment. I corrected that with six of the cane across her pert little rump, then gave Vicky four as she'd run so well and I felt she needed reminding of her place. I then demanded another photo.

Only then did I turn my attention to Rathwell. I could see he was less than happy about it, but he undressed at my order and stood patiently while I fixed him to the cross. The audience were all attention by then, giggling and whispering, even the men had smiles on their faces. To do Rathwell justice he had a fine body for his age and held himself well, obviously determined to take his punishment with dignity, just as I had once done when first bent over his whipping stool.

So I walked up and down and flexed the cane, commenting on his body and telling him how much it hurt to be caned. Finally I was ready, laying the cane across his buttocks, pulling it back, pausing, watching his buttocks tighten in anticipation and then bringing it down hard across them. He squeaked, to my utter delight. I gave him the second in the same slow, deliberate manner, really making sure he got the full benefit of being punished. He managed to stay silent for the second, so I put the third in as hard as I could and managed to make him squeak again.

Melody and Harmony were giggling behind their hands, while at the end of the row Ginny and Carrie were snickering and pointing at Rathwell. I walked around to see what was amusing them, suspecting that I knew. Sure enough, poking out from above his balls like a small carrot, was a fully hard, straining erection.

'So, who doesn't enjoy going sub?' I taunted, reaching out to stroke his balls and cock with my fingernails. 'Who would have thought it? High and mighty Master Morris, and he's all excited because little Amber's taking the cane to his bottom!'

He groaned slightly as my hand curled around his prick, then gasped as my gentle tugging motions stopped and I squeezed and pulled hard.

'Do you remember how I came after you'd had me?' I asked. 'And after you'd caned me? Do you remember how you said it showed I was your slave at heart? Well, what does this show, eh?'

I flicked his cock, then went back behind him and gave him another six hard strokes with the cane. When I went back again his cock was harder than ever. I reached out and took it in my hand, pulling gently as I gave him another cane stroke. He groaned and I gave him another, pulling harder at his cock. Somebody in the crowd started clapping, a slow rhythm that the others quickly took up. I measured my cane strokes to it, tugging at his erection as I beat him, getting harder with both cane and hand.

Suddenly he grunted and my hand was wet with spunk as his cock erupted. Before he could come down too far I reached up and put my fingers to his open mouth, watching him lap at his own come for an instant before his orgasm faded. The sight had the crowd in a frenzy, particularly Melody and Harmony, who had given up trying to restrain themselves. I bowed, taking a round of applause and then three cheers set up by Henry.

After I had caned Rathwell I was in heaven. Everybody had been congratulating me, complimenting me, hugging me, touching me up until my head was spinning and there was a wet patch in between my thighs. Rathwell had intended to go, but Henry had taken him aside and persuaded him against it, after which he was more or less his usual self. By the time Henry announced that we should be changing for the dinner he had set up, Rathwell had Harmony and Melody both naked and with a new set of six cane stripes on each well-fleshed bottom.

I went up to my room to change, along with Ginny, Ellen and Carrie. I had chosen a black velvet dress and fancy lace underwear in order to look as ladylike as possible. Ellen, having had her fill of being a pony-girl and being punished, dressed in the same deep-red silk sheaf she had worn the night I had visited her. Just seeing it brought back memories of kissing her anus and I wondered if her choice might not have been deliberate.

'Did you enjoy being birched?' I asked, keen to maintain my position as senior mistress.

'It was stimulating,' she answered, 'although I'd have preferred to have dished it out.'

'To Sven and Stefan?' I asked.

'Yes, wouldn't you?' she asked.

'I wish they'd done me,' Ginny put in.

'Maybe,' I answered, not sure that the idea actually did anything for me. 'You know why Carrie's bum's all pink, don't you?'

'Amber!' Carrie squeaked.

'She said you spanked her while your team were being watered,' Ellen replied.

'Yes,' I lied, remembering how Carrie had helped me. 'What are you going to wear for dinner, Carrie?'

'Just my panties, if that's all right,' she answered.

'Put her in a collar,' I suggested to Ellen.

'Yes, please,' Carrie answered eagerly.

'I never guessed you were such a slut, Carrie,' Ginny put in.

'I've been well trained,' Carrie answered, colouring slightly.

I didn't answer, wondering how I would have developed as Ellen's lover. Carrie had been a shy little thing at school. True, there had always been something mischievous about her, but never the openness and delight in sex that she now showed.

Ginny opted for just panties as well, flaunting herself as usual and, I suspected, intent on one or both of the young men. They had already been paying attention to her and meeting with the normal openly flirtatious response. Carrie had been less openly friendly to them once everyone had been back, evidently because of Ellen, yet I knew that at the very least she had sucked their cocks and maybe more.

By the time we got downstairs almost everybody else was

there already. Henry was running the kitchen as always, although he had allowed Francis to deal with the wines and roped in Trisha as his assistant. Rathwell had both Melody and Harmony stark naked and on leads. I greeted him with a nod and patted Melody's head, only then noting that the ring to which their leads were attached had a third one wound around it. I found myself having to swallow, knowing full well who the lead had been intended for. Rathwell smiled.

I turned away with a polite nod, aware that my lapse of composure had been noticed but I was not really bothered. After all, he was the one with the cane marks on his bottom, while mine was pristine. Feeling pretty pleased with myself, I looked around for someone to talk to. Vicky and Todd were nowhere to be seen, but I had heard tell-tale squeals and smacking noises coming from the room they were using and guessed that she was being disciplined for running so well. Sven and Stefan were both already at the table, drinking light ale out of tall glasses and admiring Ginny and Carrie across the room.

Trisha emerged from the kitchen with a great tray of canapés. She was dressed in a light dress of sheer apple-green silk. She was naked beneath it, with her nipples and the dark triangle between her legs showing. As she bent to put the tray down I was rewarded with a flash of her bottom. Her cheeks were still red from the nettles, which gave her a practical reason for leaving her panties off, and which I found an enchanting sight. Behind her came Susan, looking rather sorry for herself with her arm in a sling, but otherwise as coquettish as ever. I went to speak to her, only to be interrupted by Henry asking me to lay out place cards and handing me a list to do it by.

I suppose I must have betrayed a hint of petulance at being asked to help, because he gave me a look that I knew meant he felt I was due for a spanking. That might happen, but later. For now, it was my night. Despite that I put the cards out and helped people find their places, only then taking my own seat at the head of the table.

Dinner was excellent and went smoothly, everyone

becoming increasingly relaxed and intimate. With Ginny and Susan on either side of me I was in excellent company and was feeling completely happy and in control. Other than me, Ellen was the only female in a dominant role. I would have preferred to be the only one, but it was still a marvellous feeling. Melody and Harmony, the two fierce, powerful black girls who had wanted me as their slave were stark naked at their master's feet, having not even been permitted to sit at table. Vicky was also stark naked, and sitting a little uncomfortably on her newly caned bottom. Ginny and Carrie had on nothing but their panties, their naked breasts on display for everyone to see. Trisha had little more on and looked exquisitely submissive, while Susan was equally tempting in her starched white blouse and tiny skirt.

By the end of the main course I had made Ginny get down to the floor and take off her pants. Both Sven and I were feeding her titbits by hand, which she'd nuzzle out of our palms with her lips. Susan was cuddled into Francis's shoulder, both of them watching Ginny being fed. I was just making her beg for a choice morsel of pheasant when Henry banged on the table for attention. Ginny gulped the pheasant down and I turned to watch as the room went quiet.

'Thank you,' Henry began. 'Good evening, ladies, gentlemen and playthings. Firstly I would like to propose a toast to my goddaughter, Amber Oakley, so charge your glasses. As you know, Amber has been staying with me for some months now, and in that time I have seen her change from a shy, rather moody schoolgirl into a confident young woman with all the qualities that make the perfect pony-mistress. To Amber Oakley.'

I smiled and nodded as the entire group raised their glasses and toasted me.

'Indeed,' Henry continued, 'she has pursued her aims with the ruthless single-mindedness that is characteristic of the sexually dominant. Such is the way of the dominant woman: forceful, determined, haughty, forthright, hard to satisfy and easy to displease. Such things are truly the characteristics a slave-girl craves in her mistress. Personally, of course, being neither girl nor slave, I might argue that her character could equally well be defined as pushy, stubborn, supercilious, cheeky, impossible and sulky. In short, a brat.'

I had been about to put my glass down, but stayed with it poised in mid-air, looking at Henry with what must have been absolute horror. I knew what was coming, and couldn't really deny the justice of it. What he had said was true.

'And we all know what to do with brats, don't we?' he finished.

There was an immediate chorus of agreement, every person in the room calling as one for me to get my just desserts. I swallowed and looked around me, my bottom starting to tingle uncomfortably.

'So, I suggest,' Henry said when the clamour of demands for me to be spanked, birched, nettled, caned, cropped, peed on, dog whipped, given an enema and worse had died down, 'that in a spirit of fair-play, she should now crawl to each of us in turn, apologise and beg for a spanking. Amber?'

Well, I could have turned it down, but contrition is more than its own reward and I knew that to do so would lose me the chance of many future games. I also deserved it.

'Yes, sir,' I answered, hanging my head meekly.

'Very well, then, off you go,' he said to me, then addressed the room at large. 'Forty-eight smacks each, chaps, or we'll be here all night, but remember to make her beg first. Don't let her keep her pants up, either, I never do.'

I was blushing as I got down on my hands and knees. There were fourteen people, and every single one looked delighted by the prospect of spanking me. I decided to start with Susan, who would certainly be the mildest. I crawled to her and hung my head by her side.

'Please, Susan,' I began, with a repentance that was already fairly genuine, 'would you spank me please?'

'I might if you ask properly,' Susan replied.

'Please, Miss Wren,' I tried. 'I deserve to have my pants pulled down and my bottom spanked until I'm genuinely sorry for being beastly to you. Please do it?'

'Very well,' she answered in a bored voice that I knew was fake but still humiliated me.

She made me get across Francis's knee, peeling my dress up slowly to make me feel the full shame of exposure. He complimented me on my lacy black panties as she lifted my dress, then took one of my boobs in his hand and popped it out of my dress. With my stockings and suspenders showing, and the black panties stretched tight across my seat, I knew I made a fine sight; a sight that I intended for one or more of the girls to see as my bottom was lowered on to their faces. Now that same bottom was due a public spanking. I sighed as Susan took hold of my waistband and gently lowered my knickers. One of the men commented on the fullness of my bottom, and Francis popped my other tit out of my dress. Susan tucked my panties down around my thighs and I was ready for punishment.

'That's far enough, I think,' she remarked, snapping the elastic against my thigh. 'I can see your fat little pussy and, as you always told me, a girl's pussy ought to be showing when she's spanked.'

Then she spanked me – forty-eight stinging little slaps with the fingertips of her good hand. By the end my bottom was tingling and warm and I was beginning to feel the first thrills of the state I knew I would end up in. Francis had held me down with one hand and fondled my breasts with the other, starting to spank immediately Susan had finished. His firm, male hand quickly had me dancing and kicking over his lap, while he waited until he was finished to demand my apology.

I apologised in a kneeling position, kissed his shoes, then put my breasts back in and pulled my knickers up. There were twelve to go, which was a scary prospect, yet part of me wished it was more. Feeling warm and submissive I crawled on the floor to my next mistress, Melody. She was particularly bad, using me hard with my bottom humped up so high that half the table could see between my cheeks as I squealed and wriggled through my bare-bottomed spanking. She fingered my pussy after she'd spanked me and made me suck it before passing me on to Harmony. She was worse, giving me the same treatment but, instead of my vagina, it was my anus that she fingered. She then sat me up on her lap and made me suck the finger that had been in my bottom so that everybody could see.

After that I was in total submissive ecstasy, crawling from person to person and begging for the privilege of punishment and apology. Not one of them was merciful. Each put me through the same humiliating ritual. Apology, raised dress, lowered panties, forty-eight slaps. Most made me thank them for spanking me, and several took liberties with my bottom. Rathwell put a candle in my pussy when he'd done with me. Todd pulled my dress up to my armpits and it was left like that, although my panties went up and down like a yo-yo. Trisha was quite gentle but pushed my face in her food afterwards. Henry was the hardest, holding me tight around the waist and using all his power so that I was blubbering by the end. Vicky sat on my chest and rolled me up to do my thighs and pussy lips, which stung crazily. Ellen made me kiss her anus by way of apology, which had everyone clapping and encouraged Carrie to demand the same. Stefan and Sven did me together, each putting his cock in my mouth while the other beat me. Ginny came last, hauling me over her lap and dishing out a hard spanking with her hand twisted into my hair. She didn't stop at forty-eight, either, smacking away merrily in spite of my frustrated little kicks and squeals.

When she finally pushed me off her lap I was completely done. I made no effort to pull up my knickers or cover myself at all. I was crawling, my bare breasts dangling beneath me, my face covered in mashed potato, gravy and bits of vegetable, my bottom hot and throbbing, both pussy and bumhole feeling open and ready to be used. I badly needed to come and was going to do it in front of everyone when Henry once more called for silence.

I turned and sat down heavily on my sore behind, wondering what else they could possibly do to me. Plenty, I realised as I looked to the side. Stefan had pushed his chair back and was looking at me, an impressive erection in his hand.

'Before Amber puts herself up for general use,' Henry was saying, 'I suggest that part of Morris's suggestion needs to be honoured. To complete her lesson I think Amber should choose one of us to bugger her. Now is the time to do it, and, should she state a preference for girls, I would like to inform her that Melody has brought the required implement.'

I sat looking at him in disbelief. He knew me too well. Had he made the suggestion before I'd been spanked then I'd have laughed it off, offering some other form of submission if they were determined that I needed punishment. Henry, of course, knew full well that after being spanked by fourteen people I'd be meek and pliable. I was, and would have submitted anything other than my virgin bumhole with pleasure. As it was, the idea had my head spinning and I knew instantly that I wasn't going to refuse – or at least not refuse a woman. Melody had produced the dildo, a black thing with straps that looked at once irresistible and terrifying.

'No men, I'm afraid,' I said. 'I'm a bit precious about that. The girls could all do it, but for now . . .'

I looked round, utterly submissive, utterly wanton, deciding which of eight women to allow to bugger me with the grotesque object that Melody was toying with thoughtfully. She was out, both her and Harmony would be too rough and, after all, it was my first time. I then saw to my horror that what she was actually doing was filling the oversized testicles of the thing with cream.

'Sorry, Melody, another time,' I said. 'You too, Harmony.'

Susan I wanted, but with her arm it would have been a farce. Anyway, I wanted somebody gentle but firmer, which cut out her and Trisha too. Carrie tempted me as I knew she'd giggle and make fun of me as the dildo slid up my bum, but she'd do that anyway. Ginny had earlier offered to help me set up my business, and I knew the nights would be far from dull, so she could wait. Vicky would be nice but at that instant she was on her knees with Todd's cock in her mouth.

'Ellen,' I said, 'but you can all watch.'

'Don't worry, we intend to,' Rathwell answered.

Ellen was already on her feet, walking over to me with her heels clicking on the floor. I looked up as she approached, the monstrous dildo dangling from her hand.

'Down,' she ordered in that same stern voice that had once made me so rebellious.

Now I put my head to the floor and kissed her shoes. She made a little noise, a brief snort that signalled both amusement and contempt. I pushed my bottom up and spread my thighs until my lowered panties were stretched between them.

'Look up,' she ordered.

I obeyed. She was hitching her dress up. Like me she had stockings on, and lacy black panties. The difference was that while hers were immaculate my stockings were torn and my pants were down around my thighs. Taking up the dildo, she held the straps experimentally apart.

'It vibrates,' Melody called out.' 'Take your knickers down a little and put the egg-shaped bulge against your pussy.'

'Thank you,' Ellen replied, as politely as if Melody had been instructing her on how to use a hairdryer.

With her dress up to her tummy and her knickers a little way down, Ellen began to fasten on the dildo. Straps went around her waist and between her legs, leaving the thing protruding at the level of her crotch with the rubber balls bulging out beneath it. She pulled her panties up around the balls, making it look as if a monstrous cock was jutting out from her tiny, feminine knickers.

I swallowed, looking at the thing and wondering if my bottom-hole could take it. Henry had put a candle in me and it hadn't hurt. The plug of my pony-girl tail had stung a little. The dildo was a lot bigger than either – certainly as wide as Francis's cock – and Susan had squeaked a lot when he'd put that in her. Melody had also squeaked when I put the whip up her bottom, and she presumably took the dildo in her bum from Harmony occasionally.

'Don't worry, Amber darling, I'll be gentle,' Ellen said as if divining my thoughts. 'Carrie, come here and bring the butter. Amber, turn and stick your bottom up.'

I obeyed, even though it meant that my open red bottom was now on full display to everyone. They were relaxing, sipping their wine and watching me being humiliated, some cuddled together, others talking quietly.

'Is she really a virgin anally?' I heard Rathwell say as Carrie dropped to her knees behind me and slapped a pat of butter in between my bum-cheeks.

'I haven't buggered her,' Henry replied. 'She likes me to come over her bottom, but she won't let me try and put my cock up.'

'Extraordinary,' Rathwell replied. 'She has such a magnificent arse you'd have thought someone would have slipped one up it. Still, she's going to get it now.'

Carrie had started to rub at my anus, tracing little circles round the hole that were making me moan with pleasure.

'Does a dildo really count?' Francis asked.

'Try one up your butt, boy, and you'll say it does,' Melody answered.

'Ah,' Francis replied.

'Ssh, let's watch Ellen do it to her,' Vicky remarked. 'I want to hear Amber squeal.'

Carrie's fingers had begun to open me, pushing, then sliding inside. I groaned aloud as one, then two fingers were pushed up my bottom. Looking round I could see Ginny rubbing butter on to Ellen's rubber erection, grinning as she eyed my bottom. I grunted as Carrie slid a third finger into my anus. It stung a bit but I felt open and juicy and could feel the melted butter running down on to my pussy lips.

'I think she's ready,' Carrie said.

She pulled her fingers out. I certainly felt ready. My anus felt wide and juicy enough to have an orange pushed up, never mind the dildo.

239

'Move her round,' someone said.

A couple of slaps did the trick, leaving me side on to the table as Ellen got to her knees behind me. This was it, I realised: the moment that my bumhole was publicly deflowered. Something hard touched my anus and I tightened it automatically, only for Ellen to start rubbing it in circles. Carrie was near me, offering me something – her fingers. I opened my mouth and let her put them in, tasting myself and the butter as I sucked on them. She gave a squeak of delight mingled with disgust, making me shiver and threatening to start my tears.

'Come on, Ellen, don't tease her,' Ginny said. 'Put it in.'

Carrie pulled her fingers out of my mouth and there was sudden pressure against my anus. I squeaked aloud and tried to relax, gasping as it stretched my ring. For a moment I was going to cry red, and then it was in me, sliding up, filling my rectum, stretching and bloating me. I gave a cry, more of shame than pain, as the grotesque thing was pushed up me. Everyone started clapping and I burst into tears.

'No, no, carry on,' I gasped as Ellen automatically started to withdraw. 'Don't mind my tears, that's just how I am. Put it right in.'

Someone laughed. Rathwell I think. Ellen took me by the hips and pulled herself in, the dildo sliding up my behind until the rubber scrotum touched my empty pussy. I began gasping and panting as she began to bugger me properly. The cream-filled balls were soon banging against my pussy and I was scratching at the floor with my hands and gaping for air. I felt great, breathless and full of cock; utterly rude and utterly submissive.

'Turn the vibrator on and push it well up. You'll probably both come,' Melody advised.

There was a pause as Ellen fiddled for the switch, then suddenly it was as if my whole sex had exploded. The dildo was in my bottom to the hilt; the ridged rubber scrotum pressed hard to my pussy. The vibrations were right against my clit, making me even wilder than before. I knew I was screaming and scrabbling at the floor, calling for

Ellen and Ginny and Susan and just anyone. Hands grabbed my breasts and a cock was stuffed in my mouth, I don't know whose. Someone's hand went under me and pulled the rubber balls on to my pussy, the lace of Ellen's panties touching right on my clit. Their grip squeezed the false scrotum, squirting half a pint of cream deep up my rectum. I felt it spurt out around the shaft of the dildo and that was too much. I started to come, kicking and scratching at the floor. I was sucking desperately on the cock in my mouth, which suddenly erupted, filling my mouth with real sperm. A second, more intense climax hit me, then a third. Everything went red, then black, and the last thing I remember was Ellen calling my name as she too reached her climax.

Epilogue

So the games mistress got me in the end, but in a way that I would not have imagined possible when she first made an advance.

Ginny and I set up my saddlery business and lived together for some time, respectable businesswomen to the outside world, lovers to those who knew us. My pony-girl tack business thrived as well, and I gradually acquired a reputation for making the best tack available. I saw plenty of the people I'd come to know, both in normal life and as pony-girls, Vicky especially, who became my main model. Henry started his meets again and, once I had grown hedges to shield my field from prying eyes, I began to hold my own.

Morris Rathwell never did get me as his slave, but what would have happened had I lost that crucial race I'm not really certain. The only thing that rankled at the end was that his initial threat to tell my father had been a bluff, and a successful one. The caning I didn't mind, nor really getting fucked with my face in the mud. The second caning and buggery I feel sure I'd have taken just as well. As Ginny says, when it comes down to it I'm worse than she is. As for the week of being their slave, it's not so easy to be sure. I'd like to think I'd have enjoyed it and then gone back to my old ways, but there's always a nagging doubt . . .

NEW BOOKS

Coming up from Nexus and Black Lace

There are three Nexus titles published in December

Fairground Attractions by Lisette Ashton
December 1998 Price £5.99 ISBN: 0 352 33295 6
Beneath the glamour and excitement of the fairground there is a sinister world, undisclosed to the visiting crowds. Operating outside the restrictions of the towns they entertain, the fairground's owners are used to indulging their lewd appetites whenever and however they please. Georgia and Holly are reluctant recruits to the fairground and they soon discover the pains and pleasures of this barbarous regime, as both women endure a painful lesson in the fairground's rules. It's a lesson they will never forget. By the author of *The Black Room* and *Amazon Slave*.

The Warrior Queen by Kendal Grahame
December 1998 Price £5.99 ISBN: 0 352 33294 8
In the first century AD, the Roman army has invaded Britannia and its soldiers are sating their lusts on helpless Celtic maidens. A revolt is underway, however, led by Boudicca, queen of the Iceni. She loves dominating men as much as the Romans love dominating women, and surrounds herself with submissives who fulfil her every need, no matter how perverted. Seeking advice from a mysterious druid clan, she finds herself for the first time uncomfortably aroused by the idea of submitting to a man. Will she ever be able to satisfy her darkest urges? By the author of *The Training of Fallen Angels*.

Bound to Obey by Amanda Ware
December 1998   Price £5.99   ISBN: 0 352 33058 9
Master Francis and Mistress Lynne have appointed Caroline as their new maid. But this post requires more than the usual amount of submissiveness from the servant, and a far less substantial uniform. At times, Caroline will be expected to wear no more than a silk scarf bound tightly around her wrists. Just as she is beginning to get used to her kinky employers, Caroline finds that there are others with still more deviant proclivities – ones which she is soon to witness at first hand. This is a new edition of one of Nexus's most popular tales of submission.

The Test by Nadine Somers
January 1998   Price £5.99   ISBN: 0352 33320 0
When Rachel starts working for Michael, a high-ranking Government minister, she doesn't realise exactly what kind of job training he has in store for her. She is to be initiated into a mysterious and perverse group of female devotees of discipline; total obedience is expected of new recruits, and bizarre and lewd demands are made of them. Will Rachel pass the test?

Exposing Louisa by Jean Aveline
January 1998   Price £5.99   ISBN: 0352 33321 9
Anton and Magdalena are brother and sister, separated at birth but reunited as teenagers. The forbidden nature of their love for each other only serves to intensify their passion for experimentation – for the darkest of sexual games. Working as dancers, they fall under the spell of the manipulative Sophie and the masterful Dieter, both of whom have secret and perverse plans for the couple. By the author of *Sisters of Severcy*.

BLACK
lace

There are three Black Lace titles published in December

A Private View by Crystalle Valentino
December 1998   Price £5.99   ISBN: 0 352 33308 1
Successful catwalk model Jemma has all the wealth and status she
needs, but she can't resist taking a friend up on a dare to pose nude
for a world-famous erotic photographer. As she becomes ever more
ensconced in his bizarre world, she discovers how far his friends are
willing to go to pursue their varied sexual tastes – and how far she'll
go to keep up with them.

A Secret Place by Ella Broussard
December 1998   Price £5.99   ISBN: 0 352 33307 3
Bel is a locations scout for a film company. When a big-budget Holly-
wood movie is made in rural England in the summer, she is delighted
to be working on-set. Bel loves working outdoors – and with a good-
looking and adventurous crew of technicians and actors around her,
there are plenty of opportunities for the naughty girl to show off her
talents.

Sugar and Spice 2 ed. Kerri Sharp
December 1998   Price £7.99   ISBN: 0 352 33309 X
Sugar and Spice anthologies mean Black Lace short stories – stories
showing the power of the female erotic imagination to arouse and
excite. With contributions from women in America, Australia and
Europe, this second compendium in the series provides another dazzl-
ing variety of settings and themes. Explicitly sexual and highly enter-
taining, *Sugar and Spice 2* is the ideal introduction to the Black Lace
series.

A Feast for the Senses by Martine Marquand
January 1998   Price £5.99   ISBN: 0 352 33310 3
Claira Fairfax leaves her innocent life in Georgian England to
embark on the Grand Tour of Europe. She travels through the deca-
dent cities – from icebound Amsterdam to sultry Constantinople –
undergoing lessons in perverse pleasure from the mysterious and
eccentric Count Anton di Maliban.

The Transformation by Natasha Rostova
January 1998   Price £5.99   ISBN: 0 352 33311 1
Three friends, one location – San Francisco. This book contains three interlinked and very modern stories which have their links in fairy tales. There's nothing innocent about Lydia, Molly and Cassie, however, as one summer provides them with revelatory sexual experiences which transform their lives.

NEXUS BACKLIST

All books are priced £4.99 unless another price is given. If a date is supplied, the book in question will not be available until that month in 1998.

CONTEMPORARY EROTICA

THE ACADEMY	Arabella Knight		
AGONY AUNT	G. C. Scott		
ALLISON'S AWAKENING	Lauren King		
AMAZON SLAVE	Lisette Ashton	£5.99	
THE BLACK GARTER	Lisette Ashton	£5.99	Sept
THE BLACK ROOM	Lisette Ashton		
BOUND TO OBEY	Amanda Ware	£5.99	Dec
BOUND TO SUBMIT	Amanda Ware		
CANDIDA IN PARIS	Virginia Lasalle		
CHAINS OF SHAME	Brigitte Markham	£5.99	July
A CHAMBER OF DELIGHTS	Katrina Young		
DARK DELIGHTS	Maria del Rey	£5.99	Aug
DARLINE DOMINANT	Tania d'Alanis	£5.99	Oct
A DEGREE OF DISCIPLINE	Zoe Templeton		
THE DISCIPLINE OF NURSE RIDING	Yolanda Celbridge	£5.99	Nov
THE DOMINO TATTOO	Cyrian Amberlake		
THE DOMINO QUEEN	Cyrian Amberlake		
EDEN UNVEILED	Maria del Rey		
EDUCATING ELLA	Stephen Ferris		
EMMA'S SECRET DOMINATION	Hilary James		
FAIRGROUND ATTRACTIONS	Lisette Ashton	£5.99	Dec
THE TRAINING OF FALLEN ANGELS	Kendal Grahame		
HEART OF DESIRE	Maria del Rey		

ANCIENT & FANTASY SETTINGS

THE CLOAK OF APHRODITE	Kendal Grahame		
DEMONIA	Kendal Grahame		
THE DUNGEONS OF LIDIR	Aran Ashe		
THE FOREST OF BONDAGE	Aran Ashe		
NYMPHS OF DIONYSUS	Susan Tinoff		
THE WARRIOR QUEEN	Kendal Grahame	£5.99	Dec

EDWARDIAN, VICTORIAN & OLDER EROTICA

ANNIE	Evelyn Culber	£5.99	
ANNIE AND THE COUNTESS	Evelyn Culber	£5.99	
BEATRICE	Anonymous		
THE CORRECTION OF AN ESSEX MAID	Yolanda Celbridge	£5.99	
DEAR FANNY	Michelle Clare		
LYDIA IN THE HAREM	Philippa Masters		
LURE OF THE MANOR	Barbra Baron		
MAN WITH A MAID 3	Anonymous		
MEMOIRS OF A CORNISH GOVERNESS	Yolanda Celbridge		
THE GOVERNESS AT ST AGATHA'S	Yolanda Celbridge		
MISS RATTAN'S LESSON	Yolanda Celbridge	£5.99	Aug
PRIVATE MEMOIRS OF A KENTISH HEADMISTRESS	Yolanda Celbridge		
SISTERS OF SEVERCY	Jean Aveline		

SAMPLERS & COLLECTIONS

EROTICON 3	Various		
EROTICON 4	Various	£5.99	July
THE FIESTA LETTERS	ed. Chris Lloyd		
NEW EROTICA 2	ed. Esme Ombreux		
NEW EROTICA 3	ed. Esme Ombreux		
NEW EROTICA 4	ed. Esme Ombreux	£5.99	Sept

NON-FICTION

Please send me the books I have ticked above.

Name ....

Address ....

....

....

.... Post code........................

Send to: Cash Sales, Nexus Books, Thames Wharf Studios, Rainville Road, London W6 9HT

Please enclose a cheque or postal order, made payable to **Nexus Books**, to the value of the books you have ordered plus postage and packing costs as follows:

UK and BFPO – £1.00 for the first book, 50p for the second book and 30p for each subsequent book to a maximum of £3.00;

Overseas (including Republic of Ireland) – £2.00 for the first book, £1.00 for the second book and 50p for each subsequent book.

If you would prefer to pay by VISA or ACCESS/MASTER-CARD, please write your card number and expiry date here:

....

Please allow up to 28 days for delivery.

Signature ....